Published by Edge60
Copyright © Eric R Davidson 2015
Copyright © re-edit Eric R Davidson April 2021
The right of Eric R Davidson to be identified as the author of this work has been asserted by the author in accordance with the Copyright, Designs and Patents Act 1988.

****

The Author's Comments:

In the MILO series I have tried to create a sense of the 1970s and this may include describing situations that would not be so fitting in the 21st century. Times were different back then.
My thanks to my wife, Heather and son Adam, for their patient reading of the manuscript, correction of my mistakes and suggestions for improvements, where necessary.
My thanks also to Adam, for the original artwork on all the MILO front covers. He also designed the MILO logo. See his artwork at: **www.catchthe22.com**

The photo on the back page of the paperback was taken by my other son, Andrew, to complete a total family effort in the publishing of this book. My thanks, again, to everyone.

One final point that may be of help to anyone reading this book; £1 in 1971 is equivalent to roughly £13 today.

Eric R Davidson   (May 2015. Update April 2021)

Other books by Eric R Davidson – available in e-book and paperback format from Amazon (unless otherwise stated).

1906 – September   **(Book One in the Jake Fraser series)**

1906 – October   **(Book Two in the Jake Fraser series**

1906 – November   **(Book Three in the Jake Fraser series)**

1908 – Summer   **(Book Four in the Jake Fraser series)**

1908 – Christmas   **(Book Five in the Jake Fraser series)**

(Inspector Jake Fraser series set in Edwardian Aberdeen)

Inspector Fraser's First Case (A Short Story) – e-book only

The Varga File   **(Book One in the MILO series)**

The Assassin File   **(Book Two in the MILO series)**

The Election File   **(Book Three – due out May '21)**

The Freiheit File   **(Book Four – due out November '21)**

One Less For Dinner

The Little Boy Who Didn't Like Corned Beef

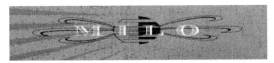

MILO logo – Copyright Adam Davidson May 2015

PART ONE

July 1948 – Rhodes Town

Hans Varga walked down the short gangway from the small vessel that had transported him, along with his wife, from Bodrum in Turkey. They both stood looking around the Mandriki harbour area of Rhodes Town and taking note of the general movement of people, both locals and visitors.

There were a number of small vessels tied up along the quayside most of them flying the flag of Greece, which was in the process of taking Rhodes and many other islands back under its direct control. Varga took a handkerchief from the top pocket of his jacket and after removing his hat, he patted his forehead.

Across the road some travellers were stepping down from a bus parked outside one of the many entrances to the Old Town. Their words were only just decipherable, but Varga could tell they were in English. It was a language he still detested. It made him feel he was in the company of enemies, even though the war had been over these last three years.

Yes, the war might be over, but no one could take Varga's memories away, much as he sometimes wished they could. It had been a war, which had started so promisingly and ended in such despair. It had set out to make Germany strong and ended with a country reduced to rubble and a population starving.

But that was all in the past now, for Hans Varga and his fellow Germans, it was all about the future.

And that future would begin with the collection of a bag he had left on the island, whilst there for two years during the war. He had been mainly in Rhodes Town and had fallen under the spell of its history.

He had read everything he could about the place.

His main interest had been with the Knights of St John who had been based on the island for around two hundred years from the 14th to 16th century. The Knights had displayed a great talent for organising themselves to the benefit of anyone who came in to contact with them. Varga wished to bring that same organisation to both his life and to the business ventures he intended starting over the coming months.

Varga's war had ended in the middle of January, nineteen forty-five, when he had realised, from the messages arriving from the Fatherland, that it was highly unlikely Germany would see victory in a war that had now turned against it.

His mind had turned to self-preservation and he had made plans to be taken to Bodrum on the coast of neutral Turkey.

It wasn't just imminent defeat that caused Hans Varga to seek escape, while he had the chance. He had done things during the war, of which he was not proud. He knew he would not be able to claim that he had simply been following orders because, in most instances, he had been the one issuing those orders.

No, he would have to accept responsibility for his own actions and get off the island before his enemies arrived. They would bring questions he did not want to answer.

One night he had packed a case, boarded a small fishing boat and turned his back on the Third Reich forever. He had lived in Turkey for a year before moving to Spain. He had never once regretted his decision to desert as he knew he owed the Fatherland nothing. He had served his country, offered it his life at times and taken only what he thought was rightfully his, at the end.

He hadn't looked upon it as stealing.

Varga had only been back to Germany for business reasons, since the war had ended. The town he'd been born in now lay in the Eastern half of Germany; he had no reason to go there again. He was grateful for the fact he had no family; there was just him now.

Varga ran his fingers through his thick, greying hair then placed his white, Panama hat back on his head. His face looked lined and his dark brown eyes were set deep in sunken sockets. He looked tired. He was the epitome of a man who was old before his time. He was a fifty-two-year-old man who looked to be at least ten years older.

He turned to his wife. "Lovely, isn't it?"

Helga Varga smiled. "Yes, it is lovely. I can't wait to see more."

Frau Varga was ten years younger than her husband and their trip to Rhodes was by way of a honeymoon. The couple had married six months ago, but this had been the first opportunity they had had to get away for a little while.

They had met, quite by chance, six months before they'd eventually married and struck up a friendship that had blossomed, rather quickly, into love. Helga had, by that time, come to the conclusion that no man would ever find her interesting enough as to ask her to marry him. She had been more than surprised when Hans had popped the question. However, she had also been more than happy to accept.

Helga took off her hat and fanned herself. She was not a woman of conventional beauty with her slightly twisted mouth, hooked nose and close-set eyes, but she cared a lot for her husband and would stick by him, faithfully, for the rest of her days.

"Which way now?" she then said.

"This way," replied her husband. "I have something to do first."

Helga fell in to step beside her husband. She had worked as a secretary since leaving school and, mainly due to the war, there had never been any opportunity to travel.

Helga's war had been greatly different from her husband's. He had maintained an element of control over his war, but Helga had had to try and get on with her life, while things slowly started to unravel around her. The propaganda machine continued to tell the German people that all was going well and that victory was still assured for the Reich.

In reality, defeat began to stare them in the face. Helga could no longer get food and stories had started to circulate that the enemy was literally knocking at the door of Berlin. Helga had prayed that the British, or Americans, got to her first. The stories about what the Red Army was likely to do were terrifying.

Their time in Rhodes Town was limited. They would soon be returning to Bodrum, where they had another three nights booked in a small, yet comfortable, hotel.

"One day I intend to live here, my dear," Hans said as they walked along passed a line of small vessels. To their right the Old Town stood proudly behind its outer wall and dominating the view was the Grand Master's Palace, which had stood there since the 14th century. Varga looked across at the building and secretly wished that, one day, it might be his. He certainly had grand ideas that benefit from having a grand palace to go with them.

They passed through St Paul's Gate and onwards in to the old Town. A road to their left passed the commercial harbour of Rhodes Town. However, Hans led his wife off to the right.

As the streets narrowed the heat became even more intense and they were both glad to be dressed appropriately. The architecture around them had much to do with the Italians, who had been on the island since 1912. They had made a number of changes though not all, in Varga's opinion, successful. The one success they could claim, however, was the Grand Palace itself.

In nineteen thirty-seven the Italian Governor of the Dodecanese began a programme of restoration for the Palace, which was completed in nineteen forty. What had been little more than a one storey ruin was now back to its former glory and had become a building that Varga coveted more than any other..

The Italians, like the Germans, were long gone and Rhodes now waited to see what the Greeks would do. What changes would they bring and would they really be for the better?

Varga led his wife in to the Street of the Knights, which he knew sloped up to the entrance to the Grand Palace. He began to talk to her about the history of Rhodes Town. She had heard much of it before but now it took on greater meaning as she was able to see for herself the buildings of which her husband spoke.

"When the Knights occupied this town, they instigated a remarkable process by which travellers could be welcomed. On this street alone there are no fewer than six Inns, representing the different Tongues, which was their way of differentiating between the various nationalities. In simple terms, my dear, if you were of German descent, then you would find the Inn that catered for the Tongue of Germany, not that that was in this street. It was such a simple idea and yet it immediately provided a new arrival to the Town with a place to visit and a friendly face awaiting."

They continued to walk up the slight incline with its rough cobbled street and better paved walkways on either side. At the top of the incline was the Grand Palace. Looking around, from the top of the hill, it became apparent that there was still work to be done in repairing some of the incendiary damage caused during the war. There was also an element of structural damage, which the Greek Archaeological Service had undertaken to repair in time.

Varga waxed lyrically about the Grand Palace, as they looked through the bars of the closed gates. He hoped that one day the Greeks would manage to re-open the Palace and allow visitors to enjoy a walk around its splendid interior. He vowed to Helga that on the day that the Grand Palace opened for public inspection, they would be first in the queue.

Having felt that he had bored his wife enough with his historical knowledge of Rhodes Town, Varga then suggested that they find a small café and enjoy a coffee. Frau Varga was delighted with that suggestion and they now walked, arm in arm, down Orfeus towards the hustle and bustle of the market area.

Many of the streets were lined with traders' stalls, some there to catch the eye of the casual visitor whilst others were providing a service for the local inhabitants. It created a colourful and vibrant sight, especially to Frau Varga who had been so accustomed to the greyness of a Germany on its knees and struggling to get up again.

They found a small café in a busy square and sat at one of the tables set up outside. A fat man with a cheery smile came to take their order. He seemed slightly disappointed that they only wanted two coffees but, none the less, he hurried off to get them.

Hans took his hat off and fanned himself again. He then glanced at his watch.

"You look restless," Frau Varga commented.

"I need to do something, my dear," Varga then said.

Frau Varga looked annoyed. "What, here? I thought we were on honeymoon; I had not expected you to have business to attend to."

Hans put his hand over his wife's and smiled. "It isn't exactly business; I simply need to visit an old friend. It won't take long."

"Then take me with you," Frau Varga added, "you know that I want to know as much about your previous life as possible. Meeting your old friends would be a part of that."

"This is something I need to do alone," Varga insisted. "As I said, it will not take long. I will be no more than half an hour. Enjoy another cup of coffee while I am away."

He then drank the coffee, which had been brought to their table, before putting on his hat again and standing up. Frau Varga made a face again, clearly showing her husband how annoyed she was at being left on her own. However, as she watched Hans walk off through the hustle and bustle of the market area, she was already attracting the waiter's attention and ordering another coffee.

*

Hans Varga walked about half a mile. He found himself checking to ensure that he was not being followed even though no one even knew he was on the island.

Old habits and all that.

He eventually stopped at a door and knocked on the rough exterior. He continued to look around until he realised his actions were probably attracting more attention than if he simply relaxed.

The door finally opened and a small, dark haired man, wearing black trousers and a stringed vest stood in the doorway. This was not the man Varga had expected to open the door.

"Is Constantine here?" Varga asked in English.

"Constantine left the island along with the Germans," the man replied in perfect English.

"Left the island?" Varga added with horror. "Where did he go?"

"I do not know. All I know is that this house was empty for a few months before we got the chance to live in it."

"The house was empty?" Varga then asked, the horror ever more apparent in his tone.

The man did not understand why this mysterious visitor should be at all concerned about how long the house had been empty; after all, it wasn't as if he was a local.

"For a little while, yes. Once it became apparent that he wasn't coming back, the house was offered to my wife and I. We had recently married and being offered the chance of a house of our own was just too good to refuse."

Varga was tiring of these tales of domestic bliss. He moved forward, almost pushing the other man aside as he did so.

"I need to look in your cellar," he said.

"There's nothing in the cellar," replied the man, trying to position himself in front of his rude and unwanted visitor.

"I do hope you are wrong in that assessment," said Varga, pushing on along the corridor.

The other man hurried after him and once more pushed himself in front, just as they reached the top of the stairs, which led down to the cellar. Varga was pleased to see that the general layout of the house had not changed since he had last been there.

"This is my house and I must insist that you leave," the man said.

Varga's anger burst from him.

"I *must* look in your cellar!" he yelled and pushed the man on the chest.

He lost his balance and tumbled down the stairs, eventually landing on the cellar floor with a groan. Varga hurried down the stairs, stepped over the groaning man and headed for the far wall of the cellar, which looked as if it had been recently whitewashed.

Varga's heart sank. All the items he had remembered lying around, were gone. His immediate thought was that the items he had come for, were gone as well.

During the war, Varga had visited the house on many occasions. He had become friends with Constantine, but it was really the company of Constantine's sister, Nana, that he had wanted.

She had been a beautiful woman, with a full figure and a healthy liking for sex. Their relationship had developed, though built entirely on lust.

Varga began running his hands over the wall. He was searching for something and the longer it took to find that something, the more concerned he became that all his plans for the future might end in that very second.

And then he found what he was looking for; a loose brick. It was closer to the floor than he had remembered and he fell to his knees and almost frantically, tore at the brick with his fingers until he had worked it loose. Behind it was a small cavity into which a cloth bag had been shoved. Varga removed the bag and opened it.

"What have you there?"

Hearing the voice, Varga looked round. The man had hauled himself to his feet, a cut visible on his head and a slight trickle of blood flowing from it. Varga knew that the man had seen more than was good for him. Varga tried to make light of what he was doing.

"It is a small keepsake that I left here during the war. It has little more than sentimental value; certainly nothing that need concern you."

"Need concern me?" repeated the man. "This is my house and anything in it should, therefore, be mine as well." He began to move closer to Varga, his hand outstretched. "Give it to me."

Varga swiftly assessed the situation in the time it took the man to close down the short distance between them. There really was only one option that made any sense. Varga put the bag in his pocket and launched himself at the man. He closed his hands round the man's throat and squeezed. His anger seemed to spur him on and his hands tightened all the more. He wasn't going to let this annoying little man take away his future.

The man was dead long before Varga actually stopped squeezing. He stepped back and the man slid down the wall and on to the floor. Varga was breathing deeply, only now aware of the effort he had put into killing the man. It had been a few years since he'd last had to do that.

Varga looked down at the body and cursed. It hadn't been part of his plan, but he knew it had to be done. He turned away and started climbing the stairs. To his horror, he met a woman at the top.

Her eyes widened on seeing a stranger coming up from her cellar. She opened her mouth to speak, but Varga had already decided that she, too, had to die. He could not afford to leave any witnesses.

He left the woman's body in the cellar along with what he assumed was her husband.

He left the house and casually strolled back to meet his wife. He acted as if nothing was wrong, hoping those who passed him would never remember he'd been there. He made his way back to Helga and found her nursing an empty cup and wearing an expression of anger.

"How was your friend?" she asked.

"He wasn't in; such a shame," Varga replied.

Helga looked at her husband. He was lying. She always knew when he was lying; his lips were moving.

November, 1950 – Hans Varga's Office, Paris

It had been a busy two years. In less than three months, after returning from Rhodes, Varga had been paid for his contraband. He had benefitted from a network of ex-German officers who were keen to help each other in whatever way they could. This rarely required them to stay within the limits of the law.

Varga, therefore, became a very rich man almost overnight. He invested his money in shipping, taking all of nineteen forty-nine to negotiate the best prices and to acquire premises for his new company. His import and export business was finally launched at the beginning of nineteen fifty. It was a time in which the world would need to rebuild and part of that rebuilding process would involve the movement of food and provisions from country to country. Varga's company was basically prepared to move anything that the client wished to move, with absolutely no questions asked.

Varga encouraged businesses to come to him by undercutting his competitors. He occasionally shipped items for less than it cost him, but he wanted the business and he wanted to be seen as the first point of contact when items needed to be shipped around the world. The tactic had worked.

Almost from day one, his business had begun to flourish, bringing an ever-growing wealth along with it.

Varga had now based his main office in the top two storeys of an office block just off the Avenue des Champs-Elysees and half a mile from the Arc de Triomphe. He still found it rather amusing to remember those photographs of Hitler as he drove along the Champs- Elysees with a smug look of victory on his face. How it had all turned sour so quickly as Hitler's insanity had become more and more apparent.

Varga had chosen Paris as he had no wish to return to Germany. For now, Spain had also served its purpose. He had bought a nice house for himself and Helga and was content with his life.

That cold, November morning, Varga was at his desk when his secretary, Marie, came in to inform him that a man, calling himself Franz Neuer, had called to see him. Varga had given the name some thought, but hadn't come up with any form of recognition.

"He said you would know him from the war," Marie continued, "He told me to tell you that he had been a fellow officer."

Varga gave the name even more thought. It still meant nothing. However, if the man really had been a fellow officer then the least that Varga could do was to see him.

"Very well, Marie, would you please show Herr Neuer in?"

Marie turned and left the room. A moment later she was back in the company of a tall man with slicked back, black hair and dark looking eyes that Varga knew at once had seen some terrible things during the war. Varga also knew at once that this man's name was not Franz Neuer.

"Would you like coffee for yourself and your visitor, Monsieur Varga?" Marie asked as she stood between Neuer and Varga's desk.

"That would be very nice, Marie, thank you, Varga replied.

Marie left the room with the visitor's eyes on her all the time.

Life's habits rarely change, thought Varga.

Varga had spoken to Marie in French, but the minute she left the room he immediately changed to German.

"Why don't you sit down Herr Neuer?"

"Thank you."

Neuer had been carrying his coat over his arm so he draped that over the back of his chair before sitting down. He crossed his legs and looked around the room. Varga studied his guest for a few seconds before speaking again.

"Do I continue to call you Herr Neuer, or would you prefer me to use your real name?"

Neuer smiled. "I have been Franz Neuer for a few years now, so perhaps it would be prudent for me to continue to use that name at all times."

"Very well, *Herr Neuer,* what can I do for you?" Varga then said.

"You have done very well for yourself, Herr Varga," Neuer began. "You obviously put the money you got from the diamonds to good effect. I, on the other hand, had to spend all my money on creating this new identity. As you know we all did things in the war of which we are no longer proud and I thought it best to change my identity before trying to build a new life for myself."

Varga did not respond to the mention of the diamonds, even though every inch of his body was keen to know how Neuer had possibly found out about them. He did not show any reaction, maintaining a calm exterior throughout.

"Why have you come here?" Varga then asked, wishing to wacto as little time on this man as possible.

"Building that new life has proved a bit more difficult than I could ever have imagined."

"I understand all that, but what do you want from me?" Varga enquired.

"I want you to offer me a job," Neuer replied calmly.

Varga looked a little surprised. "Have you any particular skill to offer me?"

Neuer brushed an imaginary piece of fluff from the leg of his trousers.

"My main talent is that I know things, Herr Varga, which means I know things about you; things that you may not want others to know."

"Ah, so your real talent is blackmail; if I'm reading you correctly, Herr Neuer?"

"A nasty word, Herr Varga, and not one that I feel correctly describes our relationship."

Varga smiled. "I wasn't aware that we had a relationship."

"We both did things during the war; which I am sure we'd rather forget. We both do not want others to know about those things and it would, therefore, be in both our interests for us to become friends, rather than run the risk of what we might do to each other, were we to become enemies."

"Is that a threat, Herr Neuer?" said Varga.

"It is not meant to be a threat, Herr Varga, just a statement of fact."

They were interrupted, at that moment, by Marie coming into the room with their coffees. Once more, Neuer was spotted looking at Marie in a somewhat lascivious manner. Fortunately, Marie had not noticed and she now made her way out of the room.

Varga pushed one of the cups towards his visitor and invited him to add sugar and cream as necessary.

"*If* we were to work together," Varga then said, "what, exactly, are you offering by way of helping to enhance my business?"

"Contacts, Herr Varga, excellent contacts."

Varga sat back in his chair. His business would rise, or fall, on the back of him making the right contacts. He had done okay so far, but were future contacts to be stronger, perhaps become a permanent part of his business, then it would certainly be worth exploring.

"Okay, I'm listening," he then said.

Neuer smiled. It was a cold, calculating smile; a smile that Varga had seen before and it still made his blood chill.

"As you know, Herr Varga, I was in the SS during the war. We were accused of many things, some of which might have been true, while others were mere fabrication."

"More of them would have been true, I'm guessing," Varga added quickly, as he reached for his coffee.

Neuer inclined his head slightly, as if acknowledging the truth of that statement. "However," he then continued, "the main strength of being in the SS was the camaraderie and the fact we swore an oath that tied us together in a way that can never be broken. That means that now, even after five years, we are still tied by that bond. I can bring you my ex-colleagues, Herr Varga. I can help build a circle of companies that will keep you in business for years to come."

Varga considered the matter for a moment. He could not deny that the SS bond was strong. They had all been mad, of course, but that madness had forced them to work together, forced them to share the burden of the accusations that followed, even after the war had ended. It was already well-known that organisations existed for the benefit of those ex-SS officers who had had to make good their escape when peacetime had arrived.

Some had been caught and punished, but many more were still at large, mainly in South America, where they continued to work for each other in any way that they could. Much as he had detested the SS, Hans Varga had to admit that their brotherhood might now be of great value to him.

In more ways than one, perhaps.

Varga considered all that in the silence that hung over the room for a moment or two. He sipped at his coffee and watched his visitor do the same, their eyes rarely breaking from staring at each other. They were like two gunfighters sizing each other up, prior to one of them pulling his gun first.

Eventually, it was Varga who spoke next.

"Perhaps, Herr Neuer, your timing has been better than you could possibly have imagined."

Neuer inclined his head again. "I am so pleased to hear that, Herr Varga."

"I need someone to run the German arm of my business," Varga then explained. "I do not wish to return to the Fatherland, it holds too many painful memories for me. However, if you do not mind working from within Germany, then I would be willing to offer you a job."

Neuer smiled again. "I have nothing to fear from returning to Germany, Herr Varga. I would be honoured to work for your company."

"I should say, Herr Neuer, that I have other plans in mind that go beyond the boundaries of the Varga Corporation. I will be looking for people who I can trust, people who will be asked to take on a dual role within my company, perhaps step outside the law in the process."

"It all sounds very intriguing, Herr Varga and I can certainly say, for myself, that you would have my full support in whatever you might ask me to do."

"Coming from a potential blackmailer, that hardly carries much weight, Herr Neuer," commented Varga.

"May I ask what you have in mind?" Neuer then said.

"You may ask, Herr Neuer, but you will not be given an answer, at least not for the moment. I need to sort out one or two things first. In the meantime, there is one thing you can do for me?"

"You only have to ask."

"Gather three men around you who can be trusted implicitly. Have them on call and bring them to a meeting that I intend organising once I am ready to launch my new idea."

"My curiosity is through the roof, Herr Varga. Do the men in question need to have any particular skills?"

"Beyond loyalty, probably not," said Varga, finishing his coffee.

Neuer took the hint that their meeting was probably coming to an end. He drank his coffee and stood up. He grabbed his coat off the chair.

"What will happen next?" he then said.

Varga stood up as well. "I will arrange for you to be put on the payroll immediately. If you would leave account details with Marie and an address at which you can be contacted, then we can get started at once. I will put a little extra into your account, so that you can keep the three men you choose in payment until I contact you. In the meantime, we will arrange for office space to be acquired, probably in Bonn. Once we have the office for you, you will be able to move there and find accommodation."

"Very good, Herr Varga," Neuer then said, holding out his hand, "thank you for giving me this opportunity."

Varga shook the man's hand.

"Something tells me that I didn't really have much option," he said.

Neuer let go of Varga's hand and turned towards the door. As he put his hand on the door handle, he turned.

"I won't let you down, Herr Varga. I will never let you down."

And with that, Franz Neuer left the room. Varga sat down again. A memory burned itself into his mind's eye. It was a memory of a cold morning with poor unfortunates being rounded up. A memory of a girl being led away to a car and the coldness of the SS officer's smile.

Hans Varga would never like Franz Neuer, but he did know that when the man said he'd never let him down, he really meant it.

January 1951 – Puerto de Soller, Majorca

There were five men in the room. They were all smoking cigarettes and there was a thickening cloud hanging just above their heads. They were drinking large glasses of brandy and there was a general feeling of contentment from the fact that they had just enjoyed an excellent meal.

The five men were Hans Varga, Franz Neuer, Wolfgang Brandt, Sigi Trautman and Helmut Breitner. Apart from Varga, the others had been in the Waffen SS during the war and apart from Brandt, had all been involved in a variety of atrocities, none of which had continued to lay heavily on their collective conscience. Few of the Waffen SS had ever had a conscience. They were, however, fiercely loyal to any cause that they attached themselves to, whether it be the Third Reich or the Varga Corporation.

In the two months since Varga and Neuer had first discussed working together, Trautman and Breitner had been offered and accepted jobs within the Varga Corporation. Brandt had been told that Varga had other plans for him and it was with those plans in mind that the five men met at Brandt's home on Majorca. It was situated high above the village, allowing a view across the water that was spectacular on a sunny day. Brandt had moved there in 1948, using money had had kept hidden in the latter months of the war, to start a new life for himself. Brandt lived in the house on his own, apart from his housekeeper, Ramona. In terms of employment, he had been rather drifting until he received the call from Neuer.

To be offered an opportunity with the Varga Corporation was something that could not be refused.

"Well, I think Kumm's work is wonderful," Trautman was saying.

He was referring to a former Major General of the Waffen-SS, Otto Kumm. He had been fighting a battle to overturn the decision taken, at the end of the war, to declare the SS to be a criminal organisation.

As long as the SS veterans were deemed to be criminals they could not claim their army pension along with comrades in other sections of the military. This meant that many men were suffering undue hardship merely from being associated with the crimes of others. As well as fighting the original decision, Kumm also wanted to set up an organisation, which would provide help to those SS veterans in the meantime.

Kumm's organisation would be known in German as the Hilfsgemeinschaft auf Gegenseitigkeit der Angehörigen der ehemaligen Waffen-SS, or more commonly HIAG.

There was a general agreement in the room that the work being carried out by Kumm was worthy of their support. However, Hans Varga had other ideas. Yes, there might be a place for contributing to organisations, such as HIAG, but he had far grander plans for what he wanted to do with his money. Of course, it helped not being ex-SS himself; he didn't have the same ties as the others, the same need to come together and protect everything they had stood for, prior to and during the war.

Brandt was the perfect host. He provided cigars and brandy, topping up glasses whenever the need arose. The atmosphere in the room was convivial, as if it were no more than a party for old friends. Only they weren't old friends. They were ex-colleagues, joined in a secret pact by their past indiscretions.

As they settled down to more brandy, all eyes kept flicking in Varga's direction. He was the reason they were all there. To some, jobs had been offered, but Varga had also hinted at something much more. He had hinted that he had plans to make Germany strong again, to put the country back at the top of successful, European countries. He was still annoyed by the way the allies had treated Germany after the surrender. He was still annoyed at the fact his country was now split, with only half of Germany standing any chance of developing as a strong and independent country.

Outside, it was now dark and from the window of Brandt's living room, it was possible to look down on harbour below, where the lights twinkled like a giant Christmas tree. It was an idyllic setting, one that belied the horrors that the men gathered in that room, had inflicted during their military service.

Varga could tell that the room was now getting restless. His fellow diners were spending more time looking his way, than they were in conversation. He felt the time had come to put them all out of their misery and to finally explain his masterplan for the future.

"If you might all make yourselves comfortable," Varga then said.

Brandt checked that all the glasses were full, then took his own seat. Silence fell. The floor had now been handed over to Hans Varga. He did not stand up; he did not feel any need.

"Gentlemen, whilst I was not a member of the SS during the war, I have always known and respected your loyalty to the oath you took all those years ago. I do not ask that you take a second oath to me, but I do ask that you give me the same loyalty as you did to the SS organisation."

There were general mutterings, along the lines of 'that goes without saying.' Varga smiled, then continued.

"Otto Kumm seeks to help ex-SS members, by providing financial support, where it is most needed. I applaud what he is doing, but I happen to think that it doesn't go far enough. Our ex-military colleagues do not want handouts; they do not want charity; they want the opportunity to work and make money for themselves and their families. They also want to be a part of a strong and hopefully one day, united Germany. We did not fight two World Wars to end up the poor relation of European politics. Germany is a proud country and we are all proud to be German. Adolf Hitler tapped into that pride, sold us a story and we all believed him. Look where his ideals got us."

Varga looked around the room and could still see an expression, on one or two faces, that took umbrage to anyone criticising the Führer.

"Anyway, I want to set about achieving what Adolf Hitler tried to achieve. I don't speak of world domination, but I do speak of a Germany that controls Europe; only we do not achieve that domination through military might. Instead, we achieve it through stealth. We will slowly take control of Europe and very few people will even see it happening."

"I like what I'm hearing," Franz Neuer then said, "but how, exactly, can we take over Europe and have no one notice?"

Varga smiled again, then drew back on his cigar and blew a heavy, cloud of smoke towards the ceiling.

"By doing it one step at a time, my dear Franz. As you all know, my Corporation is run by a Board of Directors, who remain independent of the actual running of the company. The day-to-day activities are overseen by a Chief Executive. Sigi and Helmut, this is the role you will play in Paris and Amsterdam. However, alongside the work that my Chief Executives will do for my Corporation, they will also do work for an organisation that I am going to call Freiheit. A good choice of name, I feel sure you'll agree, as we all seek that *freedom* to be ourselves again and not to have our past indiscretions constantly revisiting us."

Everyone seemed to agree with that philosophy.

It would just be nice for everyone to be able to use their real names again. It was Brandt who spoke next.

"I've tried not to be too impatient, Herr Varga, but the others in the room know that they have a future in your Corporation, whereas I have been offered nothing to date. May I ask if you have any plans for me, or are you simply here to enjoy my hospitality?"

Varga smiled. "I commend your patience, Wolfgang, and you will be pleased to know that I have come to the point where your job can now be discussed. I want you to remain outside of my legitimate business and to be the one who will oversee all that Freiheit does over the coming years. You will be my eyes and ears, reporting back on all matters pertaining to Freiheit. An organisation, such as Freiheit, can only be successful when it exists under the radar; when it goes about its business with others totally unaware that it even exists."

Brandt grinned broadly.

"I like the sound of this Freiheit, Herr Varga, but I still fail to see how we can gain control of Europe."

One step at a time, Wolfgang. The Varga Corporation allows me to base Sigi in Paris, Helmut in Amsterdam and Franz in Bonn. That gives Freiheit a foothold in three European countries before we have to do anything more. They will be Chief Executives when wearing their Varga Corporation hat and they will be known as Tongues when working for Freiheit. The term comes from the Knights of St John; look it up, you might learn something."

There was a ripple of laughter around the room. Varga then continued.

"I aim to add London and Zurich to my list of Tongues, with other cities possibly being considered as well."

"But how, exactly?" pressed Brandt. He wanted to understand but, for the moment, he simply couldn't.

"We begin by building a team beneath each Tongue. They will be made up, mainly, of ex-military colleagues, who will be grateful for the offer of a proper job and who will, also, have the necessary skills when our actions veer a little from the straight and narrow, if you get my meaning."

Another ripple of laughter went around the room. Varga continued.

"After that we will start identifying candidates for positions of authority. We will aim to help those candidates reach the very top of their chosen profession and from there they will be able to influence events in our favour. We aim for the day when every top politician, or Chief Executive, will be working for the benefit of Freiheit ahead of anything else."

Varga drank a little more from his glass and looked around the other faces. There was an excitement in their expressions, with even Brandt fully understanding what was planned. Varga spoke again.

"We start with our own Government. We slowly get people on-side with us and, hopefully in a relatively short space of time, we will have control of that Government."

"I already have a few useful contacts in mind," Neuer said, "I'm convinced we can breathe life into Herr Varga's idea almost immediately."

Helmut Breitner was the only one in the room not looking so enthusiastic about what he was hearing. Varga noticed.

"Helmut, you don't look convinced."

Breitner took a moment to speak, conscious that he might now be speaking out of turn.

"It all sounds wonderful, Herr Varga, but it also sounds expensive. Surely, we are going to have to buy a lot of support, if we want to achieve the ultimate goal of controlling every government in Europe?"

"You are quite right, Helmut, this is going to cost a lot of money and that is why, as part of your role with the Varga Corporation, you will also be required to raise funds for Freiheit. Obviously, the manner in which we fund the two organisations will differ considerably. For the Varga Corporation it will all be legitimate business, properly accounted for and with a clear audit trail, which anyone could follow. On the other hand, the money raised for Freiheit will not be accounted for in the same way. That money can come from anywhere, as long as it's in large amounts and can increase our war chest quickly. I'm guessing that Freiheit business will involve major crime; let's rob banks if we need to, just don't get caught."

Laughter rippled around the room again.

"Where will the Freiheit money go?" Brandt then asked.

"We will set up a series of accounts in Zurich and I aim to appoint someone who will be based there and act as our official accountant. You, Wolfgang, will oversee all the action that is taken in the name of Freiheit and our man in Zurich will be responsible for all the financial transactions. Of course, the two of you will be required to work closely together, so I'll let you know as soon as I find someone suitable."

Varga again looked around the room. To some extent, the others looked shell-shocked. They had expected news, but perhaps not on such a grand scale. It was Brandt who spoke next.

"Perhaps I can help to get the war chest off to a strong start."

"How so?" said Varga.

Brandt then went on to tell the room a story.

It was a short story, but it concluded with the possibility of the fledgling Freiheit getting its hands on a large amount of money.

The story involved the pocket battleship, *Graf Spee* and certain items it had been meant to take to South America and lodge in a bank there. The year had been 1939 and the items in question had been varied in size and format, but had all been worth a great deal of money. Word was that it had been Hitler's nest egg for after the war.

Anyway, the plan did not work out the way it was meant to. The British got wind of where the *Graf Spee* was and had, ultimately, chased it into Montevideo harbour where the captain, Hans Langsdorff had no alternative, other than to lodge his valuables in the bank there.

"How do you know all this?" Trautman asked.

Brandt smiled and continued.

"After lodging the valuables in the bank, Langsdorff went to the German Embassy in Montevideo and spoke to a man by the name of Edgar Held. The idea was that someone, within the Embassy, would know about the whereabouts of the valuables, in case Langsdorff didn't get a chance to tell anyone else. It was just as well he did tell Edgar because, as you all know, the Graf Spee was scuttled and Langsdorff committed suicide, all in a very short space of time."

"So, what happened to the valuables?" Breitner now asked.

"They were left in the bank and because he chose not to tell anyone, Edgar Held remained the only person to know it was there."

"Did Edgar get the valuables at the end of the war?" Varga now enquired.

"In a manner of speaking," Brandt replied with a mischievous grin. "Edgar was transferred back to Berlin before the war ended. There had been talk of him being drafted; after all, it was a time when every able-bodied man, no matter how young or how old, was being given a uniform and a gun and told to go off and defend his country. Fortunately, for Edgar, the war ended before he had to raise a gun in anger."

"Tell us about the valuables," prompted Varga, becoming a little tired of the side stories.

"I met with Edgar, quite by chance, in a bar in what was left of Berlin, in early forty-six. He got very drunk that night and he told me the story of the valuables. I pressed him for more details and he then told me that he was the only person to have the papers required for the release of those valuables. To cut a long story short, I now have those papers. If you can get me to

Montevideo, I can get you a huge payment for your war chest, minus say ten per cent for my trouble."

Varga considered the matter for a moment. He had no intention of asking what had happened to poor Edgar, that seemed obvious to everyone in the room. Finally, he spoke.

"Okay. I'll get you to Montevideo and you can have your ten per cent. How best do we then sell those valuables?"

"I have certain contacts who could be of use to us," said Brandt.

"As do I," added Sigi.

"So, between us, we ought to be able to change goods into money fairly quickly," added Brandt.

"Excellent," Varga then said. "All that I ask is you sell the valuables in such a way as to not connect the deal to anyone in this room. We need complete anonymity, is that understood?"

They all nodded.

"Meanwhile," Varga continued, "I will complete my search for an accountant and arrange for the necessary bank accounts to be opened. I'll let you all have those bank account numbers as soon as I have them myself."

Breitner continued to look concerned. Where the other saw opportunity and excitement, Breitner problems. It was he who spoke next.

"What happens to Freiheit if something happens to you, Herr Varga?"

Varga thought for a moment. "When I die, the Board of the Varga business empire will vote to elect a new Chairman. In the legitimate business world that is the natural progression of things. At the moment of my death, however, all links between the Varga Corporation and Freiheit will cease. No one else knows about it, so no one else can keep that link going. You will be denied the donations from my company, but I would hope by then, that Freiheit will be strong enough to stand on its own two feet. If I do not get the chance to select a successor, then it will fall to Wolfgang to do that. I would wish someone new to be brought in, rather than one of you step up. I hope you will ensure my wishes are carried out."

"Of course, Herr Varga," said Brandt.

"Is everyone on-board with what I am suggesting?" Varga then asked.

Brandt hurried to fill all the glasses again.

"In that case, gentlemen," Brandt then said, "I think it is time for us to drink two toasts."

With their glasses charged, all eyes turned towards him.

"Firstly," he said, raising his glass, "to Herr Varga, may he have a long and healthy life."

They all laughed. Glasses were held towards Hans Varga, as his name was shouted and a drink taken.

"Secondly," Brandt then said, once more raising his glass. "To Freiheit."

The two words were shouted by everyone and a further drink taken.

Freiheit had now been officially launched.

Friday 21st July 1961 – Puerto de Soller, Majorca

Three boats had docked in the harbour at Puerto de Soller, each one bringing two guests to the island who were destined to be living with Wolfgang Brandt for a couple of days. The harbour followed the curve of the bay and the train to Soller was just pulling out as the men gathered on the quayside.

The sky above was a cloudless blue and the sun beat down with relentless heat. The small gathering stood and waited for the cars to arrive, which would take them the short journey up to Brandt's new house on the hill, overlooking the bay. Once the cars arrived it did not take long to transport the men and their luggage up to the custom- built villa where they were each allocated a bedroom and informed that dinner would be served at seven.

Brandt had bought the land and had the property built on the proceeds he had made from Freiheit. He had even been able to build a house with a wall around it so he now felt safer, better protected from those who still sought to find and punish ex-Nazis.

The house had been built using inspiration taken from a house that Frank Lloyd Wright had designed in Bear Run, Pennsylvania. Brandt had seen photographs of the property and had loved the way it had been designed. He didn't want an exact copy, but he did ask for an approximation to the original design. He had been greatly pleased by the end product and now liked to show his home off to others, as much as he could. This would be the finest occasion yet, a gathering to celebrate the first ten years of Freiheit; giving them all their first chance to properly acknowledge the successes they had shared over those ten years. There had been no downs, only ups.

The spectre of being a wanted man still hung over most of them, but mainly thanks to the success of Freiheit, they were now rich wanted men. They could all afford the good life in whatever shape that took. To the outside world they were legitimate businessmen, holding a senior post in a highly successful company. Beneath the surface, they were making even more money, none of it legal.

Brandt had worked hard to organise Freiheit in the image imagined by Hans Varga when he had first had the idea. Freiheit now existed as a proper business, though few knew of its existence and that included many of the people working for it. Apart from the centralisation of some of the administration and the fact that all financial matters were dealt with by Gerd Seeler, in Zurich, everything else that was

Freiheit existed in the name of companies which, on the face of it, all appeared legitimate in their own right.

It was a brilliant way to have Freiheit operate in plain sight.

Of the six guests arriving that weekend, only one of them was not German. His name was Conrad Phillips, a sixty-three-year-old man who was small of stature but high on business acumen. He had been born to a German mother and brought up to regard Germany as his second home. He had managed to miss being called up for the First World War, thanks to his father getting him a job in the Civil Service.

Phillips had then been slightly too old to be called up for the Second World War although, by then, his sympathies for Germany would have been more likely to get him arrested, rather than called up. He had chosen not to voice those sympathies and that had been the only reason he had not spent much of the nineteen forties in prison.

After the war, Phillips had continued to build his business, cashing in on Germany's need for practical everything. It was as a result of the business he had done in Germany that led to Phillips meeting Hans Varga in 1952. The two men became friends very quickly and when Phillips returned to England, in 1953, Varga had asked him to become Tongue of Great Britain. Thus, making him an active member of Freiheit.

Phillips had been delighted to play any part in making Germany great again. He may have had an English name, but his heart was German. Due to the many business ventures, he was already involved in, it was agreed that Phillips would remain outside of the Varga Corporation.

The other member of the six gathering that weekend, who was not also a Chief Executive within Varga's company, was Gerd Seeler. He had been brought on-board in 1951 to be Freiheit's accountant and it had been felt that he could operate more freely, were he not tied to any other job. He and Brandt had struck up a strong, working relationship and between them they had ensured that Freiheit continued to go from strength to strength. Seeler had his office in Zurich and the sign on the wall outside proclaimed him to be exactly what he was: an accountant. It did not, however, indicate in any shape or form, that he was accountant to only one client. Everything else in his files was a smokescreen.

In fact, much of Freiheit was a smokescreen. The entire organisation was like a giant sleight of hand, while they had everyone looking in one direction, they were busy making money in another. They were also busy bringing influence to bear on Boards of Directors, Chief Executives and politicians. They had fingers in many pies, some of those fingers were already active and others were lying dormant, waiting for the day they'd be asked to spring into action.

As the men gathered that weekend they were all more than satisfied with how the first ten years had gone. Now plans would have to be made to ensure that next ten years and beyond, would be as successful. There was no time to rest on their laurels, there was still much to be done.

After dinner, on that first night, they adjourned to the sitting room, at the front of the house and occupied a series of comfortable chairs that had been laid out especially for that weekend. Drinks and cigars were offered and accepted and once everyone had settled, Hans Varga began to speak.

"Gentlemen, thank you for coming here this weekend and helping us celebrate the first ten years of Freiheit. It has been a successful ten years, a time in which we have grown to be an organisation employing a large number of people over many countries. In size, Freiheit now almost rivals the Varga Corporation and we must all thank Wolfgang for not only building that organisation, but ensuring its success."

A murmur of appreciation was heard around the room.

"I would also like to thank Gerd for his contribution, these last ten years. Without someone keeping a close eye on our finances, we would not have been so successful. Our central account is now in the millions and for that, we should be very proud. However, we cannot meet like this simply to pat each other on the back and expect to carry on as normal. If we are to maintain our success, then we need to ensure that the future is as productive as the past. Over the last five years we have developed a need for the Grand Committee to meet every quarter and at those meetings we have concentrated on current issues. This weekend, gentlemen, I want us to concentrate on the future. I want us to draw up a plan that will take us through the Sixties and onwards into the Seventies. I want us to have a clear view of where Freiheit is going. When we meet again, to reflect on the decade that was the Sixties, I want us all to still feel as upbeat as we do now. We will only do that as long as we continue forward, with clarity of thought and a desire for success. To help you give some thought to how you see our future, may I ask Wolfgang to say a few words about our present."

Brandt thanked Varga for his opening words and then launched into a rather lengthy report. He covered far more than had been necessary, even going as far as telling those in the room that Freiheit now had people building rockets and sending men into Space.

"The Americans will, of course, take all the credit, should they beat the Russians in their space research," he went on to say, "but the truth is, gentlemen, that without German technology and German know-how, the Americans would still need to put their rockets in bottles."

More laughter passed through the room.

Brandt then moved on to a more specific topic. In agreement with Herr Varga, Brandt had had commemorative medals struck, one for each of the men in that room. They were gold medals, along the same design as the old German Assault Badges. Where there had once been a swastika, however, there was now the Freiheit logo. To anyone else seeing them, the logo would have been meaningless, but to the men in that room it added meaning to a medal they were to receive with pride and renewed encouragement to carry on with the good work.

Once Brandt had stopped talking, the floor was then thrown open for ideas concerning the future of Freiheit. For the next three hours they discussed every possibility suggested and by the time they decided to call it a day, Wolfgang Brandt had, potentially, enough work to keep him busy for far more than the next ten years.

PART TWO

Early May 1971 – Reykjavik, Iceland

The small, military aircraft dropped below the cloud and circled the airport below awaiting clearance to land. On board the plane, apart from the crew, were two agents of Military Intelligence (London), more commonly known as MILO. The agency had been set up, towards the end of the 1940s, essentially to keep an eye on Germany and ensure that another Hitler did not rise from the ashes.

MILO had been formed after MI6 had announced that it did not have the capacity to watch one country, ahead of all others, if it were to protect Great Britain's security. MI5 were not interested in venturing outside British shores, so the government took the decision to have a third section, within Military Intelligence.

MILO was officially born in 1948, although an element of its work, had been carried out by MI6, until they decided they couldn't do it anymore.

In the early days, MILO employees had taken a back seat to those in MI5 and MI6. Much of what MILO did, especially through the 1950s, had been to observe, note and then pass on to its big brothers. Over the years, however, times had slowly changed and now MILO pretty much did everything, without any need to feel subservient to those big brothers.

MILO now had operatives in most of the European countries, as well as strong links with local police and other intelligence organisations. MILO was capable of picking up on their own leads and running with them, wherever those leads might take them.

A current lead involved a man calling himself Sigi Trautman. For the last twenty years, MILO had been keeping an eye on a company that appeared to be growing from strength to strength. That company had been the Varga Corporation and it had not gone unnoticed that a few of that company's Chief Executives appeared to have a past that only began as the war ended. Trautman was one of those men.

MILO had not been able to learn much about Sigi Trautman, but they had been sufficiently intrigued by the man as to place him under surveillance for the past year.

Since the early Fifties, MILO had become suspicious of the existence of an organisation they'd heard about, called *Freiheit*. At first there had been no clarity to reports about Freiheit, it had simply been a word that cropped up at various times. Eventually, a picture began to form. It was still sketchy, but it now seemed possible that Freiheit was connected to ex-SS officers. Was it possible, therefore, that the Varga Corporation and its employees might be connected to Freiheit, in some way?

It had been with that question in mind that MILO had taken to keeping an eye on Sigi Trautman. All had gone well until five days ago.

A MILO agent had rather given himself away one day, as he'd followed Trautman from shop to shop. Later that same day, the men in the MILO monitoring room, realised they were getting nothing but silence from Trautman's home. He was supposed to be there and yet he was making no sound at all.

After an hours silence, the senior officer in the monitoring room had ordered two of his men to visit Trautman's home and confirm he was still at home. He wasn't.

A check of airports and railway stations eventually confirmed that no one, using the name Trautman, had apparently left Paris. However, one eagle-eyed airport employee reported dealing with a man who had acted very suspiciously while having his paperwork checked. When shown a photograph of Sigi Trautman, he confirmed it was the same man and that he was travelling under the name Herman Langsdorff.

Anyone going as far as carrying false identification had to have something to hide. Sir Tavish saw this as a major lead and dispatched his two best men to catch up with Trautman and to, hopefully, get answers to the many questions that still surrounded the man.

Those two agents sat, side by side, each looking out of their side of the plane. Ben Ward was thirty-five years of age, ruggedly good looking and with dark hair that he kept in a modern style, which was far longer than might have been expected for a Government employee. He had been with MILO for ten years having been recruited direct from Oxford University. The Ox-Bridge joke had always been that only Intelligence Agents and Russian spies got jobs after leaving Oxford and Cambridge.

Mike Brown was looking out of the window on the other side of the plane. Mike was thirty-two years old and had been with MILO for seven years, four of which had been as Ben's partner. Mike's hairstyle was shorter and his hair almost black. He had been told that he looked like the actor Ralph

Bates, though he had never really seen the likeness himself. At six feet tall, Mike was two inches shorter than Ben. Both their height difference and university education were a constant reason for them having somewhat heated discussions at times.

They both also enjoyed success with the ladies. Mike, for the moment, was between relationships, but Ben appeared to be getting serious over Camilla Carter, a woman he'd been seeing for a little while now. Mike was concerned that his partner might be thinking of engagement rings and weddings. He hoped that marriage would not be a reason for Ben leaving MILO. They worked well together, as well as being mates.

Clearance was given to land and the small aircraft did one final circuit of Reykjavik Airport before straightening and slowly descending on to the tarmac. It was a perfect landing. The plane taxied to the airport buildings and drew to a halt.

Ben and Mike climbed down from the plane and now stood on the tarmac stretching limbs and slowly bringing life back to aching legs. The airport had been there since nineteen thirteen, although it had been modernised and upgraded during the war by the British and Americans who had been based there. Iceland had been seen as a strategically good location for the Atlantic shipping and the Allies had occupied it before Germany could make a move.

There was a black, official looking car sitting on the tarmac around sixty feet from where the two agents were standing. Leaning against the car was a fair-haired man, wearing a black suit and sunglasses. He looked like a professional hit-man but Ben and Mike presumed that this was their official lift in to Reykjavik.

They crossed to the car and the fair-haired man stood up and smiled. "Welcome to Reykjavik, gentlemen. My name is Haddur."

They shook hands and got in to the car. Overhead the clouds had parted sufficiently to let the sun shine through, which made Haddur's sunglasses at least appropriate, if not fashionable. They left the airport and drove the two kilometres in to the heart of Reykjavik with its brightly coloured houses and quaint shops. They followed the road round by the water and then continued a short distance further until they arrived at a white, wooden fronted, symmetrical building with a short stair leading up to the front door. The back of the building looked out across the water. They stopped in the car park and a cool air greeted Ben and Mike as they got out of the car.

Another man was waiting for them at the door of the building.

"Welcome, gentlemen, my name is Petur Jonasson and I am the Deputy Commissioner within the Icelandic Intelligence Service."

"Ben Ward."

"Mike Brown."

They shook hands.

"Welcome, again, to you both. Do come in, I have coffee ready for you."

Both Ben and Mike were struck by how perfect the Deputy Commissioner's English was. He spoke with a clarity that was seldom heard amongst the many local dialects of Great Britain.

"This is a lovely building," Ben said as they entered the front door.

"Yes it is. Your Ambassador used to live in this house and Sir Winston Churchill famously visited it during the war, as did Marlene Dietrich I believe."

"Not at the same time, I hope," commented Mike. The other two men smiled at the very idea.

They were shown in to a large room at the back of the house which had a row of windows along one wall, providing a great view of the water. Between the house and the water was a road, though it did not seem greatly bothered by traffic. Within the room was a large, conference table with seventeen chairs set around it.

In the corner of the room, under the window, sat a trolley, on which the coffee and cups had been placed.

Petur went over and poured three coffees. He took them back to the table, along with milk and sugar.

"Do sit down," he then said to his visitors.

Once they were all seated, Petur started to speak.

"Your organisation asked us to pick up on a man using the name Herman Langsdorff. From what we were told, Langsdorff has been using the name Sigi Trautman, since the war, but there is every reason to believe he'll turn out to be a war criminal, trying to hide his past."

Ben nodded. "We don't have a great deal more to add. He is a Chief Executive with the Varga Corporation and a man who, as Sigi Trautman, has only existed since the war. Although we've been watching him for a while, we really haven't learned that much. If it hadn't been for his non-existent past and the fact he did a runner the minute he clocked one of our agents, we wouldn't be here."

Petur now nodded. He shuffled a selection of papers, which lay on the table in front of him and pulled one to the top.

"We've checked the information at the airport and can confirm that Herman Langsdorff *did* arrive on a flight that had originated in Paris. However, as far as we can ascertain, no one of that name has ever been on the island before. As you might expect, everyone tends to know everyone else and a stranger, no matter what nationality he may be, does rather stick out in our communities."

"So, we've lost him, for the moment," said Ben.

"Perhaps not," added Petur, moving another sheet of paper to the top of the pile in front of him. "Around twelve years ago, we received a tip from contacts within the West German police, that we may have had a war criminal in our midst. His real name was Jürgen Maier, an ex-SS officer wanted for a number of atrocities carried out in the latter stages of the war. We knew of two Germans living on the island and immediately had them both checked out. One of them turned out to be too old to have ever served in the Second World War, but the other interested us greatly. He was calling himself Martin Goetze and he lived in a cottage, pretty much miles from anywhere. However, as soon as we showed any interest in him, he disappeared. We came to the conclusion that he must have left the island on a boat, as we found no trace of him at the airport."

Petur then took something from within the pile of papers and slid it across to Ben. It was a photograph.

"That is a picture of Jürgen Maier," he then said.

Ben studied the photograph. It wasn't the greatest quality, but he was pretty sure he was also looking at a photograph of Sigi Trautman.

"This is our man, I'm sure of it."

Mike took the photograph and looked at it. He agreed immediately. Petur sipped at his coffee and rearranged the papers into a tidier pile.

"In that case, gentlemen, we need to take a little drive. Maier's home, as I said, is well away from civilisation and, to be honest, was a little rundown the last time I visited. However, if he is back on the island, I can't believe he would have gone anywhere else."

The three men finished their coffee and then headed out to the car again. Petur spoke to Haddur in Icelandic and then turned to look at Ben and Mike.

"You'll be heading up towards the Gullfoss," Petur now explained. "That's where Goetze had his cottage. Haddur will drive you there and provide you with the necessary authority to have a proper look around. I only hope you find him there."

"The Gullfoss?" repeated Ben.

"Yes, in English it would be the Golden Falls. They are a delight to see."

Ben and Mike climbed into the back of the car and Haddur had a further conversation with his superior. He then got in behind the wheel and started the engine. The clouds had gathered again and the sun was hidden from view, casting a greyness across the land.

They drove out of Reykjavik and their route took them through terrain that was almost other-worldly. Nearer to the Gullfoss, the land began to look even more like another planet. Here was where geology came to the surface of Planet Earth, where holes were ripped in the earth's core by the movement of the tectonic plates. It was a wild and rugged domain in which Man was probably never meant to survive. However, when did Man ever listen to Nature? Where there was a heat source there was a possibility for Man to build himself a home and put down his roots.

Martin Goetze had done just that. Around half a mile off the only road for miles he had acquired a single-storey home for himself along with a garage at the back.

Haddur stopped the car outside the house just as rain now started to fall. Even in the wet, the area had its own picturesque look to it, though none of the three men really had time to take in the scenery. They were more interested in the half-ruined property that stood before them. They were also very interested in the fact a car was parked at the side of the house. Was someone else already there?

Haddur led the way to the front door. Mike was looking around outside. Haddur called out, giving any occupant the chance to come to the door. They waited, but there was no reaction,

"Do either of you have a gun?" Haddur then enquired, looking from Ben to Mike and back again.

Ben and Mike shook their heads.

"Neither do I," added Haddur, "so here's hoping Herr Maier isn't armed."

Haddur put his weight to the front door and pushed it open. Inside, the house was a mess. It looked as if no one had been there since Goetze had walked away from it all those years ago. They split up and each took a different part of the house.

"In here!" came the almost instant cry from Mike. The others hurried to join him. He was upstairs, in the front room. He was standing inside the doorway, looking up a man hanging from the main beam that ran the length of the room. The rope around his neck had pulled tight, squeezing the last of any breath out of him. His face was discoloured and his tongue protruding. He was dead, but maybe not for that long.

"Is it Trautman?" Ben asked.

"Can't be sure," said Mike. "but it looks like it could be."

"I'll arrange to have him taken back to Reykjavik," Haddur then said. "We can get him formally identified there. I have a radio in the car, if you'll excuse me."

"Do you think he could have come back to Iceland to kill himself?" Mike then said to Ben.

"You don't go on a trip to kill yourself," replied Ben. "There must have been unfinished business here, which he needed to attend to; then he killed himself." Ben looked around the derelict building, "But what could that have been?"

While Haddur was still outside, using the car radio, Mike and Ben continued searched the house, ever hopeful that they might find something useful. In one of the back rooms, they found floorboards pulled up and a space that would have been big enough to conceal a number of items.

"Maybe, what he came back for was in there," said Mike, nodding down at the hole in the floor.

"Found it empty and decided to end it all?" added Ben, with little in his tone to indicate he even believed that himself.

It didn't make much sense to either of them. They finished looking around the rest of the house and then ended up back at the front door, just as Haddur was coming in. He explained that others were now on their way and that he would have to remain there until they arrived. That, of course, meant that Ben and Mike would have to remain there as well.

Ben told Haddur about the possibility that Trautman had come back for a specific item, citing the hole in the floor of the back room as evidence that *something* had definitely been hidden there in the past. However, that something clearly wasn't there now and nothing had been found lying around the house. That meant it hadn't been Trautman who had found it, unless another person had been there to take it away for him. But why go to all that trouble and why the need for him to kill himself? Was it purely because he knew he had been compromised?

"I took a closer look at the tyre tracks out there," Haddur then said, "and there's evidence of more than one car having been here recently."

"So, there's every chance that Trautman *did* have company," said Ben.

"Came here to meet with someone," added Mike. "And that other person took away whatever was hidden here."

Ben looked around and thought for a moment.

"That all fits, but why then would Trautman feel the need to kill himself?"

"Fear of being caught?" suggested Haddur. "A lot of these ex-Nazis choose to kill themselves rather than face trial."

Ben nodded. He knew that to be true of many of them, but he still couldn't see the sense in Trautman travelling all that way to then kill himself. Ben then turned to Haddur.

"How quickly could a post mortem be carried out on our friend up there?" he asked.

"You thinking it's not suicide?" added Mike.

"We have to consider the possibility that Trautman's guest was here to collect whatever had been hidden, but also to clear up any loose ends. Knowing he was under scrutiny might have been what sealed his fate."

"I'll arrange for a post mortem to be conducted as quickly as possible," Haddur then said, "though it'll be tomorrow before you'll get a report."

Ben was happy to wait.

Eventually, the forensic team arrived and Haddur took the time to tell them exactly what he wanted of them. The body was to be taken for a post mortem. Haddur would arrange for the post mortem to be carried out, though there was every chance they'd have to come from outside of the island. Iceland was not abundant with pathologists.

They had then driven back to Reykjavik, taking their time so that Ben and Mike could appreciate a little more of the island. It was now too late for them to return directly to London, so rooms were booked for the night.

Over an evening meal they discussed their excitement at the fact Sigi Trautman might yet prove to be the strongest lead MILO had had in a long time. If someone deemed him to be such a risk that they needed to kill him then surely that meant he was hiding an even bigger secret than even MILO had thought.

Might that secret be Freiheit related? Had the inadvertently come across a major player in the Freiheit organisation?

Both Ben and Mike seriously hoped so.

*

The following day, Ben and Mike returned to London. By then, they knew the body they'd found was that of Sigi Trautman, real name Jürgen Maier. They also knew he'd definitely been murdered. There was evidence of garrotting under the rope around his neck. Someone had clearly wanted Trautman silenced forever.

The information gathered on Iceland had given MILO its first clear link between the Varga Corporation and ex-SS war criminals. Did it also, however, give them the first clear link between the Varga Corporation and Freiheit?

*

That same day, Wolfgang Brandt had received a telephone call. Only the word *done* was spoken and the call ended, but it was enough to tell Brandt that his colleague and acquaintance, Sigi Trautman, was now dead.

He put the phone down and poured himself a drink. From the day he'd been appointed to the job he did for Freiheit he had taken responsibility for the major decisions. That included terminations. No one was above being terminated if it was deemed necessary. Poor Sigi had become a necessary termination the minute he'd try to run.

Trautman had phoned Brandt from Iceland and explained why he was there. In doing so, he signed his own death warrant. A member of Brandt's clear-up team was sent to Iceland with simple instructions:

Remove any damaging evidence and terminate Sigi Trautman.

Over his drink, Brandt thought about two things. The first was that he would now need to find a new man to work out of Paris; for that he would need to speak with Herr Varga. The second thought, however, was of far greater concern. It now seemed clear that MILO was beginning to be an even greater nuisance. They would all need to be a lot more careful from now on, there would be no place for complacency.

Monday, 31st May 1971 – MILO HQ, Central London

The offices for MILO were situated on Leadenhall Street in the City of London. There were five floors to the building but only the first three were explained by the brass sign affixed to the wall outside. The first two floors were owned by the National Westminster Bank and the third floor was a company of lawyers who specialised in commercial law.

The top two floors were not accessible from the street.

The casual visitor was met with a door on the staircase that was permanently locked and only meant to be used in the event of a swift evacuation.

Access to this part of the building was actually from next door. The third floor of that building was occupied by the staff of a fashion magazine. At least that was how it appeared. In reality, it was a security check for anyone visiting MILO. Behind the façade of typists and journalists was a security team with some of the most sophisticated equipment available to them.

All visitors, passing through those security checks, were then escorted through to the MILO offices. No one visited without being accompanied.

Ben Ward had arrived there at a little after eight o'clock that Wednesday morning. He walked through the typing pool and noted that most of the women were already at their desks, fingers clattering on the keyboard of their typewriters and cigarettes smouldering in the ashtray beside them.

One or two of the typists glanced up as Ben passed, a smile playing on their lips as they did so. Ben tried not to stare; it wasn't gentlemanly. Even Ben, on a daily basis, was checked by security before continuing next door. Recognising someone was no excuse for not checking their credentials thoroughly.

The MILO offices were clean, bright and modern in terms of both the décor and the equipment being used. The lower floor was where most of the technical staff worked. The upper floor was where Ben had his office and also where the rest of the senior employees were based. It was often said that the top floor did the thinking, but the floor below did all the *doing*.

Ben made his way to the office he shared with Mike and entered. He hung his jacket over the back of his chair and sat down at a desk that was already looking a mess. Overnight, items thought to be of interest to Ben, had been left on his desk by various colleagues. MILO maintained a staffing presence, twenty-four hours a day, for the entire year.

There was always someone on call, always someone ready to jump into action..

Mike put in an appearance at quarter to nine. He had brought in two coffees, one of which he offered to Ben. The offer was accepted and Ben took the coffee with him, when he went through to see the Old Man, as he was affectionately known.

Sir Tavish Viewforth's office was two doors down from where Ben and Mike worked. As befitted the Head of the Department, Sir Tavish's office was twice the size of anyone else's, though measured against the office space afforded to the Heads of MI5 and MI6, it was still modest. Ben found Sir Tavish hunched over his desk, his blue eyes peering through spectacles that had been placed towards the end of his nose. He was reading the contents of a file. As Ben entered the room, Sir Tavish looked up.

"Good morning, Ben. Sit down."

Sir Tavish Viewforth was a fifty-nine-year-old Scotsman, thought by many to be a trifle dour but also reminding others of the actor James Robertson Justice, due to his heavy build and full beard. Most things in Sir Tavish's life were deathly serious and though he did have a sense of humour it remained well hidden, especially during working hours.

Sir Tavish had lived a full life to date. Born in nineteen twelve to a mother who would dote on him all her life and a father who was to die in the trenches before he even had the chance to properly bond with his son; young Tavish grew up believing in the futility of war and forever wondering why his father had to be one of the casualties. However, when the Second World

War began in nineteen thirty-nine, Tavish Viewforth had been one of the first to sign up.

He had joined the Royal Air Force and was soon flying above Britain doing all that he could to prevent German bombers from reaching their destination. Unfortunately, he had only been flying for six months when he was shot down and had to bail out over the green fields of Kent. He was badly wounded and after a suitable period of recuperation he was told he would never be able to return to the Royal Air Force or, indeed, combat of any kind.

Instead of flying, Tavish Viewforth was directed to Military Intelligence. If he could no longer fight the Germans with his body then he would do so with his mind. He had gone on to help the likes of Ian Fleming to come up with various ways and means of confusing the Germans. He had proved to be very successful at what he did. He was an ideas man; but he also had the ability to communicate those ideas to others. He could also be very persuasive where necessary, but without ruffling feathers in the process.

He was well liked and the work he did soon brought him to the attention of a number of important people in both the military and political worlds in which he moved. He further added to his profile by playing a major part in the deceit that surrounded the D-Day landings. Viewforth had proved himself to be a master of the half-truth. He fed information to the Germans, which could so easily have been true but which, in fact, had been designed purely to have them look the other way.

Winston Churchill went on record to give credit to the men and women of the Intelligence Units who had provided the Germans with puzzles, throughout the war. By keeping the Germans tied up with things that weren't going to happen it made it easier for others to get on with planning events that would. Tavish Viewforth became better known for the work he did in Military Intelligence than he would ever have done flying Spitfires.

By the end of the war, he had shown himself to be an able intelligence officer who had risen a few ranks in the process. When the new Military Intelligence (London) section was started in nineteen forty-eight there was only one name put forward to be its Head. Tavish Viewforth had spent the last twenty-three years in charge of MILO and in that time he had been knighted, in nineteen fifty-nine, in recognition for the work he had done for his country.

Ben sat down. They had a morning meeting every day that they were both in the office. Ben, as lead agent, had the responsibility for keeping Sir Tavish up to date with events. In return, Sir Tavish would tell Ben the things he had learned from the corridors of power. It was an exchange of information rather than a boss talking to a subordinate.

That morning, however, there had been little to discuss and the meeting had not lasted very long. Ben had returned to his office and seconds after he had left Sir Tavish, the door to Sir Tavish's office had opened again and his Personal Assistant, Ralph Steadman, had entered. Steadman was a young man dressed in old man's clothes. His suits always looked like they had been made in the forties and his hairstyle and general appearance made him look twenty years older than he was.

"Sir Basil Jenkins is here to see you, Sir Tavish," Steadman said.

"The sun must be shining, Ralph, if Sir Basil has come out to play."

Steadman smiled at the rare flash of humour from his boss.

"Are you free to see him now?"

"Best show him in, he tends to sulk if we keep him waiting."

Steadman left the room but was back, moments later, with a man a few steps behind him. Sir Basil Jenkins was the Head of MI6. Although on the same level as Sir Tavish, Sir Basil lorded over a bigger building and occupied a bigger office. If he could have got away with it, he would have lorded over Sir Tavish as well. Sir Basil was a small man with a round face atop a round body. He exuded an air of pomposity, which usually led to others giving him a wide berth, if at all possible. Unfortunately, for Sir Tavish, he had no means of escape on this occasion and thus found himself rising from his chair and preparing to have a conversation with a man that he simply didn't like.

"Would you like coffee, Sir Tavish?" Steadman asked as Sir Basil passed him and headed for one of the vacant chairs.

"Would you like coffee, Basil?"

Basil Jenkins made a face. "Foul tasting stuff. Bring me a cup of tea, please. Milk and two sugars."

"And a coffee for me, Ralph," added Sir Tavish as he sat down again.

Once the door was closed Basil Jenkins began to speak. "I came here myself as there have been a few incidents, which I think fall more into your domain, than mine."

"I'm intrigued, Basil," Sir Tavish added as he sat back in his chair.

"I lost an agent last week," Sir Basil then said.

"I'm sorry to hear that. What happened to him?"

"From witness reports it would appear that his car was forced off the road."

"Then he was murdered?" commented Sir Tavish.

"So, it would seem."

"What had he been working on?"

Sir Basil took a packet of mints from his pocket and popped one in his mouth. He then put the mints back in his pocket before saying anything further.

"That's just it, his current workload involved nothing in particular; certainly nothing serious enough to get him killed. Anyway, after his death I sent a couple of agents to his flat just in case there was evidence of him working on something that we hadn't known about. They found his flat ransacked. Someone else had clearly been looking for something, though we've no idea if they found it."

"Where was this agent based?"

"Berlin."

"So, it could be the Russians?" Sir Tavish suggested.

"I doubt that very much, Tavish. West Berlin may be entirely within East Germany but there is little movement from the Russians; they seem happy to keep to their side of the fence as it were."

"Have you any idea who might have killed him?"

"Nothing concrete. However, and this is the bit that will interest you most, amongst the items found in the man's flat, was a notebook. A number of pages had been torn from the book, but it was still possible to read an imprint on one of the blank pages. The word *Freiheit* was clearly visible."

Sir Tavish sat forward; his interest grabbed by that one word.

"Was your man working on anything related to Freiheit?" Sir Tavish now asked.

"Good Lord, no. We have no interest in such matters. Far too busy than to be concerned with the possibility that Freiheit even exists. That, my friend, is very much your domain."

Sir Tavish was pleased to have at least been given his place, but the sad fact was that even *he* had no proof that Freiheit *did* exist, only a lot of suspicion and the fact the word kept cropping up in the strangest of places. Like in a notebook owned by an MI6 agent who wasn't supposed to be investigating anything of interest.

"Tell me more about this man you've lost?" Sir Tavish then enquired, though the answer was delayed by the arrival of Steadman with the beverages. Once he had left, Sir Basil began to speak.

"The agent's name was Sam Halliday. He'd been in Berlin for just under two years, but was very low in the pecking order. I mean, Sam shouldn't have been involved in anything dangerous, certainly nothing that might have got him killed."

"So, why would he have any knowledge of Freiheit?" Sir Tavish then asked.

"He shouldn't have had any knowledge of anything," came the rather blunt reply. "Look, Tavish, what do you think this Freiheit is anyway?"

Sir Tavish drank a little of his coffee.

He then placed the cup back in its saucer. He sat back in his chair and pondered on how brief he could make the reply.

"We believe it to be an organisation set up mainly by ex-SS. Exactly what they do, we're still working on, but we have reason to believe that they may have people working within companies around Europe. Their exact intent is also still unclear, though gaining an element of control would appear to be their driving force."

"What do you think they seek to control?"

"Europe probably," said Sir Tavish. It was half in jest, though the comment had not been meant as a joke.

Sir Basil scoffed. "Sounds a bit dramatic to me."

"Maybe so, but don't underestimate the effect they could be having on just about everything that we do. I mean, if Freiheit were behind Sam Halliday's death, then they've arrived at your door already."

Sir Basil drank his tea and considered that point for a moment. He then provided Sir Tavish with a little more background information on Sam Halliday and left a thin file on Sir Tavish's desk. The two men then finished their hot drinks over more general conversation.

Before Sir Basil left, Sir Tavish returned to the subject of Sam Halliday.

"I presume you're okay with my men visiting Berlin and snooping around a little?"

"No problem. I'll tell my people to be as helpful as possible and ask that you make sure your men are very careful while they are there. Whatever he was involved in, it cost Sam his life."

"My people are always careful," said Sir Tavish.

"That's the point, Tavish, so are mine and still one of them gets killed."

"Point taken," conceded Sir Tavish.

He briefly reflected on the fact that danger lurked around every corner as his staff carried out their daily assignments. They worked in the murkier corners of society, regularly coming across people with secrets to hide and those with secrets to hide were usually dangerous. There was always a danger of someone getting killed, Sir Tavish was just grateful that it had not happened very often in the time he had been the Head of MILO.

Sir Basil left and Ralph Steadman accompanied him back to the security level. While he was doing that, Sir Tavish was on the phone asking Mike Brown to come through and see him.

Wednesday, 2nd June, 1971 – Berlin

Two days later Mike was in Berlin. He had been given access to both Halliday's flat and also his desk at work. A search of both proved fruitless though he did find another reference to Freiheit on a sheet of paper in Halliday's desk drawer. No one at work could explain why Sam might have various references to Freiheit. Beyond knowing what the word meant, no one could answer any of Mike's questions either with regard to Sam, or Freiheit.

Mike had pulled together a pen picture of Sam Halliday. He had been with MI6 for ten years, but always in a relatively junior capacity. Sam had never shown any real desire to move upwards in his chosen profession, always appearing happy to take orders and have someone else do the worrying. His colleagues all spoke of Sam being a quiet man who pretty much kept himself to himself. He was a nice man and a good colleague; one they could always depend on. No one had ever considered the possibility that Sam might have been conducting his own investigation; he just didn't do things like that, they all said.

Mike had also spent time speaking to the neighbours closest to Sam's flat. One or two of them had spoken about a team of decorators turning up on what was now known to be the day after his death. These had, presumably, been the men who had ransacked the property. But why would anyone feel the need to ransack Sam Halliday's flat? What would he have had that was so important? Mike wondered if the information might have been related to Freiheit and that they had sent in the decorators.

Had Sam Halliday stumbled on something that had needed removing? Had that been why he'd been killed?

Many questions but few answers. After two days in Berlin, Mike returned to London knowing little more than when he had arrived..

Same day – Bonn

Franz Neuer stood at the window of his office, looking out across the centre of Bonn and giving thought to what he had just been told him. After weeks of believing Sigi Trautman had committed suicide here he was, being told that the man had been murdered and all in the name of protecting Freiheit.

Neuer turned and went back to his desk. Sitting on the other side of that desk was Wolfgang Brandt.

"Was there no other option?" he then said.

" I don't believe so. With MILO on his tail, he could have led them anywhere."

"And what did Herr Varga have to say about the action you took?"

"He wasn't very pleased; however, he did see the light after I explained how we must protect Freiheit at all costs. This organisation was not set-up to crumble the first time anyone starts sniffing around us. We were set-up to survive and if that means a few casualties along the way, then so be it."

Neuer thought for a moment.

"Who is to replace Sigi?"

"Herr Varga has asked for suggestions, no one knows as yet."

Neuer thought for a moment before speaking again.

"And what about MILO?"

"With Sigi dead, that lead has died with him. MILO have nothing else on us and they can continue to monitor the Varga Corporation as much as they like, they'll learn nothing about Freiheit doing that."

Neuer looked worried.

"Too many of us have hidden pasts. Do you intend killing us all, if MILO were to get too close?"

Brandt smiled. "No need to worry, Franz; MILO won't get close to anyone else. Sigi was just unlucky."

"Okay, Wolfgang, let me put my question a different way," Neuer then said. "If I, too, were to be *unlucky*, would you order my death as well?"

Brandt's expression turned to stone.

"Of course, I would Franz. We are all dispensable."

"I thought we'd lost the need for killing our own" Neuer almost snapped.

Brandt laughed. "Good God, Franz, you're the last person I would expect sentiment from. You cared little for who you ordered to be killed, back in the day. This is no different."

A part of Neuer wanted to argue, wanted to speak up for poor Sigi. However, the other part of Neuer, the part that had controlled most of his actions during the war, could see the sense in what Brandt was saying. The organisation had to survive at all costs, which mean that no one individual could ever be allowed to put the many at risk.

"Maybe I have more to lose than you, Wolfgang," Neuer finally said.

"All the more reason that you should accept and understand my methods, Franz," countered Brandt. "My past isn't so colourful as some, yet even I don't like the idea of an intelligence agency snooping into it. I want all those close to me to die in their beds in the arms of a beautiful woman, not on the end of a rope."

Neuer smiled. The thought of being in the arms of a beautiful woman certainly appealed. In fact, at his age he'd settle for *any* woman.

"Very well, Wolfgang, I accept that you may know what you're doing." He spoke with a smile and Brandt accepted the comment on that level. "Tell me, though, why did Sigi go back to Iceland?"

"He had gems to collect. They were to pay for yet another change of identity."

"And what happened to them?"

Brandt smiled. "They have now been converted to hard cash and added to Freiheit funds. Even in death Sigi was able to contribute to the cause."

Neuer sat back in his chair. "Has there been anything else happening?"

"There was an incident in Berlin, but we dealt with it."

Neuer sat forward again, concern once more etched across his face.

"An incident? What type of incident?"

Brandt took a moment to answer, as if he hadn't really wanted to talk about it. However, he'd been foolish enough as to raise the subject, so he was rather stuck with explaining himself.

"An MI6 agent was becoming a nuisance, so we had to deal with him."

Neuer looked outraged. "Does *dealing* with people always mean having to kill them?" he then said, sounding rather exasperated in the process.

"As I said, Franz, Freiheit has to be protected at all times."

Neuer heard what Brandt was saying, but in this instance, it didn't make him feel any better. Killing, in itself, had never bothered him, but having friends and colleagues killed was a different matter altogether.

Wednesday 2nd June, 1971 – MILO HQ

Sir Tavish was on the phone.

He was speaking to Abner McQueen, Head of the MILO Section within the CIA. Set up at the same time as the MILO HQ in London, the Americans had decided to leave it as a part of an existing intelligence agency, rather than start up something completely new. Abner had autonomy, but no real status. He was still viewed as Head of a small fry section, dealing with small fry problems. Accordingly, Abner's team was small, only around fifty in total. He occupied a corner of Langley that had once been used for the stores and any technology that was available to him, was ultimately the property of the CIA and not MILO.

Sir Tavish always enjoyed his chats on the phone with Abner. The two men felt that they had a close working relationship and a deep respect for each other. They had rarely met face to face, but had never allowed that to sour the working relationship in any way. Most of their business was done over the phone. On this day, Abner had phoned Sir Tavish and after the usual pleasantries he was finally getting to the point of the call.

"I'm sending you someone," Abner said.

Sir Tavish was leaning back in his chair, a cup of coffee in front of him and the thought of going home still uppermost in his mind.

"What do you mean, you're sending me someone?" he said.

"Exactly that," added Abner. "She's a great kid, you'll like her."

The word *kid* did not sit well with Sir Tavish. Americans might use the term to cover a multitude of things, but to Sir Tavish it meant one thing and one thing only; trouble.

"Who is she and why are you sending her here?"

"Amy Clinton. She's been with us four years, you must at least remember her name," said Abner.

At that precise moment, Sir Tavish didn't.

Instead, he waited for the *why* to receive an answer. Abner now provided that.

"We just need her away from Washington for a little while."

"A little while?" said Sir Tavish, not liking anything that he had heard so far.

"Yeah, maybe a month or two."

Sir Tavish nearly fell off his chair. *A month or two.* What was he expected to do with a visitor for a month or two? Abner hadn't realised how unique he was; Sir Tavish didn't usually make friends with Americans. He had never been a fan of Americans and was always happiest when a whole ocean separated them from him.

"Why do you need to get her away from Washington?" Sir Tavish now asked, though he wasn't at all sure that he really wanted to hear the answer.

"Oh, don't worry, Sir Tavish," Abner replied, "Amy's not done anything wrong. As I said, she's a great kid and a great asset to the MILO organisation."

"I get the message, Abner, you like her. Now, would you kindly tell me why you need her out of Washington."

"Amy has a rather outspoken uncle who is a Congressman. His views on the Vietnam War are somewhat adrift from the rest of us and there are those, in the corridors of power, who feel he needs to be brought under control a bit. I don't want Amy around at a time like, it might pile undue pressure on to her. I'd rather she was with you, being kept busy."

Sir Tavish thought for a moment. In truth, he didn't feel as if he had much option, other than to agree to Amy Clinton coming to London for however long it might take.

"Okay, Abner, when were you thinking of sending her?"

"She's in the air as we speak," replied Abner. "Should be in your office tomorrow."

As usual, Abner McQueen had been one step ahead of Sir Tavish from the very beginning of their conversation.

Friday, 4th June, 1971 – MILO HQ

Ralph Steadman looked in on Sir Tavish.

"Security tell me there's a stunning blonde asking for you."

"Ah, that'll finally be the elusive Miss Clinton. She was supposed to be here yesterday. Go down and collect her, please, Ralph."

"Of course, Sir Tavish."

A few moments later Steadman was back. Behind him walked a beautiful woman, with long blonde hair and perfect skin. She wore a white blouse and blue jeans. She had a bag over her shoulder and was carrying a jacket over her arm. When she was introduced to Sir Tavish, she lit up the room with the most radiant smile, showing off, as with nearly all Americans, a set of perfect teeth.

Amy was invited to sit down, which she did.

She then opened the bag she'd been carrying and took out a folder, which she now handed across to Sir Tavish.

"Mister McQueen wanted you to have this, I believe it is very important."

"Thank you," said Sir Tavish, opening the folder and taking out three sheets of paper. He cast an eye over them and immediately noticed the Great Train Robbery getting a mention.

" What is this?" he then asked.

"The CIA is in the habit of sending agents down into parts of South America in the hope that they'll pick up on some useful intel. One of their agents got talking to a local and the rest is in that report."

Sir Tavish tutted rather loudly. "So, that's all the CIA can do with themselves, eh?" he said, an air of disgust in his voice.

"You'd be surprised what they learn, Sir Tavish," Amy said.

"Like what?" Sir Tavish pressed.

"If I tell you the CIA agent had been talking to Ronnie Biggs."

Sir Tavish's eyebrows went up slightly at the mention of Biggs' name.

Biggs had been one of the Great Train Robbers. He had escaped from prison in 1965, after serving fifteen months of a thirty-year sentence. In 1970, he had arrived in Rio Di Janeiro where, presumably, he had bumped into an undercover CIA agent on the hunt for useful information.

"And?" Sir Tavish said, still not looking that interested.

"And Ronnie got a bit drunk on a few occasions," Amy said with a grin. "It seems that Ronnie liked to talk, especially to anyone buying him drinks. He said that much of the funding for the job came from an unknown source. Ronnie heard that that source was either German, or came from German money. The investment was repaid handsomely. Ronnie also claimed that they stole far more than the official figures quoted. He reckoned the authorities would have had even more egg on their face if they'd admitted to the true amount stolen that night."

"They've hardly recovered any of it," commented Sir Tavish, "so I don't suppose anyone need ever know the true amount."

"If there was a mystery investor then he must have been repaid many times over," Amy then said.

"It would have helped immensely if Ronnie had been able to tell your CIA alcoholic who that mysterious investor had been," Sir Tavish then said. "Whether he'd been German or not."

"There's every chance Ronnie wouldn't have known anything about investors, or planners, or anyone else for that matter," Amy now said." He was just one of the foot soldiers, surely?"

Sir Tavish thought for a moment and then reached for one of the phones on his desk. He punched in two digits and waited.

"Yes, Ben, would you come through for a moment."

Ben was in the room, almost before Sir Tavish had replaced the receiver. Sir Tavish noticed an attraction between Ben and Amy, which was allowed to pass as quickly as it had arrived.

"This is Amy Clinton, from our Washington office," Sir Tavish then said. "Amy, meet Ben Ward, you'll know him to be the lead agent around here."

Ben and Amy shook hands and then Ben sat down. They now both turned towards Sir Tavish, keen to hear what he might say next.

"Amy has brought us some interesting information, Ben, which I would like both of you to run with, just to see if it takes us anywhere."

Ben looked interested. He glanced at Amy, who smiled, and then they both were back listening to Sir Tavish as he continued to speak.

"It seems that Ronnie Biggs likes to tell the locals, where he now drinks, about his escapades with the other train robbers.

He's been telling tales of rich Germans benefitting from the proceeds of The Great Train Robbery netting them a whole lot more than has ever been admitted."

"Do you want us to find Biggs?" Ben then asked.

"I don't see any point in doing that," countered Sir Tavish. "We'll leave that to others. In the meantime, let's accept that what Ronnie said was true and that it really was a rich German who financed the job. Could it have been Hans Varga?"

"Hans Varga?" repeated Amy with a questioning tone.

"I'll leave Ben to bring you up to speed later," Sir Tavish said, looking at Ben for an answer to his question.

"It might be," was the answer eventually offered, "but, on the other hand, it could be anyone."

It wasn't the answer Sir Tavish had been hoping for but even he realised it was the best he was going to get at that precise moment.

A few moments later, Ben and Amy were leaving the room and heading for Ben's office. Nothing more was said until Ben had unlocked and opened the bottom right-hand drawer of his desk. He took out a folder and handed it to Amy. Written on the front, in heavy, black letters was:

THE VARGA FILE

"A little light reading for you," he said with a smile. "I'll take you somewhere quiet and you can study it."

Ben took Amy to Room 314. It was usually used for team meetings, but on this particular day it was empty. Ben turned and left the room. Amy put her jacket over one of the chairs and hung her bag over another. She then sat down and pulled the file closer to her. She then took a notebook from her bag, along with a fancy looking fountain pen with gold initials engraved on the side. Not surprisingly they read *AC*.

As Amy made her way through the contents of the file, she made notes. An hour later she felt that she knew all anyone might know about Hans Varga.

She sat back in her chair and stretched the ache out of her limbs. She'd been sitting in the same position for two long and her body didn't like it. At that moment, the door opened and Ben came back into the room, He was carrying two mugs of coffee.

"Hope you like it black," he said, placing one of the mugs in front of Amy.

"I'm an American, I can drink coffee anyway you present it to me," she replied with a grin.

Ben sat down.

"So, now you know about Hans Varga."

"He buys ships after the war," Amy said, spinning her mug round to grab hold of the handle. "Where did he get the money for that?"

"We don't know, just like so many other things about the man."

"And you don't know if he's Freiheit, or not, either?"

"Not at the moment. Lots of suspicion, no evidence. We've found an excuse to go over the company accounts nearly every year since Varga came on to our radar and every year it's the same; not as much as a figure out of line. There is no indication of any financial irregularities anywhere."

"I note the Varga Chief Executive in London is a guy called Gerald Taylor; what do we know about him?"

"Nothing more than what the company will allow us to know," said Ben. "It's the same with the other Chief Executives in Bonn, Amsterdam, and Paris. "

"And the other Chief Executives are all German?" said Amy.

"Yes."

"Then why be different with Taylor?"

"No idea," said Ben.

Amy was about to speak when the door opened and another, rather good-looking, man came into the room.

"Ah, Mike," said Ben, "let me introduce you to Amy Clinton, all the way from the States."

"Always good to put a name to the face," said Mike, shaking Amy's hand then sitting down.

"The Old Man wants Amy and I to have another look at Varga in light of some information Amy's brought with her."

Mike was then informed of the Ronnie Biggs connection, which he found more amusing than potentially helpful.

"Well. good luck with that," Mike then said. "As for me, I'm still working on Sam Halliday. I can't find any obvious link between him and Freiheit, but I'll keep digging."

Mike left the room and Ben returned to talking about the Varga Corporation with Amy.

"We know that Varga's company is connected to the SS due to the fact that three of his Chief Executives were all in the SS. One of those is dead now. He was found dead in Iceland and we believe Freiheit had him killed because we were on to him. We later confirmed his true identity to be that of Jürgen Maier, a known war criminal."

"So, Franz Neuer and Helmut Breitner could well be war criminals as well?" suggested Amy.

"They could be," agreed Ben, "but without their real names, there's no way of checking."

Amy drank some coffee.

"Okay," she then said, "what's the plan?"

"No plan, as such," replied Ben, "just a list of questions we hope to answer as out investigation unfolds"

"What do we do first?" was Amy's next question.

"Two main objectives," said Ben. "Firstly, we try and put find the real identities of Neuer and Breitner and secondly, it would be nice to know where Varga got the money to buy his first ships."

Friday, 25th June, 1971 – MILO HQ

Three weeks had gone by since Amy had arrived from America and been assigned to work with Ben.

In those three weeks it had been announced that the new Chief Executive for Paris was going to be Sebastian Diefenbach, a name known to MILO, but only in a minor capacity. Amy had been given the job of filling in the gaps on Diefenbach's past. She had been able to find a complete history for the man from various sources. He had, like Varga, been Wehrmacht during the war and there seemed to have been enough prior links to Varga to give a clear indication as to why he'd been chosen for the job. He was fifty-two years of age and had been working, within the Varga Corporation, for the last ten years.

As far as the MILO report on him was concerned, there seemed no cause for concern. Diefenbach appeared to be exactly who he said he was.

As far as other matters were concerned, little had been learned. Another member of the team, Sarah Jones, had been given the task of finding out from where Varga might have got the money to start his business. She had pulled together every piece of paper she could find that was related to the financial records of the Varga Corporation. Everything had been looked at before, yet Sarah felt it was worth revisiting them.

To assist her, Paul Manson from the MILO Finance Department, had been seconded. Sarah would have been the first to admit that she needed all the help she could get, when it came to making sense of figures.

Ben and Amy were still trying to put another name to Franz Neuer. They had collated lists of war crimes and the people who had perpetrated them. They also began with the assumption that Neuer and Varga had to have known each other before Neuer started working with the Corporation.

It made sense to further assume that their initial contact would have happened during the war.

To that end, they had gone back to Hans Varga's war record. There was less fiction and a lot more fact in what was recorded of his war. The best they could find, however, were occasions when Varga had worked alongside the SS. Unfortunately, the account did not include the names of any SS officers.

Of course, Varga and Neuer could have met over a drink in Berlin for all Ben, or Amy, knew. They'd maybe never crossed paths in any military sense at all.

Basically, Ben and Amy were drawing a blank. Sarah and Paul, meanwhile, were confirming that Hans Varga certainly had a business brain. He had started with a major investment (source as yet unknown) and moved forward in leaps and bounds. His decision-making had been exemplary; Paul, in particular, had been very impressed with the way in which the Varga Corporation expanded and increased its business.

The more Paul read, the more he began to admire Varga.

Friday, 25th June, 1971 – Tongue of Great Britain's Office, Central London

As with all the Varga Chief Executives, Gerald Taylor had two offices. Varga and Freiheit business was never allowed to mix. Each office was staffed with different people. Taylor had considered using his secretary, Hannah Kennedy, for both locations, but had concluded that it might put both her and his own position in danger of being uncovered. For now, at any rate, Hannah helped him with his Varga work only.

The Varga office was little more than an administration centre; a place from which to pay staff and make decisions. The main work was done from a series of buildings spread around the entire country. As Chief Executive, Taylor was never expected to be in his Varga office all the time, which left him with a lot of time to get on with his Freiheit duties.

On that Friday morning, Taylor was at his Freiheit desk, reading through paperwork and drinking a coffee. Sitting across from him was a girl from the typing pool. She was there to take note of any letters, or replies, which Taylor felt were necessary. There were usually very few, however, in the world of Freiheit. The less paper floating about, the less chance of anything damaging being discovered.

All Freiheit work was carried out behind a veil of secrecy. They were like cuckoos, always occupying someone else's nest. The building might be occupied by a firm of lawyers, but in their midst, renting a little office space, would be Freiheit. Anyone employed by Freiheit would, officially, be employed by the lawyers. No formal record; nothing to give them away.

Taylor finished dictating letters and told the typist she could go. As she opened the door to leave, another woman stuck head into the room.

"Mister Taylor, you are remembering Rosa Weber will be visiting today."

Taylor looked up at her and grimaced.

"How could I ever forget," he said, in a tone heavy with sarcasm.

Rosa Weber was Wolfgang Brandt's hatchet woman. Her role, basically, was to tour round the Freiheit Tongues and kick ass. She was a woman rarely pleased with anything. She had a face that could sour milk and a chip the size of a boulder on her shoulder. Her attitude, towards everything and everyone, was always hostile. She was one hundred per cent Freiheit, caring little for anything else.

Before the woman at the door could leave, Taylor spoke to her again. "Is Tony around at the moment?"

"He's in his office. Will I ask him to come through?"

"Please."

Taylor spun his chair to allow him to look out of the window that ran the length of the wall behind him. The view of central London never ceased to bring joy to his heart. He was a London boy, born and bred. He had drifted into a job with the Varga Corporation, almost by accident. Early in his career, he had been identified as a possible recruit for Freiheit.

Taylor had connections with organised crime, only they were deep-rooted and anything but obvious. Due to Varga's desire to get Taylor involved in Freiheit, he fast-tracked him through the Varga Corporation until he had become the Chief Executive in Great Britain. By that time, Taylor also knew that he would be Freiheit Tongue of Great Britain as well.

He spun back to his desk and gave some thought as to what he would discuss with Rosa today. She liked to hear nothing but good news; he hoped he could bring her some, but first he'd have to talk with his Number Two; Tony Rutherford.

Tony was a good man to have around. He had fingers in many pies, most of them lucrative. He also had connections, though he didn't have to hide his as much as Taylor had to do.

The door opened and Tony came in. He was carrying a coffee.

He sat down on one of the spare chairs.

"The dragon's here this afternoon, I assume," Tony quipped, laughing at his own humour.

Before Taylor could respond, the intercom on his desk buzzed. Taylor picked up the phone. A woman's voice spoke in his ear.

"Call from Paris, Mister Taylor."

"Thank you, Put it through."

Gerald Taylor found himself listening, rather than talking. He was listening to a voice he hadn't heard before. The man introduced himself as being Sebastian Diefenbach and he was the new Tongue of France."

Taylor had heard that Diefenbach had taken over from Sigi Trautman, but he had not had any prior cause to speak to him. Diefenbach wasn't phoning simply to say hello. However; the call was to inform Taylor that Hans Varga had been diagnosed with terminal cancer and had only a few months to live.

As a consequence, Varga had asked for a meeting of the Grand Committee to be organised as soon as possible. The meeting would be at Varga's new home on Rhodes. Further details would be sent once a date had been finalised.

Taylor put the phone down and sat dazed for a moment or two. Tony Rutherford put down his coffee. He could see that his boss had been greatly bothered by the call.

"The dragon's not coming early is she?" he asked, trying to lighten the moment.

"Herr Varga has cancer; he'd dying."

"Oh, my God," responded Tony. "How will that affect the work we're doing here?"

"Varga has called for a Grand Committee meeting to be organised; they'll send me details later. As for the work we do, nothing will change. Freiheit may have started with Herr Varga, but it has moved on and now lives and breathes for itself. We'll need a new Grand Master, but I feel sure that Wolfgang will keep the ship afloat during any period of transition."

"But the Varga Corporation will cease to fund Freiheit in anyway?" Tony added.

"Yes, which will mean Rosa will be even more adamant that we all start injecting more money into the cause," said Taylor. "She will be in a ball-breaking mood today, I guarantee that."

Tony grinned. He was only too happy not to have to deal with Rosa Weber on any level. He spoke next.

"I might have news that you can pass on to the lovely Rosa; maybe even put a smile on her face."

"I don't believe in miracles," quipped Taylor and Tony laughed again.

Tony Rutherford looked as if he'd stepped out of a rock band. He had shoulder-length, fair hair and blue eyes. He was a little over six feet three in height and possessed the gift of the gab, something he used incessantly on the ladies. He had what might be described as matinee looks and definitely attracted attention when he walked into a room.

He picked up his coffee and sat back in his chair. As he did so, he began to speak again.

"I have more information with regard to the bank raid, we've been planning."

Taylor sat forward; it did sound like good news was coming.

"Go on," he said.

"We have a team in place; all we need now is to finalise the plan."

"And that moves us on how, exactly?" snapped Taylor, expecting to hear much more than that.

"It takes time," Tony said, remaining calm under an attack from Taylor's anger. "We need finance in place to pay for everything. There'll be equipment, people to be bought off and information to be acquired. We've selected the two banks we intend hitting, but because it will be two jobs at the same time, we need to make sure the plan is fool-proof."

"When do you think they'll be ready to go?" Taylor then asked.

"Another six months at least. There really is no point hurrying things; that would just lead to everyone being arrested. No, we take our time, make sure we've covered all eventualities and then simply walk away with the cash."

Much as it annoyed him to be kept waiting for what he hoped would be a massive pay day, Gerald Taylor could see the sense in what Tony was saying. The end product would be the biggest donation to the Freiheit central account since the Great Train Robbery.

Suddenly, something Tony had said, fully registered with Taylor.

"Wait a minute, you said you'd selected *two* banks, I thought we were only aiming to hit one?"

"Slight change of plan thanks to an excellent piece of intelligence which happened to come my way. There's apparently a lot of very interesting material hidden away in the safe-deposit boxes of the Moorgate Branch of Barclays Bank; better even than what we're told is in Lloyds of Baker Street. At first, I thought about switching banks, but we're too far on with the planning for Baker Street. It makes more sense to do them both, only we'll approach each job in a totally different way."

"Will we hit them both exactly at the same time?" Taylor then enquired.

"That's the intention. We have a date pencilled in for September, which might be tight seeing as there's still a lot of preparatory work to be done."

"How much do you reckon we will scoop in the way of cash?" Taylor then asked.

"I'd reckon over a million in Baker Street alone. However, if the contents of the safe-deposit boxes are as dynamite as we are led to believe, then the world is your oyster with regard to the blackmail potential."

"Any idea what's in them?" Taylor enquired with growing interest.

"Word is there are items relating to the Government and perhaps even the Royal Family. Apparently, there could be Government Ministers who would physically shit themselves if the contents of those boxes were to fall into the wrong hands."

Taylor whistled. "Really?"

"That's what we're being told," added Rutherford. Lighting a cigarette as he spoke.

"And this can be done by the end of September?"

"That's what we're aiming for, at the moment," Rutherford then said.

Taylor noted a reminder to himself. "Okay, set up the bank transfer papers and I'll sign them. Set aside what you think you'll need, but don't go overboard, or I'll have Fraulein Weber ranting in my ear, and that's the last thing any of us want."

Tony puffed on his cigarette and smiled. "Bet she loves you really."

"No way. The woman hates all men, believe me."

"Okay, I'll meet with my people and come up with a figure. I'll come to you once I need a signature."

"Good. Could I ask that you have a little more detail for me before I go to Rhodes?"

Tony nodded. "I can certainly have a brief report prepared by then. Anything else?"

"No, that's it for just now."

Tony stubbed out his cigarette in the ashtray and picked up his empty mug. He stood up and made his way from the room. There was much to do and not a great deal of time in which to do it.

Taylor, meantime, sat back in his chair and pondered on how good he was going to look in the eyes of the other Tongues. His star was in the ascendency and not even a visit from Rosa Weber could spoil the mood he was in now.

*

Rosa Weber was shown into Taylor's office at a little after three o'clock that afternoon. Weber looked her usual efficient self, dressed in a trouser-suit of grey with a white blouse beneath. Her hair was cut quite short and, as was usual, she had a rather intense expression on her face. Taylor had never seen her smile, let alone enjoy a proper belly laugh. She appeared to have no sense of humour, whatsoever.

Taylor had always found it difficult to estimate Rosa Weber's age. If pushed, he would have guessed she was in her sixties and yet, there were times when he might have thought she was slightly younger. Taylor had heard tales of Weber being active during the war, so knew her to at least be in her fifties. He also knew her to be hard as nails.

He offered Rosa a chair and asked if she would like a coffee. She accepted the coffee and then sat down, crossing her legs as she did so. Although he was not facing her, Taylor knew that the annoying, little woman would be looking around his office with her usual expression of disapproval. He knew that she did not like him, though he did not know why.

Taylor returned to his desk with two cups of coffee.

Rosa did nothing to acknowledge what he had just done for her. No thank you and no nod of acknowledgement. She picked up her coffee and took a sip, making a face as if she even disapproved of that as well.

She put the cup back on the desk and picked up the briefcase that she had brought with her. She opened the case and took a bundle of papers from it. She then put the briefcase down on the floor and started to look through the papers.

"Herr Seeler seems pleased with the returns being shown by London," she said. Her tone let Taylor know that Rosa Weber wasn't pleased, however.

"That's good to, hear," Taylor said.

"*I*, on the other hand, am of the opinion that you could be doing even better."

Ah, thought Taylor, *Freiheit's accountant is happy with me, but Freiheit's Rottweiler believes otherwise.*

Rosa Weber adopted an expression similar to that of someone experiencing an intense and extremely distasteful smell, wafting around their nostrils. Taylor felt obliged to argue his corner.

"What, exactly, is wrong with London's figures?"

"Oh, nothing if measured against previous figures coming out of London, which, I am sure, is what Herr Seeler was doing. I, on the other hand, look at the bigger picture, look at the figures being produced by all the Tongues. When viewed that way, London could be doing better."

"There will always be discrepancies across Europe," said Taylor. "Some Tongues have better access to organised crime, others don't. As it is, we all do the best we can; you can't really ask any more than that."

"Oh, but I can, Herr Taylor. I can ask you to do a lot better and I *will* keep asking until you respond. Herr Phillips, for example, always produced excellent figures from London."

"He had the benefit of the proceeds from the Great Train Robbery," countered Taylor. "None of the Tongues could ever compete with that."

"Perhaps not to the same level," conceded Rosa, "but there is still room for improvement."

It was time, thought Taylor. *Time to hint at what lay ahead.*

"Well, actually," he began, laying the cup down again, "I do happen to have a plan, which although in its early stages, promises to put millions into the Freiheit account."

Weber sat up in her chair. "That sounds very interesting," she said. "Tell me more."

Taylor told her as much as he was prepared to say, which didn't actually amount to much. However, Rosa Weber had heard the word *millions* and really didn't need to hear more.

Gerald Taylor had instantly moved up in her estimation.

If he could deliver on his promise then the year would be good for Freiheit and very good for Rosa Weber. Her bonus was paid as a percentage of Freiheit profits. The more the organisation made, the more she made.

Friday, 9th to Sunday, 11th July, 1971 – Hans Varga's house, Rhodes Town

Hans Varga sat in the courtyard of his house in Rhodes Town and looked up at the sky. It was that lovely colour of deep blue and he rejoiced in the fact that the last few months of his life would be spent here. He would now only have occasional visits to the offices in Paris; he was happy to hand the reins over to someone else and concentrate on enjoying what little time he had left.

He was drinking a glass of red wine and Franz Neuer was sitting with him. It was mid-afternoon and they were awaiting the arrival of Brandt and the other Tongues. Rooms had been prepared for everyone and Varga had employed extra staff for the weekend. He wanted everyone to be comfortable and to enjoy their few days away from normal business.

One of the maids crossed the courtyard. Neuer's eyes followed her. She reminded him of happier days when he might have stood some chance of attracting such a girl.

But those days were long gone. His thoughts, however, had brought a smile to his face, one that had not gone unnoticed by Hans Varga. His eyes now turned towards the girl as well.

"Oh, that we could, eh Franz?" commented Varga.

"Sadly, those days are gone," said Neuer. "However, it does an old man good to remember what it was like to bed a beautiful woman."

"To bed *any* woman," quipped Varga and the two men laughed.

They drank more wine and their minds wandered.

The courtyard was a suntrap and they sat under a striped umbrella, which spread over the table at which they sat. The house itself surrounded them on three sides, the fourth side of the courtyard being a wall with a gate set into it. Varga had only been there a matter of months. As soon as he knew how ill he was, he set about finding a property in Rhodes Town.

He had known, for a very long time, that he had wanted to die there.

The house had newly come on the market and he had been able to buy it at a price which was slightly below average. The deal had been struck quickly and the sellers had been able to move out at once. Varga had wasted no time in moving in. He still had his home in Paris, though he was already of a mind to sell it and just take a room in one of the hotels, were he ever to go back for business reasons.

He knew that the Board of Directors had a meeting arranged for the first week in August when, at his request, they planned to elect a new Chairman. They had thought it a good idea for the new man to be in place *before* Herr Varga died, so that matters could be discussed, if necessary,

Varga put his glass down and looked across at Neuer.

"At least I can die a happy man," he then said.

"Oh come, Hans, you're not quite there yet."

"I'll be lucky to see the year out, my doctors tell me the cancer is spreading and there is nothing anyone can do to either stop it, or even delay the process. I don't mind, I've had a good life."

"But have you really managed to do all that you set out to do?" Neuer then asked.

Varga thought for a moment. Strangely, his mind suddenly filled with memories of Helga. She had died, a little under two years ago, when the car she'd been travelling in had collided with a delivery van. The drivers had survived with hardly a scratch, but Helga's side of the car had borne the brunt of the impact.

She had died at the scene.

Varga had taken her death badly, probably more so than he might have thought. He had loved his wife, though never in a passionate way. Their love for each other had bubbled under the surface, never quite showing itself at any given time.

Varga eventually provided Neuer with his answer.

"Yes, Franz, I believe I have done it all. Obviously, I wish Helga was still here. Maybe we'll meet again soon."

Neuer saw the distant look in Varga's eyes. There might even have been a little moisture in those eyes, not the old man would ever have admitted to crying.

At that moment, both men were distracted by the arrival of a third man. He came in through the gate, wearing a light-coloured suit and panama hat. He was carrying a small suitcase and a bulky looking briefcase. It was Wolfgang Brandt. Brandt was now seventy-six years of age, though he had retained a good head of hair, all be it completely white now. His hair almost matched his suit.

As he crossed the courtyard, Varga noted how strong Brandt still looked. How he envied that strength.

"Wolfgang, how are you?" Varga announced. There was a cheerfulness in his voice, which Brandt had not expected, given the news.

"Tired," came the reply, as Brandt sat down beside the other two. "I'm too old for all this travelling."

"I'm too old for *everything*," said Neuer and the three men laughed.

"How are *you* feeling, Hans?" Brandt then asked, as he laid his briefcase at his feet, next to the suitcase.

"Not too bad, considering. I'll feel a lot better after this weekend, once I know the future of Freiheit is settled."

"Are you finished with Paris now?" added Brandt.

"I should think so. Maybe a meeting or two, but certainly no daily grind; I've had enough of all that. Would you like a drink, my friend?"

"A glass of wine would be lovely, thank you."

Varga picked up a bell, which was lying on the table. He rang it and almost immediately, another girl appeared from one of the doors. She, too, was dressed in a black dress with a white apron over the top.

She looked quite timid as she approached the table at which the men were sitting.

"Three more glasses of wine please, Sofia," Varga said.

The girl went away. Brandt spoke next.

"How much input will you be having this weekend, Hans?"

"I will observe as much as anything," came the reply. "I will, of course, offer my thoughts, where necessary."

Brandt nodded. He had enjoyed a great deal of autonomy, since being given the role of leading Freiheit and he really didn't want Hans Varga interfering at this late stage

Varga continued.

"There is a large room in the house, which I've had prepared for our meeting. I don't want to take up the whole weekend with business, so I rather hoped that we might use Sunday for our business discussions and enjoy the island tomorrow."

Brandt saw no need to argue with the arrangements. He saw the meeting more as him talking and the others listening anyway, so he wasn't expecting the business element to take that long.

"It seems as if you have thought of everything, Hans," Brandt then said.

The three men then fell silent, choosing to say nothing even after more drinks had been brought out to them. They were just three old men, sitting in the sunshine and enjoying their memories.

*

Outside the gate of the courtyard was a lane that zig-zagged back to the Street of the Knights. On one of the dog-legs was a rather insignificant door, currently looking the worse for wear and anything like the entrance to a property. Normally, it would have been lying empty, but not at the moment.

Word had reached MILO ears that the senior Chief Executives of the Varga Corporation were to be meeting on Rhodes, to discuss the future busines of the Varga company. It had also been made public knowledge that Hans Varga had terminal cancer and was now to take a backseat in all matters pertaining to his own company.

Sir Tavish had found it rather strange that Varga's replacement as Chairman would soon be decided by the Board of Directors and yet the Chief Executives had been called to a meeting with Varga at his new home on Rhodes. Sir Tavish had thought it strange enough as to send Ben and Amy to Rhodes to keep an eye on proceedings.

A property had been acquired and a team sent in to renovate and bring it up to a level where someone could live there for a few days. In case anyone enquired, Ben and Amy were posing as newly-weds, awaiting the completion of the house, which they would then use as a holiday home. They were visiting the island to check on how well the builders were doing. Everything about the house was a front for MILO activity.

As Varga, Neuer and Brandt sat enjoying their wine, Ben and Amy were in the house, not fifty yards away. Unfortunately, it had not been possible to find a way to get bugs into Varga's home, so Ben and Amy could watch from afar, but could neither see, nor hear, anything of use to them.

Not that they really knew why they were there. The Varga Corporation had not hidden the fact that there was to be a meeting, even though it would have made more sense for Varga's replacement to hold such a meeting.

Ben, in particular, thought it was all a waste of time.

He would rather be back at Headquarters, digging ever further into the past of Varga's Chief Executives. Ben was convinced the answers lay amongst their war records, not in a courtyard in Rhodes Town.

To Ben, this was nothing more than a jolly and he was prepared to look upon it on that level and nothing more. Having unpacked their things, Ben suggested they went for a walk by way of getting their bearings. He really just wanted to be out in the sun.

They walked down to the harbour, bought an ice cream and then sat down to look at the many boats tied up along the quay. As they were sitting there, one particular vessel caught their attention. It tied up and a small group of men made their way down the gangplank. Ben recognised them as being Varga Chief Executives.

"There they are," he said.

Amy followed the direction of Ben's waving arm. She watched as a minibus pulled up and the men climbed aboard.

How unnecessary, she thought, *the house is within walking distance.*

Such were the delights of being rich that even walking had become an unnecessary chore. Ben and Amy watched the bus drive away. They finished their ice-creams and took their time strolling back to the place they'd call home for a few days.

*

On the Saturday Ben tried to follow the group as they toured around the island. At one point, however, they all boarded a boat and set off for what turned out to be an hour-long trip around part of the island's coastline. He got back to the house, late afternoon, filled with a sense that the day had been an even bigger waste of time and that neither he, nor Amy, had any right to be on the island at all

Come Sunday, Ben was still fuming at the fact he and Amy were achieving nothing, except topping up their sun tan. He had tried to look into the courtyard, but saw nothing of interest,

What Ben hadn't known, was that all Varga personnel were sitting in one, large room, enjoying an endless supply of cold drinks and discussing matters that had absolutely nothing to do with the Varga Corporation.

In the centre of that room was a long table. Hans Varga sat at the end of the table, with the others sitting down either side of it.

Varga wanted them to discuss the future of Freiheit, beginning with his replacement.

It made sense, to Varga at any rate, that that replacement ought to be Wolfgang Brandt. He was all but doing the job of Grand Master anyway; it was just a matter of now giving him the title. Brandt was sitting at the table exuding his usual self-confidence and looking every inch the leader. Varga was more convinced than ever that he was making the right decision.

Varga eventually sat forward and rattled a pen off the side of his glass. The room quietened and all eyes now looked in his direction. His opening remarks were brief. He thanked everyone for all they had done and for the loyalty they had shown him. He then said it was time to hand over the reins and that it should be Wolfgang Brandt who would now take control of Freiheit for the next few years.

No one saw it their place to question Herr Varga's decision, even though Brandt's age obviously created a problem in its own right. How much longer could a man of his age remain active?

"And now Wolfgang," Varga had said, "you may have the floor."

Brandt inclined his head slightly in acknowledgment of what had just been said. He then began speaking. At one stage he mentioned Rosa Weber's name and there was a collective groan around the table. It did not go unnoticed with Varga, who immediately sat forward. He raised his hand and Brandt stopped talking.

"Do I detect that Rosa Weber might be a problem?" Varga said.

No one seemed prepared to answer at first, but eventually it was Gerd Seeler who took it upon himself to offer a response.

"Rosa clearly sees herself as doing an important job within the organisation and I appreciate she means well."

"However?" said Varga. "I sense a 'however' coming along."

"However," Seeler then said, "she rarely does anything for reasons other than her own. Her motives are driven purely by the bonus she receives at the end of the financial year. She seeks more from the Tongues even when I have already made it known I'm happy with the way things are. I'm sure she thinks she is doing a lot of good but, quite frankly, her actions are counter-productive."

Everyone, apart from Brandt, was nodding in agreement. Varga now turned to Brandt.

"Why *do* you use Rosa?"

Brandt looked a little flustered. He had not expected to be questioned, by Varga, about anything. He took a moment to offer a reply.

"I believe we need to keep a certain amount of pressure on the Tongues; I also believe it pays to have at least one individual constantly reminding them that they work for each other, as well as the good of Freiheit."

"But why pay her a bonus?"

"To give her an incentive to do a good job," Brandt replied, in a tone that seemed to conclude with the words *why else?*

"But, if I am understanding what Gerd is saying then, clearly, she *isn't* doing a good job," said Varga. He then turned to Gerd Seeler and asked for him to elaborate on what he thought of Rosa Weber.

"She's a menace," Seeler now said, feeling he could say a bit more now that he'd discovered that Varga wasn't a great supporter of Rosa either. "She does nothing that I cannot do myself. I guarantee you could lose both her and her bonus and it wouldn't make any difference to Freiheit's profits."

Brandt started to speak in Rosa's defence, but was silenced by Varga raising his arm again.

"I rarely interfere, Wolfgang," he said, "but I feel I must insist that you either get rid of Rosa altogether, or else you place her under Gerd's direct management. We can't have her interfering in the way that she does, especially as she has no *real* place in our organisation.

The bonuses will, of course, cease immediately."

Brandt, rather reluctantly, agreed to terminate Rosa's employment and was given authority to give her a final payment, equivalent to three month's pay.

With the problem of Rosa Weber resolved, the meeting seemed to adopt a more relaxed tone. Much was discussed and, by the end, Hans Varga was a happy man. He also felt that he had maybe managed to clip Brandt's wings a little in the process. If he was to be the new Grand Master then he had to learn to accept that post with humility and a better understanding for the people working with and for him.

Two major decisions were reached that afternoon. The first was that the men round that table would now spend more time on Freiheit business. Over time they would step away from their Chief Executive role and concentrate fully on Freiheit. Only the future of Freiheit mattered.

The second decision, though simple in its wording, was rather more difficult to bring into action. It was agreed that each Tongue would now be given sole responsibility for one aspect of the Freiheit organisation. Gerald Taylor, for example, would now be the Tongue responsible for transport. That would include planes owned by Freiheit as well as the many cars, vans and buses they had around the world.

With each of the Tongues having such a responsibility it ensured they were even more dependent on each other, thus making it harder for any one of them to declare unilateral independence and try to take total control.

Even Brandt, as the new Grand Master, would always need the support of *all* his Tongues.

As the meeting broke up and they all went off to prepare for dinner Hans Varga, in particular was happy with the way the day had gone.

He was certainly leaving with Freiheit in a better place.

PART THREE

Monday, 12th July, 1971 - Durham Prison and London

The year had just passed its midpoint and MILO continued to be frustrated in its investigation into Varga and all things related to his company. The one lead that continued to remain unresolved, was that of the possible German investment in the Great Train Robbery. Both Ben and Sir Tavish felt there was more to uncover there and with that in mind, Sir Tavish and Ben hatched a plan that might hopefully provide them with more information which would strengthen that lead.

Efforts had already been made to make contact with those in the criminal underworld who were prepared to 'sell' information to the intelligence agencies. The word on the street was even more convinced that there had been a major investor in the Great Train Robbery and that that investor was, almost certainly, not British. Beyond that, nothing could be confirmed, but Sir Tavish had still felt they had enough to merit spending more time on it.

It was agreed that Ben would go to Durham Prison and interview Bruce Reynolds. Meanwhile, Viewforth himself, would speak with ex-Detective Chief Superintendent Frank Williams. If anyone knew anything about the funding of the robbery, it ought to be them.

Amy, meanwhile, had been told that she would remain in London for the foreseeable future. Abner had wanted her to be given a cover story, but Sir Tavish had taken the decision to tell her the truth. She had been outraged to have been packed away, like some errant child who didn't know how to behave in company. She told Sir Tavish that her uncle had never been that close to her and that it really wouldn't have bothered her to have carried on with her job, whilst he was being investigated. However, having got her gripe out of the way, she then went on to tell Sir Tavish that she was really enjoying her time in London and was happy to remain there for as long as she was being useful.

It was decided that Amy shouldn't go with Ben when he interviewed Bruce Reynolds. Sir Tavish thought it would place her in a difficult position, being a woman wandering around a men's prison. Mike would have been sent with Ben, but he was already in Berlin, once more following up on a half-lead regarding Sam Halliday. A second bank account had been found, in Halliday's name, which contained more money than might have been expected for an MI6 operative. The concern now was that Halliday had been on the payroll of Freiheit and Sir Tavish wanted that possibility investigated immediately.

Sir Tavish did not want Ben interviewing Reynolds on his own, so he came to an agreement with MI5 to be loaned one of their agents for the day. Although they were really there riding shotgun, Sir Tavish thought it only wise to involve MI5, just in case other domestic security issues arose as a result of what Reynolds might say.

The agent chosen was Terence Lambert, a man already known to Sir Tavish. Lambert met Ben at King's Cross Station, prior to boarding a train to Newcastle. They had met before, but this would be the first time actually working together. They shook hands and set off for a compartment that looked reasonably quiet. There wasn't one and they had to make do sitting with two clergymen and a young mum with her baby for company. As a result, work was not discussed at all during the journey.

The meeting with Reynolds was scheduled for two o'clock that afternoon. Ben was looking forward to it. He had always taken a close interest in the stories behind the Great Train Robbery and he knew that if anyone could be classified as the brains behind the robbery, then it would probably be Bruce Reynolds. Of course, as the *money* behind the robbery had never been identified, it was perfectly possible that the real brain was actually sitting with that money. For the moment, Reynolds would have to do.

Reynolds had been in prison for three years. The police had taken their time in catching him. It had been Reynolds running out of money that had been the major factor in his arrest. He was now looking at spending a great deal of time in prison. Many had commented that the train robbers would have been given lighter sentences had they murdered someone. Given the length of every sentence handed down, it was to be assumed that the Establishment had not liked the idea of a robbery taking place in their own backyard.

Ben and Lambert arrived in Newcastle station, where a car was waiting for them. Ben drove through to Durham, arriving with enough time to grab lunch before making their way to the prison. Lunch was light and both men decided to steer clear of any alcohol. They wanted a clear mind for what lay ahead.

After lunch, they made their way to the prison and passed through the necessary security checks, before being led to an interview room, which was furnished with a table and four chairs. There was a small window at ceiling height and a door at either end. They had entered through Door A and Bruce Reynolds was eventually led through Door B. He was dressed in prison garb. He was a handsome man, though his heavy framed spectacles did make him look a bit like Hank Marvin. Reynolds was accompanied by two prison guards who now took him over to one of the spare chairs before taking up a standing position either end of the room. Reynolds looked at Ben and then at Lambert.

"You two ain't coppers," he then said. "This must be serious."

He smiled at his own attempt at humour, then sat back a little from the table and crossed his legs. Ben took the smile to be more of a sneer. Most major crooks had little time for any form of officialdom. Reynolds eventually settled on Ben again.

"I'm surprised there's anyone interested in speaking to me."

"We're here because one of your old fellow-robbers has been shooting his mouth off," Ben said, leaning forward across the table.

"That'll be good old Ronnie," said Reynolds. "He must be the only one of us still on the outside. Where is he these days?"

"South America," replied Ben. There seemed no need not to answer the question.

"I tried some of that, but it wasn't for me. I like eels and warm beer too much. Talking about what I like," Reynolds then added, "any chance of a smoke?"

Lambert glanced at one of the guards who inclined his head slightly. That would apparently be okay. Lambert took out a cigarette and handed it to Reynolds. He then held his lighter out and Reynolds leaned forward to light the end of his cigarette. He drew back hard and sat back in his chair, eventually allowing smoke to escape down his nose. The nicotine hit was immediate.

Ben allowed this little scene to play out and then spoke again.

"Word at the trial was that you were the mastermind behind the robbery."

"Can't take all the credit," came the instant reply and Ben thought, for a moment, that Reynolds might be about to say more. As it was, he inhaled more smoke and appeared to find greater interest in looking at the floor, rather than his visitors.

Lambert took up the questioning, though not with much thought towards honesty.

"One of our lads heard something very interesting the other day."

"Really?" said Reynolds, not looking at all interested.

"Seems you only pulled off that train robbery because you had backing. We've heard that backing was from the Germans. What do you have to say about that?"

Reynolds smoked a little more, then looked.

"That story has been going around ever since we pulled the job. I'll tell you this; no job ever goes smoothly unless it has been well funded and well thought out. We did both and that's as much as you'll hear from me."

"How much did you get away with?" Ben then asked.

"A lot," came the reply, "In fact, too bloody much. We had no idea what to do with it all."

"So, your backers got a windfall," commented Ben.

"Suffice to say, everyone did alright out of it," said Reynolds.

Lambert now leaned a little closer to Reynolds.

"We've done a little digging, Mister Reynolds, over these last eight years and we can't find anyone, in this country, who would have had the money to finance a robbery like the one you pulled off. I'm not even sure if there's anyone in Britain who could have planned such an audacious act. We're certain you got help from abroad and everything we've learned, seems to be pointing in the direction of Germany. Now, I realise there's no way you'd give us names, in fact you probably don't even know any names, but surely you can at least either confirm, or deny, whether or not that help did come from Germany."

Reynolds finished his cigarette. He then looked from Ben to Lambert and back again, a slight smile playing around his lips. "Tell you what," he eventually said, "I'll neither confirm, nor deny, what you've just said. How will that do?"

From the look on Reynold's face, Ben took that answer as being a yes. This was Bruce Reynolds way of giving them an answer, without actually giving them an answer. Reynolds continued speaking.

"Anyway, gentlemen, do I get told which departments you represent?"

"MI-Five," said Lambert.

"MILO," added Ben.

"My God, the big guns, I really have gone up in the world. Can I go now?"

Ben nodded and Reynolds stood up. The two guards hurried to be at his side and then led him out of the room. As they reached the door, Reynolds paused and turned back.

"Give Mister Williams my best," he said and then left the room.

Satisfied that they had learned all that they would ever learn from Bruce Reynolds, Ben and Lambert made their way out of the prison and began their journey back to London.

*

As Ben and Lambert began their journey back from Newcastle, Sir Tavish Viewforth was at his Club sitting in the smoking room with ex- Detective Superintendent Frank Williams. They were enjoying a brandy, with cigar, and Williams was talking about his retirement from the police and the fact that he was now working for Qantas, the Australian airline.

"But I am assuming you didn't invite me here to talk about the job I'm doing now," Williams eventually said. "There is only ever one reason why anyone wants to talk to me these days; it's that damned train robbery."

"Guilty as charged, Frank. I would have spoken to Mister Butler, had it not been for his rather untimely demise."

Williams had insisted on Sir Tavish calling him Frank. Sir Tavish, however, was to remain Sir Tavish, he needed to know someone far longer than one lunch before dropping his hard-earned title.

"Tommy worked himself to an early grave."

"Indeed. I'll come straight to the point, Frank, did you ever consider the possibility that foreign money was behind the robbery?"

"We never really thought much about who funded the job; we were too busy trying to catch the men who did it. You have to remember, the Establishment took the robbery as a personal insult and demanded the perpetrators not only be caught, but be seen to be punished and punished severely. Resources were thrown at us and high-ranking police officers and politicians watched our every move. It was not a good time to be a police officer in our little corner of the Force."

"But you must have considered the possibility that you never actually came that close to catching the real brains behind the robbery; much as Bruce Reynolds would like to take all the credit."

Frank Williams put his brandy glass down and flicked cigar ash into a rather ornate ashtray that lay between them. As Sir Tavish watched him do it, he couldn't help thinking, if only fleetingly, that in Frank Williams there was a look of Ron Greenwood, the West Ham manager. It did seem to Sir Tavish, however, that Williams appeared to be coming across as a far more serious individual. It was a rare smile that crossed Williams' face, just before he spoke.

"Sir Tavish, how much do you know about the Great Train Robbers?"

"Just what little I've read."

"And how much do you know about the aftermath of the robbery?" Williams then said.

"Not as much as I probably should," Sir Tavish admitted, finding comfort in a sip of his brandy.

Frank Williams leaned a little closer.

"Once our merry band of robbers had nicked the money they drove to a farmhouse and remained there for what turned out to be far too long. They basically had no exit strategy. They could have driven to London and lost themselves in an environment of which they were all familiar. They could even have driven to a private airfield and been out of the country before anyone even knew the money was gone. In short, there were a number of options they *could* have taken, but the reality is that they went to a remote farmhouse and played Monopoly. If there *had* been a Mastermind then I feel sure he would have come up with an exit strategy of some kind. We never believed there was a Mr Big, there was just a bunch of semi-incompetent thieves who got lucky in terms of the cash they nicked. No one had really thought it through, which meant that the moment they drove away from that stricken train, they were out of their depth. There were fewer brain cells than people in that farmhouse, Sir Tavish and the truth of the matter is, they were always going to get nicked, it was just a matter of time when."

Sir Tavish considered what had just been said.

"Okay," he eventually said, "let's forget the notion of a Mastermind, as such. However, they had to have had money to buy the people, information and equipment that they would have needed to pull off the job. Did you ever get to the bottom of where that money came from?"

"These were career thieves, Sir Tavish," Williams then said. "They could have had money set aside from other jobs, or they maybe even pulled off a few smaller jobs to finance the big one. There is no reason to believe that anyone else was involved."

"Even though stories of a mysterious German have been floating around since the day they pulled off the job," said Sir Tavish.

"Stories is the operative word, Sir Tavish."

"How much did the gang get away with?" Sir Tavish then enquired.

"Just over two and a half million. They probably thought they were going to get a quarter of that, when they hit the train."

"And how did you come to that figure?" Sir Tavish now asked.

Frank Williams looked a little confused at this line of questions.

"The banks gave us all the information we needed."

"So, the figure of two and a half million came solely from the banks?"

"Of course, but why should that matter?" asked Williams.

"What if the banks underplayed the amount that went missing," Sir Tavish now suggested.

"Why would they do that?" replied Williams, looked ever more confused.

"To save face. It was bad enough that they admitted to sending nearly three million pounds through the night, on a train with no security. How much worse would that have sounded if, say, five million had been on that train?"

"Do you know something in particular?" Williams now asked.

"No, I'm merely suggesting that the gang might have got away with a lot more than has ever been made public and that that extra money went to the financial backers, which I'm further suggesting, took it out of the country."

Williams pondered on what had just been said.

There was obviously no evidence to support what Sir Tavish was saying but it certainly sounded possible. The Post Office had, previously, admitted that they sometimes transported anything up to six million on occasions and there had also been some doubt, amongst the banks, as to exactly how much might have been on the train that night. The banks had always said the estimate of their losses had been conservative. Williams finally spoke again.

"I concede that your theory may well be correct, Sir Tavish, but there could be no way to prove it."

Sir Tavish smiled.

"Thankfully, I do not need to prove my theory, Frank. Only for the purposes of a court of law does one need proof. In my line of work, proving something is rarely required.   We work beneath the radar and that gives us certain freedoms, which you never enjoyed as a police officer."

"It all sounds very mysterious, Sir Tavish," Williams then said. "I wish you well with your line of inquiry and if you learn anything more about the robbers, I'd appreciate an update someday. In the meantime, let me say just one more thing. As I said, we were never convinced that there ever was a Mastermind, as such, but we were always firmly of the belief that there was an inside member of the team. The gang knew too much and, of course, there was the little matter of the security vans in which the money was transported."

Sir Tavish looked a little confused. "But I heard the train wasn't pulling any high-security coaches."

"Because they were all, rather conveniently, out of commission, for one reason or another, that night," said Williams. "I think that's a little more than coincidence."

"Yet, no one had ever been caught," said Sir Tavish.

"The Post Office investigators spent months digging into every aspect of the train robbery. They checked out all the staff involved and probably many who weren't. They turned over every stone and yet no one crawled out. There is no evidence, anywhere, of an insider helping the gang and yet there simply had to have been. One of life's mysteries, I suspect," added Williams.

"Well, if I learn anything that I think might be of interest to you, Frank, I'll give you a call."

"I'd appreciate that, Sir Tavish," said Williams, sitting back to enjoy the last of his cigar.

Tuesday, 13th July, 1971 – West Berlin

Mike Brown was sitting at a small café enjoying a strong coffee and reading the morning paper. It was ten o'clock and the sun was shining brightly from a clear sky. He had been in Berlin for three days now and had yet to find any evidence that Sam Halliday's second account had anything to do with Freiheit. Mike had even met with some animosity from Sam's colleagues, for even suggesting such a thing.

Though no one could explain why Sam should even have a second account, irrespective of how much might be in it, equally no one was prepared to suggest that their colleague might be crooked. A few even went as far to suggest that Sam was too low down the food chain to interest anyone, let alone a foreign power. One colleague did, however, give Mike a lead. He knew of a woman whom Sam was in the habit of seeing; her name was Maria. Mike then found Maria's name on a piece of paper, nestling inside a notebook, which had been left in the bedside drawer. There was a phone number beneath the name.

Sam's superiors had frowned on the fact that Sam had, apparently, been conducting a clandestine affair with a German woman. All MI6 operatives were under threat of being sent home, if they were found to be fraternising with what was viewed as the enemy. It wasn't German women in general that was the problem; it was the threat of Stasi agents being sent from East Germany to seduce unsuspecting agents to gain information from them. Many a wrong word had been uttered between apparent lovers.

Mike had said that he wasn't bothered about the affair, as such and that he only wanted to speak to Maria. He wanted to hear her side of the story before he started accusing Sam Halliday of anything. With that in mind he'd phoned the number on the piece of paper found in Sam's flat. Surprisingly, his call was answered, though he'd had to work hard to stop her from putting the receiver down again.

Initially, Maria had been reluctant to meet with Mike, but he had finally persuaded her that he only had Sam's best interest to heart and that he wasn't MI6, which meant he had no ulterior motive for wanting to see her. Maria had cried when Sam's name had first been mentioned; it seemed clear to Mike that she'd really cared about him. It didn't sound like a Stasi honey trap.

Eventually, Maria had agreed to a meeting, though she insisted that it be outside and in full public view. Mike suggested a possible location and Maria seemed happy to meet there. A time had been agreed for the following day and that was why Mike now found himself sitting at that outside table, reading a newspaper.

It was now nearly twenty minutes past the time they'd agreed and Mike was beginning to think she wasn't going to turn up. He was on to his second cup of coffee before he finally saw a woman heading, rather slowly and possibly reluctantly, in his direction. He tried to keep eyes on her without appearing to stare too hard. He didn't want to scare her away now. Eventually, she arrived beside Mike and he was able to see her properly for the first time. She was very pretty, with long, auburn hair that fell over her shoulders in ringlets. She wore a short coat over jeans and a tee shirt. Mike could immediately see why Sam would have been attracted to her. She approached him with caution and when they started speaking to each other, it was in German.

"Mike?" was all that Maria said at first.

Mike stood up and held out his hand. "Yes it is. Thank you for coming, Maria."

He wanted to use her name quickly, it was his way of putting her at her ease. Mike could tell the woman was nervous; she kept looking around like a frightened bird sensing danger all around. Mike moved a little closer and touched her arm.

"It's okay, there's no need to be afraid. I've been sitting here over half an hour and I've seen no indication that we are being watched or, for that matter, that you were being followed."

Maria continued to look uncertain. Mike smiled, then spoke.

"Please, have a seat and I'll order coffee."

Maria looked around, seemingly unwilling to take Mike's word alone. She moved to the other chair at the table and sat down. She hooked her bag over the back of the chair, all the time looking around.

"They could be following me," she said.

"I was watching; there's no one there," insisted Mike. "Now, can I get you a coffee?"

Maria said yes.

Mike now attracted the attention of a waitress, who had come out to clear another of the tables. Once the waitress had gone away, Mike leaned a little closer to Maria.

"I really do appreciate you agreeing to see me. I won't take up any more of your time than is necessary, so perhaps you could tell me how long you'd known Sam."

"About a year."

"How did you meet?"

Maria now looked at Mike as if he were an idiot.

"You *do* know what I do for a living?" she then said.

It was more her expression, than the words she'd spoken, that caused the penny to drop. Mike now realised that Sam had probably been paying for their relationship. That being the case, there was every chance that Maria wouldn't be able to help. If all they had done was meet for paid sex, then she wasn't likely to have got to know him that well at all. However, there had been those tears when his name had first been mentioned on the phone. Surely, that meant she had cared for him more than her other clients.

"Sorry, I didn't know," Mike then said, feeling his face redden a little with embarrassment.

"Well, you know now," added Maria, turning to fish in her bag for what turned out to be a packet of cigarettes. She put one between her rouged lips and lit the end of it. She drew back on the end and seemed rejuvenated by the hit she got from the nicotine coursing through her body.

"You sounded upset on the phone," Mike then said." I can't believe that Sam meant nothing to you."

"Sam was my ticket to a better life," Maria replied. "When I was with him I could forget what I did for a living. He had stopped being a client; he was my lover, plain and simple."

"You loved him?" pressed Mike, finding it hard to believe that a call girl could love anyone in particular.

"I never admitted to myself that I did until I heard that he was dead. I've known for a little while that Sam loved me. He would have done anything for me."

As Maria spoke about Sam she was smiling.

"You said that Sam was your ticket out of the life you live," Mike then said, "did that mean you were giving up on your other clients?"

"I make far too much money to ever consider that," replied Maria. "No, what I meant was just the fact I felt different when I was with Sam. He reminded me of the fact I was a woman with my own needs. He met those needs and more; we were really good together and I don't just mean the sex."

"How did you first meet Sam?" enquired Mike, as the waitress came back with the coffee.

Maria waited until they were completely alone again, before answering the question.

"I met him at a party. I go to a lot of parties, as you might imagine."

It was already clear to Mike that Maria was way above being a prostitute, she was an escort and one that would never have been cheap. Her clients, in the main, would all be rich men with a need for female company other than from their wives. They would be men prepared to pay for everything, which usually included having sex in ways that wives would rarely agree to.

"I would have thought you'd move in circles that were well above those visited by the likes of Sam Halliday?" Mike now said.

Maria smiled again. It made her look even prettier and Mike could clearly see why she would be so popular as a choice of escort. Turning up at a party, with Maria on your arm, would have made an impression in itself.

"I wondered myself why Sam was at that party, but he just laughed and said he'd gate-crashed it which, of course, he wouldn't have done. The parties I'm taking about were strictly supervised; no one attended without an invitation, or being in the company of an invited guest."

"Sounds like a strange kind of party," commented Mike. "The kind I go to tend to be open-house, rather than invitation affairs."

"My clients tend to be powerful men and powerful men always have a need to hide secrets and maintain their anonymity. I am part of that anonymity; when they are with me, they can be whoever they want. Men like that don't want to go to parties where just anyone might turn up. They like to know who will be there; like to know there won't be any prying journalists for a start."

"So, these powerful men, do any of them have names?" Mike then said.

"They all have names," replied Maria, adding sugar to her coffee, "but you won't get any of them out of me. The main element to my job, beyond being amazing in bed, is that I keep my mouth shut."

"Okay," said Mike, "let's leave names to one side for the moment. Tell me about what *kind* of men went to those parties, outside of them being rich and powerful that is."

"There's nothing much more to say about them, other than they were very rich and, in their own way, very powerful. Most of them were old, at least in my estimation. I'm talking about them being seventy at least, maybe older. Half of them couldn't get it up, but they still liked the thrill of having a beautiful woman on their arm as they walked into the party."

"And then there was Sam," said Mike, "where in God's name did he fit in?"

"At first, he didn't," replied Maria. "He was just there, wandering around the party like a spare part. It was mainly because of the fact he didn't fit in, that I started speaking to him in the first place."

"So, why was he there?" pressed Mike.

"Same as the rest of us, he'd been invited."

"By whom?"

"No idea, but I have a suspicion that I know why," Maria then said, sipping at her coffee and still checking around for anyone showing more interest in her than she'd like.

Mike's curiosity was suitably aroused. "I'm listening," he said.

"When Sam and I started to see each other, he never said a word about the job he did. In time, however, he opened up about the fact he worked for MI6, but he also hinted that he was working for someone else and I believe it was that someone else who invited Sam to the parties."

Mike was a little confused. "Why would you think that?"

"Because the parties I attended were not normal affairs," explained Maria. "Half the people at them weren't who they claimed to be and the other half seemed more intent on taking instructions, than enjoying themselves. It was as if the main reason for the party was to pass on information. I believe that Sam was a middle-man in that process."

"But who was passing on information and about what?" Mike then enquired.

"Again, I have no idea. I do know, however, that what appeared to be very important men would turn up and have clandestine meetings while we girls were left to powder our noses, or enjoy the odd glass of Champagne on our own."

"Was Sam ever at one of those meetings?"

"Good grief, no. Sam was just a messenger, nothing else. He waited with us for an update and then he'd go off and, no doubt, pass on what he'd been told."

"Did you ever know who any of those very important men were?" Mike now asked.

Maria shook her head. "No, they were never in our company."

Mike could hardly believe that. A man, obviously accustomed to getting his own way, turns up at a party where there are a number of highly attractive call-girls available and they didn't take the time to mix. If they really were only there for business purposes, then that business had to be ever so slightly dodgy, at least in Mike's estimation. No one conducts business and sends out runners from a party if everything is legitimate and above board,

"Did Sam ever say anything about his second job?" Mike then enquired.

"No. He did say it would help towards his pension, but he never went into any detail."

"And were you to be part of his retirement plan?" said Mike.

Maria smiled again. Another happy memory had come and probably gone.

"We spoke about being together. Whether that would ever have happened, we'll never know. He certainly wanted to be with me, but I was perhaps too attached to my lifestyle."

"How did you find out that Sam was dead?" Mike enquired.

"I was phoned by one of those powerful men I spoke about earlier."

"To tell you Sam was dead?"

"Yes."

"How had he known?"

Maria looked puzzled. "I have no idea' he just did."

"What did he tell you?"

"That Sam had been killed in a car crash and how sorry he was. He knew we'd been close and thought it best to tell me, before anyone else did."

"Can you tell me the name of this man?" said Mike.

"I'd rather not; client confidentiality and all that."

"Had Sam been acting differently recently?" was Mike's next question.

Maria thought about the question. "A little nervous, perhaps. He told me there were things going on at work, things he didn't want to worry me with I didn't think anymore of it."

"It wasn't really a car crash, you know," Mike then said.

Maria looked confused. "What do you mean?"

"He wasn't involved in a collision, as such, he was forced off the road."

Maria now looked scared. "What do you mean, forced off the road?"

She was looking around again, her eyes nervously darting in one direction and then another.

"Just that," said Mike, realising he was scaring her, but feeling he had to continue. She had to know that she was now in danger. From the way she was acting, Mike could see that she'd probably worked that out for herself. Her eyes widened as she said:

"You mean, someone killed him?"

Mike took a moment to reply. "That's exactly what I mean."

"Oh my God," Maria then said, the tears now flowing down her cheeks and a handkerchief being produced from her bag. She eventually gained control of her emotions enough to say: "They'll come for me next. They'll think I know something and I don't. Oh my God," she then said again, standing up and looking around, now convinced she might be being watched. "They could be watching us at the moment; they could be seeing me here with you. You've put me in even more danger."

Maria grabbed her bag off the back of the chair and started to walk away. Mike quickly took money from his pocket and left it under a saucer. He then hurried after Maria and as he did so, he noticed, for the first time, movement in a car a little way down the street. Two men were getting out of the car and Mike sensed they were coming after them.

He didn't want to alarm Maria, but he took her by the elbow and moved a little closer.

"In a minute," he said, "we're going to go through a department store. We're not looking for anything, just making sure that no one could be following us."

He noted the look of fear in Maria's eyes.

"It's just a precaution," he added, briefly glancing back and noticing the men were beginning to close on them.

Mike steered Maria through the store, taking various detours and eventually, exiting through another of the many doors they could have chosen. Mike quickly led Maria to where he had parked his car and practically threw her in the back seat, telling her to stay down until he told her otherwise. He then got in to the driver's seat, started the engine and set off towards the MILO offices.

As they passed another of the exits to the department store, Mike noticed the two men who had been following them, were now standing on the pavement, looking up and down and probably cursing loudly.

Tuesday, 13th July, 1971 - MILO HQ, London

Ben met with Sir Tavish at a little after two in the afternoon. The purpose of the meeting was to exchange information they had gathered on the Great Train Robbery.

"Did you get much from Reynolds?" Sir Tavish asked.

"Not a lot. I'm guessing he isn't a fan of people in authority, so he was never likely to be very forthcoming."

Sir Tavish nodded. "Once a thief, always a thief."

"You could say that," agreed Ben. "Anyway, even though he didn't actually *say* anything of any consequence, he did allude to something very interesting. I asked him, outright, it he had known of any German money behind the train robbery. I couched the question in terms of whether he would confirm or deny a German presence. He said he would neither confirm, nor deny it. I think that was his way of telling me that there had been German money and perhaps even German input I'm more inclined to believe that Freiheit could well have been the source of that money and that the payback they got from it was far more than even they might have expected."

Sir Tavish nodded again. He was beginning to think the same way. Proving it would be tantamount to impossible, but if they adopted the working theory that Freiheit had been behind The Great Train Robbery, then the next phase would be to find someone who could not only confirm that, but also provide a clearer picture of how, *exactly*, they had managed to get in tow with a bunch of small-time crooks.

"Was Frank Williams any help?" Ben then asked.

"He did tell me that the estimate regarding how much was stolen, wasn't very specific and could have erred on the cautious side. To be honest, I'm not sure if anyone really had the first idea as to how much money was on that train. It had been as high as six million on occasions. If it had been that, on this occasion, then millions went unaccounted for and someone could be sitting on a nest-egg that no one is actually looking for."

"In short, the perfect robbery," said Ben.

"Certainly, one that no Mastermind could have planned in such a perfect way. If the banks weren't sure how much money was on that train, then how could the robbers ever have known how much they were driving away with that night."

"And there's no way they could have taken the time to count out six million pounds," said Ben.

"They would have set aside the money due to go back to the investors," said Sir Tavish, "and then had a stab at counting the rest. Some of the gang may not have been that bright, however, so who knows what total they came up with."

"Has anyone had any thoughts on who might have been the brains behind it all?" enquired Ben.

"Williams would have us believe there never was a Mastermind," answered Sir Tavish.

"Why would he be so sure?" Ben then asked.

"Because of the lack of an exit strategy," explained Sir Tavish. "Williams believes that, if someone had really come up with a plan, then they'd have had an exit strategy. As it was, those men took the money to a farm and waited. What the hell were they waiting for?"

"Maybe that *was* the exit strategy," Ben then said.

"I don't follow," said Sir Tavish.

"Collect the investor's cut and then let the gang be caught," said Ben. "No one in the gang would have known who the investors were and with at least a large percentage of the money back, the police investigation would have been reined back."

Sir Tavish nodded. It wasn't a totally insane notion. He spoke again.

"If we take the view that those investors were connected to Freiheit then we have to hope that somewhere, amongst the low-life of London, that someone would be able to confirm it. Get the word out on the street that we're prepared to pay good money for information concerning anyone involved in the planning of the Great Train Robbery. It has to be *useful* information, mind, I'm not paying for any old rubbish."

Ben was still smiling as he left the room.

13th July, 1971, MILO Offices – West Berlin

Maria Bauman sat in a small room, with only a small, insignificant window to break up the monotony of three of the walls around her. The fourth wall had a door in it. There was a thin covering of lime green paint on the walls and the floor was covered with a darker green cutting of linoleum. In the middle of the floor was a table, with four chairs set around it.

Maria was drinking a mug of coffee and Mike now arrived with two bacon rolls he'd acquired. He placed one in front of Maria and sat down with the other still in his hand.

"You'll feel better if you eat something," he said, pointing down at the bacon roll. Maria eyed hers with suspicion, as if she had never seen anything like it before. It might have looked a bit strange, but it smelled inviting, so she picked it up and bit into it.

"It's okay," she then said, sounding surprised.

Mike smiled. "I can cook more than that," he said. "But it'll do for just now."

They finished their food in silence.

Mike then leaned forward, across the table. Maria started to look concerned again and it was she who actually spoke first.

"We *were* being followed, weren't we?"

Mike saw no point in lying to her, especially as he now had her in a safe environment.

"Yes. I was hoping you'd be able to tell me who they were?"

Maria shook her head.

"I don't know. I've thought there were men following me before, but I could never prove it."

"Tell me a little more about the work you do?" Mike then said, moving his mug a little closer and cupping it with his hands.

"I'm not proud of what I do, but it pays the bills."

"I'm not judging you, Maria, far from it. I simply want to get a better idea of the world you moved in and maybe, from that, get a better perspective on what Sam was really doing."

Maria digested what had just been said and then nodded.

"As I said, I'm an escort. I don't like being called a prostitute because what I do, does not always lead to sex. Sometimes I'm just there for company and to look good."

"Is it normally the same men who pay for your time?"

"Usually."

"And do you get a feel for who these men are? I mean, do they ever talk about themselves?"

Maria laughed. "All the time, but they do it in such a way that they don't actually give that much away. They'll tell you how much power they have and how nice they can be to me. They'll tell me how good they are in bed and how they can give me a good time. They'll make it sound like paying for a woman's company is the most natural thing in the world. They'll even tell me they have a wife and family, but they will never tell you anything about them. They will never talk about their work and they will never tell me anything that might be wholly personal to them. It is as if they have only a small piece of themselves that they are willing to give to me. It means I end up knowing next to nothing about them."

"Yet, you said they appeared to be at those parties more for business reasons, rather than anything personal?" Mike then asked.

"That was the impression I got. There really was an awful lot of talking done amongst the men and not much action at times."

"But you never even for the slightest inclination as to what they might have been talking about?" Mike added.

Maria shook her head again. "All the talk was done in other rooms. We girls were never part of any of that."

"So, why have you there in the first place?" Mike enquired.

Maria smiled. "I told you, we were there to look good. We were window dressing for the party, often there to be looked at but rarely touched. That's why I said that what I do doesn't always lead to sex. Many of my clients are too old. If I'd really given them a good time we'd have been calling for an ambulance before the end."

Mike laughed. Maria laughed as well and for a brief moment the atmosphere in the room lightened with their mood. Mike drank a little coffee and then continued with his line of questioning.

"Did you ever pick up on any clues as to who the men at your parties might have been?"

Maria thought for a moment. "Sam once joked that he thought many of them might have been ex-SS. They certainly acted as if they might have been part of that brotherhood."

"You said these men rarely told you much about themselves," Mike then said, "could that have come from the fact they were accustomed to hiding their past in front of others?"

"They were certainly accustomed to hiding secrets. I mean, as far as their families were ever concerned, *I* was one of those secrets."

"And Sam was working for these men of secrets?" Mike then said.

"In some capacity; yes."

"And getting paid for it?"

"That would appear to have been the case; yes."

Mike decided to take Maria down a slightly different route. He asked her to have a look through a book of photographs, just in case she recognised anyone from the parties she had attended. Had those parties been Freiheit connected, or even just a meeting-place for ex-SS, then there was every chance that somewhere amongst their number would be faces already known by the authorities.

Maria looked worried. She asked if she was now in even greater danger.

"Not as long as you're in my charge," said Mike. "You're safe here and I'll make sure you remain safe. I'm guessing we'll have to get you out of Berlin, but we can keep you safe, don't you worry."

"But I am worried. I don't know anything, but I'm worried that they, whoever *they* are, might think I do."

"*They* can think what they like," said Mike, "I promise, I won't let anyone hurt you."

Maria looked at Mike for a little while and then she smiled.

"Okay, I believe you," she then said. "Do you want to show me that book now."

Tuesday, 13th July, 1971 – Hamburg, West Germany

Ralf Dinger was not a happy man.

As Head of Security for Freiheit he was forever dealing with problems, the solutions for which usually involved other people. He got annoyed, therefore, when those other people failed to play their part in solving Dinger's problems. Obviously, he could not do everything himself, but on occasions he truly wished that he could.

He had just received the call from West Berlin. Maria Bauman had disappeared, whilst in the company of a strange man, who seemed too street-wise to just be some random client she had met. There was every reason to believe that she was now in the company of an intelligence agent, country of origin unknown.

Dinger assumed it was the British. They were the biggest pain in his arse, the most likely to be poking their collective noses into matters that should not be concerning them. If it were the British, did it mean that MILO were getting closer, or was it just MI6 working on matters relating to Sam Halliday?

As soon as he'd realised that Sam was going to be a problem, he'd had him dealt with. A trifle crude, perhaps, but efficient none the less. Germans took a pride in being efficient; they did not like to waste energy on lost causes. They had all thought Sam to be a colleague, but that had not been the case. He had turned against his master and under no circumstances could that be allowed.

Dinger felt sure he had nipped the Sam Halliday problem in the bud, having him killed before he had been able to tell anyone anything. Not that Dinger even knew what Sam might have learned. It ought to have been nothing, but he couldn't be sure.

His thoughts turned to Maria Bauman. Lovely girl. Great in bed, from all accounts and someone well versed in keeping her mouth shut. The men he'd put on her, were only meant to observe. They were under instructions not to get too close, but they were also under instructions not to lose her. Now she was in the wind, did that make her a more serious threat, or had she actually not known anything in the first place?

It boiled down to how little, or how much, Sam might have told her. Dinger remained confident that Sam Halliday had never known that much to tell her. Dinger had had Maria's flat bugged and spent many an entertaining night listening to her having sex with a variety of men, some of whom were known to Dinger, while others weren't. He knew Maria to be a vocal participant in bed, letting her men know what she liked and, in turn, ensuring she did to them what they liked. Dinger had often pictured himself in bed with her, as he had listened to those many recordings.

Yes, lots of noise during the sex act, but nothing of any consequence away from it. Maria had not been in the habit of saying much to anyone and all the recordings of her with Sam had shown that they had enjoyed each other's company, but never spoke about anything on a personal level. It was as if Maria wanted to keep the real her hidden from the clients, even those clients she allowed to get a bit closer than others.

She didn't *seem* to know anything, but did that really mean that she *didn't* know anything. Recordings only captured the spoken word, what if she had been holding on to papers for Sam? What if she had *read* more than listened? What if Sam had been all too aware that her flat was bugged and had, effectively, played those who were listening? Were that the case, then Maria could be anywhere, by now, telling them the whole story.

But what could that story possibly be? What could Sam have learned that would be particularly damaging to Freiheit? He might have picked up on the off name, but they wouldn't have led anywhere. Most of the men at those parties were living under an assumed name anyway. Maria might recognise faces but, again, that would only lead back to an assumed name and a concocted life history. The more that Dinger considered the matter, the more he convinced himself that

Maria Bauman could know nothing that would directly affect Freiheit and the people within it.

However, just to make sure, he made another phone call. He would send the West Berlin heavies to check-out Maria's flat. Their instructions were simple:

"Tear the place apart and if you find anything even remotely connected to Freiheit then destroy it immediately. If there is anything that might be connected to Sam Halliday then take it away and let me know. For the moment, however, don't concern yourself with Maria Bauman herself. I do not see her as a threat."

Satisfied that he had done all that he could, for the moment, Dinger then poured himself a large whisky and sat back to read through a variety of reports that had come in from various corners of Germany. He liked to keep up to date with developments within Freiheit, so that he could continue to feedback, with an element of accuracy, to Herr Brandt at the end of each month.

Tuesday, 13th July, 1971 - MILO Offices, West Berlin.

Maria stopped turning the pages of the book she'd been given.

"That's one of them," she then said, pointing at the photograph of a man at the top of one of the pages.

Mike swung the book around and pointed at the photograph.

"This one?" he said.

"Yes."

Mike took the picture from between the clear sheets in which it was trapped and read the name written on the back. *Mayr Scheer. Might be Karl-Heinz Achen, though no proof of such meantime.*

"We have his name as being Mayr Scheer, does that ring a bell with you?" Mike then enquired.

"I told you, I never got the names of any of them. I do remember him being a regular at the parties though. I saw Sam speaking to him on more than one occasion."

"Excellent," said Mike. "Anyone else you recognise?"

Maria began working her way through the remainder of the book. The only other photograph that she selected was of Sigi Trautman. However, with Trautman now dead it didn't help as much as it might have done. It did point to the parties being meeting places for ex-SS, which would have been the perfect arrangement for keeping everyone up to date with Freiheit business at the same time.

After they had finished with the photographs, Mike then asked Maria if Sam had ever given her anything, no matter how insignificant the gift might have been. She said he'd never given her anything. Mike then asked if Sam was at Maria's flat much. She confirmed that he had been.

"We made love there," Maria then said, a smile crossing her face as she remembered happier moments.

"And he never left anything at your flat?" said Mike.

"Not that I'm aware of."

"Would I be able to go and have a look around?" Mike enquired.

"Do you think Sam *did* leave something?" Maria asked in reply.

"Even after the little I've learned about Sam; I'd still expect him to have kept some record of what he was doing and yet we've found nothing."

Maria took a set of keys from her bag," Feel free to go and have a look; just don't mess up the place, okay?"

Maria was smiling as Mike took the keys from her. He smiled back, she seemed to be relaxing a little in his company. Mike then asked one of the female staff to keep Maria company, while he was away. He then met up with a colleague and set off for Maria's flat.

*

Mike knew something was wrong as soon as they got there. The front door was slightly open, the lock having been forced. He carefully pushed the door open and waited to see if anyone reacted to his shout. There was nothing. He entered the hallway, his colleague close behind and both men already feeling the surge of fight or flight adrenalin. Each room they visited had been trashed. Whoever had been there, had been through the entire flat and emptied drawers, cabinets, wardrobes; the lot. The floors were strewn with papers, garments and assorted other items.

The question springing to Mike's mind was: *had they found anything of value?*

The next question, which followed closely behind was: *is it worth us now looking?*

Mike decided that it was. They took half the property each and checked everywhere they thought Sam might have seen as a safe hiding place. It had to have been somewhere that Maria was unlikely to go herself, he would not have wanted her to be aware that he was hiding something that could put her in danger.

Mike stood back at one stage and thought things through, once again. His eyes fell on the French windows that led out on to the balcony. The doors were still closed and locked. It seemed obvious that no one had been out there, certainly not recently. Mike had a quick look around for a key, but couldn't find one. He went into the hall and picked up the phone. He reconsidered using it, almost immediately. There was every chance it would be bugged; possibly for some time. He shouted to his colleague that he'd be back as soon as possible and then hurried out the door.

He walked a short distance to a café, which was situated on a nearby corner. There was a phone at the back, which he now asked to use. He flashed his identification card, which obviously looked official enough to gain the necessary permission from the café owner, without them really looking at the content of the ID card.

He phoned the office, spoke to Maria and then headed back to the flat, now armed with the knowledge of where the balcony key was kept. Within moments of arriving back at the flat, Mike was out on the balcony and approaching the pot in the corner. He lifted the plant out and checked underneath. Success.

A small, black book, wrapped in a polythene bag, was lying there. Mike picked it up and replaced the plant. He didn't pause to look closer at what he had found, but merely pushed it into his pocket and went back into the flat. He locked the doors behind him and put the key in his pocket beside the book.. If others wanted to check the balcony now then they'd have to work a lot harder for the privilege.

Before leaving the flat, Mike took the time to pack a suitcase with items he knew Maria would need. A circuit of the property failed to come up with her passport, or any other personal paperwork. Either she kept them somewhere else, or the previous visitors had removed them.

They left the flat, pulling the front door shut behind them. It wasn't locked, but it at least *looked* secure. They crossed the road to their car and Mike got into the passenger seat, throwing the case on to the back seat.

On the journey back to the office, Mike had already began thinking of a way to get Maria out of West Germany. Somehow, he needed to get her back to the UK, where he felt they could protect her better.

*

Mike got back to the MILO offices and found a room where he could read through the contents of Sam's book. The less people who knew he had it, the better. Not that he had any reason to believe that amongst his colleagues lurked a spy.

He took the bag from his pocket and then took the book out of the bag. He opened it with growing excitement at what might be inside. Unfortunately, it turned out not to be much. Only a few pages had writing on them. He began to read what there was:

I am not a traitor.

I'm sure many were beginning to think that I was. Please believe me, I'm not.

They contacted me around six to seven months ago. I was approached one night in a pub. They knew who I was; I had no idea who they were. They said they could help me; they could speed the path to promotion and better days. In return, all I had to do was a few favours when required.

I saw it as an opportunity. I was never going to play their game, but I did think I might be able to learn more about them, maybe even get a few names.

From Day One I knew I was dealing with Freiheit. They never said who they were; I just knew. I bet old Viewforth will be annoyed to learn I was inside the Freiheit organisation and said nothing to anyone. If MILO are involved now – sorry.

I was never asked for MI6 information. I was never actually asked for anything. All I did was pass information on. It was all cryptic stuff, so I never understood the meaning of any of it. However, it did get me to the parties and that is where we'd learn a lot, if we could only breach the inner sanctum. There is a strict hierarchy within Freiheit. Everyone knows their place and as I was a lowly subject, I was never going to be told very much.

I really thought I could make a difference. I really thought that I would stumble on a strong lead, but it never happened. My hopes of playing the hero were dashed by a group of men who all seemed to know how to keep a secret.

I have two names. Not much, but perhaps a start.

Mayr Scheer. *Seems to be quite high up in the Freiheit organisation as he arrives at parties with information, which is then disseminated to the other guests. Never within my hearing, of course, always in a quiet room somewhere. Scheer, I feel sure, is actually Karl-Heinz Achen. One guest let slip his first name at one party and another spoke of his time in Finland and Lithuania during the war. Achen was certainly in both countries and is still wanted for atrocities in both. Both men fit the same description and the one photograph of Achen that I was able to see did look a lot like Scheer. These ex-SS pay good money for their new identity, but I can't seem to find anything to do with Scheer prior to the war starting. Achen, on the other hand, was a right charmer.*

The other name is **Sigi Trautman**. *Have only recently started working on him, but feel pretty sure that Trautman's real name is Jurgen Maier, another charmer wanted for deeds committed in the war. He works for the Varga Corporation and I still have a feeling that Freiheit and Varga are connected, though I haven't been able to find out how. Maybe it's the fact that the Varga Corporation grew so big so quickly that it makes one assume there was illegal shenanigans somewhere.*

Maria Bauman knows nothing. She may love me, in her own way, but she knows nothing about either what I've been doing, or Freiheit itself. She is nothing more than a beautiful woman who has found herself caught up in a world of nasty men with concealed pasts. She probably doesn't even know that the parties she's been attending have, at the very least, been a breeding ground for SS dogma and a means to ensuring that the SS brotherhood never dies.

They are all still as mad as they were thirty years ago. They still believe in Adolf Hitler and they still believe in the superiority of a powerful Germany.

It is definitely the parties you need to watch. I was told about them on the phone. I never had face to face contact with anyone, I think that's the way they work. Freiheit seems to be a well-oiled machine in how it has been organised. It is designed to survive a certain amount of damage, so if you want to destroy Freiheit you'll need to cut off its head, or cut out its heart. Possibly both.

Sorry I couldn't be of more help. Please look after Maria. I assume I must now be dead, if you are reading this and I can only hope the good guys got to this book first.

Sam Halliday (No Traitor)

Mike put the book back in the bag and the bag in his pocket. Sam Halliday had been right; it wasn't much. In fact, Mike didn't think it was anything like enough to have cost him his life. Freiheit must have suspected he'd known a lot more. Did that mean they would now feel the same about Maria? Was her life now in danger? All the more reason to get her out of West Germany.

At least Sam had confirmed what Maria had already told Mike; namely Meyr Scheer was a guest at those parties. He also now confirmed that Scheer was really Karl-Heinz Achen, so it was time to set the dogs on Achen and have him arrested for crimes committed during the war. At least the arrest of a major war criminal would be some success for Sam Halliday, even if it had cost him his life.

Mike now found a phone and made a few calls, all of which cleared the way for Maria and himself being on a plane that night, taking them to England.

Friday, 16th July, 1971 – London

The man calling himself Barry Gibb slowly climbed out of bed, trying hard not to disturb the woman lying beside him. The blankets were pulled up and all that was visible was her curly red hair. In the company of this woman, the man was known as Barry Gibb, but he was actually Tony Rutherford.

The woman was Gill Potter. She had always thought of herself as being a bit of a plain-Jane. Her more glamourous friends had always got the boys first, Gill often getting no more than the sympathy vote. She usually got the boy no one else wanted. It had often been better than nothing.

Gill had done well at school and by the time she left, she'd even found herself in a relationship with a boy who'd told her he loved her. She'd believed him and tumbled into bed one night,

after a few drinks at a party. She'd thought that he was the one; the boy she'd marry and have a long and happy life with.

He left her three weeks later. She never forgave herself for being so stupid and vowed never to make the same mistake again.

Her now jaundiced view of men had gone a long way towards Gill keeping her image downbeat. She never dressed to directly attract anyone; she was quite happy to wear what she liked and enjoy her own company. Who needed men anyway?

On leaving school, Gill had worked in a couple of offices, learning general administrative skills. She had then seen a job advertised for Barclays Bank and had applied.

Which was why she was now the secretary to the manager of the Moorgate Branch of that bank.

Six weeks ago, Gill's opinion of men had been changed. She had been out with a few of her friends from the bank and she'd been undergoing the usual experience of seeing those friends attracting the attention of men, while Gill was pretty much left alone to enjoy her drink.

And then Barry Gibb started speaking to her. She couldn't believe her luck; he was gorgeous. All her *I hate men* notions departed the moment he flashed her a smile and offered to buy another drink. She had been swept away by his charm. Life, for Gill Potter, was definitely on the up.

In the time that had passed, they'd seen each other at least half a dozen times. They'd spent much of those times in bed. Gill had never experienced sex like it. Here was a man who really seemed to care for her; who really wanted to do all that he could do to please her. She'd had to pinch herself, on more than one occasion, to make sure she wasn't dreaming.

Gill pushed back the covers and focussed on Tony, as he got out of bed. He looked back and smiled.

"Just going for a wash," he said and made his way to the bathroom.

Tony relieved himself, then turned to face the sink. There was a mirror above the sink and Tony now saw his own face looking back at him. He wasn't sure he liked what he saw but, then again, a man had to do what a man had to do. Gill Potter was important to him and if it required a little deception to ensnare her, then so be it.

He knew she was beginning to love him.

He knew she'd be shattered when the truth finally came out, but he couldn't afford to care. It wasn't as if he would ever have loved a woman like Gill Potter. He needed her purely for information, the fact he'd managed to add a little sex to that had been a bonus.

He began washing, his mind running over the plan for the bank raids once again. These raids would not be so much about money, they'd be more about the contents of safe-deposit boxes. It needed a lot more planning, but the end product would make it all worthwhile.

Tony had other contacts working in various banks around London. They'd all provide a little information here and a little there. Like a jigsaw the pieces would slowly fit into place until the perfect bank raid was just waiting to happen. Gill Potter would be required to provide some of those pieces.

It was just a matter of finding the right time to tell her.

Tony finished drying himself off. He brushed his teeth and then returned to the bedroom where he found Gill out of bed and dressing. He looked at her as he entered the room. Although she wouldn't normally have been his type he had found it less of a chore to seduce her than he'd first thought. She'd been good company and a quick learner in bed. He'd quickly come to the conclusion that there was a passionate woman inside Gill Potter, only she chose not to release her unless prompted.

"There's plenty hot water," Tony said, pointing back towards the bathroom.

"I need to get home to change," Gill replied, "I'll have a wash there."

Gill finished zipping up her dress and now looked around the room for her bag. They had been rather amorous the night before and their clothes and personal items were lying everywhere. She eventually found her bag kicked under the bed. Her jacket was hanging over the wardrobe door; neither of them could remember how it got there.

"Will I see you later?" Gill then said.

Tony moved closer and they kissed.

"I'll be there at the usual time."

Gill smiled. "I'll have food on the go. You can bring the wine."

"Deal," said Tony.

He watched Gill leave the flat and sat down. He knew it would be the last time he'd see her happy.

After tonight, he thought, *it'll be nothing but hatred.*

Friday, 16th July, 1971 – MILO HQ, Central London

Things had moved on a little since Mike had returned to London with Maria. There was still uncertainty as to how safe Maria would be in London, assuming that Freiheit were still interested in her. Sir Tavish had considered using Maria as bait, hoping to draw Freiheit operatives out of the woodwork, but he had quickly decided against that; Maria deserved better. She was, after all, just a pawn in someone else's game.

Sir Tavish decided, instead, to put Maria in a safe-house, situated just outside London. It was a large house in the country with garden space at the back that would allow her the opportunity to get much-needed exercise and still remain within a protected environment. She had two MILO agents for company and Mike also intended spending as much time with her as he could.

Mike, in the meantime, had set about looking into the life of Karl-Heinz Achen. Firstly, he had found out that Meyr Scheer did, in fact, have a job with the Varga Corporation, though in a relatively minor capacity. As with many of his ex-SS colleagues, his identity as Meyr Scheer did not start until 1946. His photograph, however, did confirm that he and Achen were one and the same person.

Achen's name was connected to a number of atrocities, which had been committed in various Eastern European countries throughout the war. He was a big fish on the list of war criminals and the right thing would have been to report what they knew, immediately.

Instead, Sir Tavish decided to wait a little longer, just in case the Achen link brought them closer to Freiheit.

Mike had also tried to get more information on the parties Maria had attended. It turned out that all the properties, which Maria had been able to identify, had been taken on short leases. One party and move on. No audit trail left behind. Freiheit were the best at covering their tracks. Mike began to realise why Sam Halliday's interfering had so annoyed the organisers of those parties. There they were, taken such measures as to protect their anonymity and in their midst was a man intent on bringing them all down. No wonder they'd decided to kill him.

Ben, Amy and Mike were sitting in room 314. A coffee percolator bubbled in the corner. A half-finished bottle of whisky lay beside it, though it was too early in the day for anyone to be contemplating a nip of Scotch.

They were searching for links. They were searching through the timeline of those men they *did* know about; in the hope they might find information on others that they didn't. It was a long-winded way of getting nowhere fast, but it was all that they had meantime.

They started with Karl-Heinz Achen and Jurgen Maier. Maier had been killed for fear of MILO getting too close to him. Achen, on the other hand, didn't even know he was on MILO's radar. The only concern was that Freiheit might also link Achen with Maria Bauman, which would put her in even more danger.

The usual search had been done on Hans Varga's war record to see if Achen turned up at any point. He hadn't.

They also had Franz Neuer. He was little more than a name at the moment, but it seemed fair to assume that if Achen and Maier, two men with changed identities, were working for the Varga Corporation then Neuer might also be working under an assumed identity.

If that were the case then what was Neuer's real name?

Amidst much shuffling of paper and the odd note being taken, Ben suddenly looked up, as if a light had come on above his head.

"Maybe these men were connected *before* the war," he said, "in which case, we haven't gone back far enough."

Amy looked horrified. "Jeez, we have a lot of names to work through as it is. If we go back a full ten years then what's that going to add?"

"In which case we break up the list even more and bring in as much help as we can," said Ben. "There has to be a connection and it would help immensely if we could find it."

Ben left to visit the Computer Room. They'd have to provide a lot more information before the team could move forward with his latest theory. With Ben away, Amy took the opportunity for a little small-talk.

"How is Maria doing?" she asked.

On hearing her name, Mike smiled broadly.

"She's holding up. I'm going to see her this weekend, there's a few points I want to clarify with her."

Amy turned on him. "Oh, for God's sake Mike, you can't only see the girl when you have questions to ask. She needs to feel her life is getting back on track so take her out, let her enjoy herself."

Mike was a little taken aback by Amy's sharp words. He was about to challenge her when the thought struck him that she might be right. He'd never considered taking Maria out and yet there was no reason why he shouldn't, other than her not wanting to, of course. He'd speak to her that weekend and take her for a meal, if she was in agreement.

By the time Ben returned to the room, Amy had moved on to another part of Varga's war record. Ben had just sat down again when Amy spoke.

"Here's something that might at least be a blemish on Herr Varga's otherwise untarnished reputation."

As she spoke, Amy moved a few sheets of paper around. She had notes on them all, making it difficult to tie things together in a hurry. She started reading from one sheet.

"There was an incident on ninth of September, nineteen forty-three, in Parma when Italian troops rose up against the German forces sent to control them. It was one of those occasions where both Wehrmacht and SS units were definitely in the area at the same time."

Amy then found another piece of paper.

"Varga was definitely in Italy at that time, though I don't have him specifically in Parma. Seems a number of Italian soldiers were executed along with innocent locals who were hanged from the nearest lamp-post simply to send out a message to their fellow countrymen."

"We need more information on those incidents and if possible, we need the names of the SS officers who were in charge around the time that those atrocities took place."

"Let's spread the search a little further," Amy then suggested. "I'll start looking for anything prior to the war starting, and you two can concentrate on the war years themselves."

They agreed that that was a good idea. A central list was to be started. Any names that showed potential would go on that list and be further checked at a later time.

Friday, 16th July, 1971 – Gill Potter's Flat, Clapham Common

Dinner had been a success. Gill could certainly cook; Tony had always thought that. The dishes were left to fend for themselves in the kitchen while two glasses and another, newly opened, bottle of red were taken through to the living room. Tony sat on the settee and Gill put the bottle on a table by the settee, before sitting down beside him.

She'd noticed earlier that this new man in her life seemed preoccupied, as something were preying on his mind. She feared he might be building up to ending their relationship. It certainly wouldn't have surprised her.

"There's something bothering you, isn't there?" Gill eventually said. If this was to be the end, then best get it over with.

Tony took one last drink from his wine glass and then laid it down, a little distance from where he was sitting. If she was going to get violent then he didn't want wine all over his smart clothes. He drew breath, then began talking.

"I've not been entirely honest with you, Gill, in fact I've been entirely *dishonest* with you to date."

Gill looked puzzled, but said nothing. Tony continued.

"I only really brought you into my life because I need you to help me."

Gill's confusion deepened, but still she chose to let him do all the talking.

"I need you to get me certain information from your branch and I need it fairly quickly."

Finally, Gill spoke. It was only one word and it was almost stuck in her throat.

"What?"

"I ask you to do this as a favour to me," Tony then said, "but if you were to consider saying no, then I'm afraid I've done something which I feel sure would make you think again."

The confusion was back on Gill's face. This time she did manage to speak again.

"What the hell are you talking about?"

"I want you to get me copies of the front door and vault keys for your bank. In return for doing that you'll be well paid."

The horror on Gill's face was now evident. She put down her wine glass and stared even harder at Tony.

"What would make you think I'd help you with anything, let alone something illegal? You might be decent in bed, Barry, but you're not that good. I *can* live without you."

"Yes, Gill, I know that; only I can't move on with my plan unless you get me the information I need."

"Then your plan won't be going anywhere, because I'm not prepared to risk my future for you."

Tony stood up.

"I pretty much expected you to say that, which is why I took out a little insurance on you."

Gill's expression was now one of concern mixed with fear.

"What have you done?" she asked, though a part of her didn't really want to hear the answer.

"At the Fleet Street branch of Barclays Bank, I have had an account running for the last eighteen months or so. A young lady, who is an acquaintance of mine, has been paying in money on a monthly basis and also keeping some items in a safe-deposit box. The account is currently in the name of Melanie Fleming."

"This is all very interesting," said Gill, "but what's it got to do with me?"

"I'm coming to that," Tony said, sitting down again, but maintaining distance between them. "After I'd met you, I arranged for my lady acquaintance to put certain fresh items into the safe-deposit box and to also ensure that more paperwork was completed at the bank. In short, there are now papers in the safe-deposit, which explains that Melanie Fleming is actually Gill Potter. My friend is pretty good at forging, she'd managed to sign the name Melanie Fleming in the style of your writing. I think it looks pretty authentic."

"What difference does it make if people believed this second account was actually mine?" Gill then asked, still not fully understanding what this man was saying.

"Ah, of course, I forgot to tell you the part that really causes you problems," Tony then said.

Gill looked worried again. She waited for him to explain himself.

"The account has five thousand pounds in it. The safe-deposit box now contains evidence that that money was made from immoral earnings. You've left a notebook there with client names, appointments and payments made. Once again, I believe the handwriting looks quite authentic and though someone might eventually see through my little game, your reputation would be in tatters long by then."

"You bastard! Gill practically shouted at him.

"Sadly, I can't disagree with that assessment," Tony said. "However, I need the information that you can bring me and I had to make sure you wouldn't say no. Do as I ask and all this goes away, except the five thousand pounds, which is yours to do with as you please."

"Why?" Gill then said, the tears running down her cheeks.

"I've told you why, Gill. This is nothing personal, if it's worth anything at all, I do really like you and to be honest, I never thought that would be the case."

"You fucking bastard!" Gill announced again and she threw herself at him.

Tony fought her off and pushed her back to where she'd been sitting.

"There's no point in you expending energy trying to fight me, Gill, you'll never win. I have you stitched up and the only way out is to get me the information I want."

Gill was weeping openly. Tony picked up his wine glass and sat some distance from her again. He waited for her to calm down. As she did, she asked another question.

"How do I know you're not just making all this up?"

Tony smiled. He went over to his jacket and took something from an inside pocket. He handed a piece of paper to Gill. It had the address of the Fleet Street branch at the top. The content of the letter referred to the safe-deposit box and also to the fact the current balance was £5,432.00p. Once she had read that, he handed another sheet of paper to her. This time it contained what appeared to be details of meetings and payments.

Gill's blood froze. The handwriting could well have been her own. It seemed she was being told the truth. It seemed she was now trapped between a rock and a hard place.

"What, exactly, do you want me to do?" she then enquired, feeling she had no way out, other than to co-operate with this man.

Tony smiled again and returned to his jacket. This time he took a bag from another pocket and took it across to Gill.

"I want you to get me impressions of the front door key and the vault door keys. Those are small tins with plasticine in them, all you have to do is press the key into them and I'll do the rest."

Gill looked at the bag, then back up at the man still standing over her.

"You never had any feelings for me, did you?" she then said.

"Not to begin with, no. However, I can now honestly say that I really do like you Gill and I'm truly sorry to have to do this to you. However, there really is no other way."

Gill sat and thought some more. She wanted to pick things up and throw them at him. She wanted to punch his chest and call him all the names under the sun. She wanted to do so much and yet she knew it would all be meaningless. He had planned everything to a point where only she would suffer now. She couldn't afford that.

"Okay," she eventually said, "I'll do what you ask."

"Thought you might," grinned Tony.

"Only, there's one major problem with your little plan."

The grin faded and for the first time Tony looked worried.

"What do you mean, a problem?"

"I can't get you impressions of the vault keys."

"Why not?"

"Because I'm never near them. They don't come within fifty feet of my working day, sorry."

It was now Gill who was smiling.

"I hold the trump cards," Tony then said. "It's your reputation that's on the line and only you can stop me going public with the contents of that safe-deposit box."

129

"But I really can't get at those vault keys," Gill insisted.

"Then think of a way. I don't care how you get them, just get them, okay?"

"When do you need the information by?" Gill then enquired.

"End of August at the latest."

"It seems I have no other option than to do what I can."

"Good girl."

"I'll be in touch. Now get out."

PART FOUR

Thursday, 29th July, 1971 – Hans Varga's home on Rhodes

Two decisions had been made, earlier that week. The first was that Ben and Amy should arrange to interview Hans Varga. Sir Tavish had decided to go straight to the horse's mouth and see what came out.

One of Ben's police contacts had also been in touch to say that he'd heard from one of his informants that Conrad Phillips had put money into the planning of the Great Train Robbery. With Phillips dead, it wasn't the most productive of leads, but Sir Tavish decided, nonetheless, to put Gerald Taylor on their list of Persons of Interest. If a previous Chief Executive could be involved in criminal activities, then maybe the current incumbent could be the same.

It was the Thursday before Ben and Amy could get the chance to see Varga. They arrived at his home a little before two in the afternoon. They were shown to a room at the back of the house, which was mercifully cool, certainly compared to the baking heat outside.

A few moments later and two men came into the room. Both Ben and Amy assumed that the older man was Hans Varga.

The younger man was immaculately dressed in a light suit and carrying a briefcase that had probably cost more than Ben made in a month. This had to be the lawyer.

Everyone sat down and Varga asked if they would like a cold drink. The offer was universally accepted and Varga rang a small bell to attract the attention of one of the maids. Once she had brought lemonade for everyone and left them to their discussion, Varga sat forward, leaning his elbows on the table as he did so.

"I have to say that I never expected to draw the attention of any of the intelligence agencies. I am a legitimate businessman, so what could you possibly want with me?"

"Just one or two points of interest that we hope you can clear up," said Ben.

"Well, if I can," said Varga.

"Where did you get the money with which to start your business?" Ben then asked. It was blunt, but it was meant to be. They were trying to get a reaction. They didn't.

Varga sat back; still quite relaxed, still very much in control.

"That is well documented. Surely, you read up on that already?"

"It just said 'unnamed silent partners,' which seems a bit vague," commented Ben.

"They wouldn't be silent partners if we named them," said Varga with a smug smile.

He was very much in control, much to Ben's annoyance.

"We know you came here in forty-eight," Ben then said. "Was that your first time back since the war?"

"It was. Helga and I used the trip as a honeymoon. She died in a car crash, but I'm sure you'll already know that."

"And then, not long after that trip to Rhodes, you had enough money to start a business," Ben then said. It was more of a statement than a question, but Varga responded nonetheless.

"No connection whatsoever. I had my honeymoon, then got down to starting my business. Certain individuals were happy to back me. They have all been paid handsomely for the faith they placed in me."

"Around the time you were on Rhodes, in forty-eight, there was a double murder," Ben now said.

"Was there?" said Varga, sounding less than interested.

"According to the police records, the murder took place in the house of a man whom locals believed to be a Nazi sympathiser. His name was Constantine Bavros, does that name mean anything to you, Herr Varga?"

Varga's expression did not change. "Not that I recall."

"Constantine had a sister; she was called Nana. Ring any bells?"

Varga picked up his lemonade and took a drink. "None whatsoever," he then said.

"The police reckon the reason for the murder was burglary."

"Do they now?" Varga then said. "Look, I admit to being here in forty-eight but I did not stop off to kill someone; I was here on my honeymoon, nothing else."

The information concerning the double murder had only just come to Ben's attention. A local police officer had uncovered details of the murders along with a local man who claimed to have information about the previous occupants. He told the police about Constantine and Nana and also the fact Hans Varga had been a regular visitor.

The police had investigated Constantine and Nana further, learning that Nana had been killed in Turkey within three months of leaving Rhodes.

Constantine had apparently disappeared altogether; they could find no trace of him.

"So, you definitely didn't know either Constantine Bavros, or his sister, Nana?" Amy now asked, taking up the questioning.

There was now a slight twitch at the side of Varga's left eye. He looked away, just for a brief moment, but it was still the act of a man most likely to now tell a lie.

"From your tone, you seem to think otherwise," he finally said.

Amy continued. "We have it on good authority that you did know both Constantine Bavros and his sister, Herr Varga. Locals remember you and they remember you as a regular visitor to the house."

Ben was now studying Varga closely, as Amy asked her questions. He had the look of a man being reminded of something painful, even though he continued to deny knowing what Amy was talking about.

"I'm afraid that your good authority has rather missed the mark," Varga then said. "I used to visit quite a few ladies when I was on this island during the war. They were little more than playthings, a mild distraction at a time when death might be just around the next corner. I bedded them with no thought as to who they were and consequently, I have no memory of them as individuals. Nana may have been one of those women and Constantine her brother, but the names ring no bells, I can assure you of that."

"So, you continue to deny knowing them?" pressed Amy.

"I believe my client has already said so. Perhaps, you could move on to something else," the lawyer then said. He still had not been formally introduced.

Ben looked at the lawyer. "Your client continues to contradict information that we've been given. We have the right to press him a little harder for a more truthful response."

Ben looked back at Varga, who was glancing in the direction of his lawyer. It was as if he was deciding how much more he was prepared to say. Maybe, in giving any answer, he was simply digging a deeper hole for himself. However, he did eventually provide an answer.

"Very well. I do remember Nana, but I do not remember her brother. Nana *was* one of the many women I visited when I was here. We had sex, that was about it."

"And yet you arranged for her to leave the island," Amy added.

Varga looked at her, as if he hadn't wanted anyone to know that.

"The locals knew of our assignations; I thought she might have been in danger after I left."

"And yet she died anyway," said Amy.

"Apparently so," conceded Varga.

Ben thought he saw real emotion in the old man's face. He decided to change the subject completely.

"Tell me about Conrad Phillips, Herr Varga?"

Varga looked puzzled.

"He's dead, what more can I say?"

"Oh, I'm sure you can tell us a lot more, Herr Varga," Ben said, his tone almost rebuking the old man.

Varga looked at Ben for what seemed like a long time. He said nothing, but Ben could almost see the cogs turning inside the man's head.

"What do you want to hear?"

"Did you ever have any reason to question Conrad Phillips work ethic?"

"I really don't know what you mean by that."

"Did you ever think that Conrad Phillips had done anything illegal in the name of the Varga Corporation?"

Varga sat forward. When he spoke, there was venom in his tone.

"If I had ever thought such a thing of the man, then he would not have died while still in my employ; I would have sacked him on the spot."

It sounded believable and Varga's reaction had seemed perfectly natural. Of course, the man had lived most of his life telling lies, so what difference would one more make.

"Why do you ask such a question?" the lawyer then chipped in.

"We have our reasons," was all that Ben would say. He hoped that by creating an air of mystery, he might make it sound as if he knew more than he did.

"And they might be?" pressed the lawyer.

"We have reason to believe that Conrad Phillips helped fund the Great Train Robbery."

Varga laughed. "What nonsense," he said.

"And you have proof of this?" enquired the lawyer, in a tone that clearly shouted, *but of course you don't.*

Ben chose to ignore the question, mainly because he didn't like the answer he would have had to give. The lawyer continued.

"If, as you say, Mister Phillips were to have been involved in funding the train robbery, are you also implying that he may have benefitted from the proceeds at the same time?"

"It would be fair to assume that, yes," said Ben.

"But, surely, all the proceeds were accounted for."

"Not necessarily. No one really knew how much money was stolen that night; it could have been significantly more than the banks ever admitted. If that were to be the case, then millions of pounds could have gone elsewhere and only the banks would know."

"Or, maybe, this is all a figment of your overblown imagination," added the lawyer. "Either way, I think we are done here. You, obviously, have nothing of any consequence to say to Herr Varga, so perhaps you should be on your way. My client is not a well man, he needs his rest."

Varga stood up and made his way out of the room. The lawyer followed, but paused in the doorway. Ben was close behind.

"How sick is your client?" he then asked.

"Very sick. He may only have a matter of weeks now; the cancer has spread and there is nothing anyone can do. I ask that you now leave him alone to die with dignity."

"Don't worry, it's unlikely we'll be back," Ben then said and he led Amy out of the house.

On the drive to the airport, Ben turned to Amy.

"Well, what did you make of that?"

"I think he's lying, I'm just not sure about what."

"Probably about everything," added Ben.

There really wasn't a lot more to add.

Monday, 2nd August, 1971 – MILO HQ, Central London

Two new lines of inquiry had been started since Ben and Amy had got back on the Friday. Mike was now looking deeper into the affairs of Gerald Taylor, whilst Sarah had been asked to look back on the life and times of Conrad Phillips. Amy, meantime, would soon be on her way back to Rhodes. They had received word, from the local police, that they had moved on a little with their investigation into the double murder of 1948. They felt it might be in MILO's interests to work more closely with them. Amy had been assigned to the task and was already at home packing.

Meanwhile, Sir Tavish had received material from the computer room, within MI5. A list of questions had been sent to them and now, a few days later, the replies had come back. Sir Tavish had called the meeting to update the team on what he had received from MI5.

The main gold nugget, within what was really a lot of mud, was the uncovering of two reports, both dealing with the same incident. The incident had occurred in November, 1938 and both the Wehrmacht and the SS had written a report to cover the action taken that night.

The SS account said that men had been called to two blocks of flats, in the early hours of the morning, to break up a group of residents who had been causing trouble and chanting anti-Government slogans.

The Wehrmacht report, on the other hand, spoke of an SS truck load of soldiers systematically ransacking peoples' homes and carrying off their belongings. The officer, making the report, also mentioned the fact that the SS officer, that night, had also taken a girl away in his car. There was a signature at the bottom of the Wehrmacht report; it was Hans Varga's.

Everyone now showed interest in the name of the SS officer who had taken the girl away in his car. It was given as Gunther Weiss; a name that meant nothing to anyone currently sitting in the room.

The question now was, who was Gunther Weiss?

Monday, 2nd August, 1971 – Gerald Taylor's Varga Office, London

Gerald Taylor sat at his desk, pouring over a mound of papers, all of which had arrived within the last couple of days. There was a Chief Executive meeting in three days and he needed to be fully focussed on Varga business. There had been occasions when he had let Freiheit business take precedence, but now that they were completely separated, he could no longer allow one to rule the other.

His main source of interest remained the upcoming bank raids. There seemed a greater excitement to making money illegally.

The intercom on his desk buzzed. Taylor picked up the phone. Hannah spoke.

"Mister Taylor, I have your wife for you on the line."

"Put her through please, Hannah."

"Gerald," the voice of his wife, Helen, now said, "I couldn't remember if you were going to be home for dinner tonight."

"I told you before I left this morning."

"Maybe you did, but I was half asleep and didn't really hear what you said."

"I said I'd be home for dinner, though I might be a little later home than usual."

"That's okay, I'll just have dinner ready for eight, instead of seven."

"Very good," said Taylor.

"See you later then, darling," said Helen and put the phone down. Taylor put down his receiver and sat back. The memories positively flooded into his mind.

He had met Helen at university. She had been far more intelligent than Gerald, studying a science-based subject, while Gerald chose History. They had seen each other across the hall at one of the dances and Gerald had eventually plucked up the courage to ask Helen to dance. He had thought her the most beautiful girl in the hall and had been firmly of the opinion that she would tell him to get lost. She didn't. They danced, then they danced again. They had then gone for a drink and that was them set for life. They remained together through university and then Gerald proposed.

They were married in 1962 and Gerald had got a job in the Varga Corporation in 1963. He had worked quite closely with Conrad Phillips, almost from day one. When Phillips died, the decision was taken to promote Gerald, even though he was younger than many of his competitors for the job. Helen had been so proud of her husband's achievements in the world of business, but she had never, at any point, wanted those business matters to invade their personal time.

They did not have children. It hadn't been planned that way, it just seemed that nature did not want them to be parents. Not that that bothered Gerald very much, although he had always been of the opinion that Helen's desire for children had always been stronger.

Gerald returned his attention to the papers in front of him, but was almost immediately interrupted again by a knock at his door. He called whoever it was into the room and Tony Rutherford put in an appearance. He was wearing a beige, three-piece suit with brown boots and a cream shirt, open at the collar. He looked as if he had just stepped out of a fashion catalogue. Without being invited, he came right into the room and sat down.

"We're nearly there," he said with a smile. "I have someone on the inside who can get us copies for the front door and vault keys for Barclays Bank in Moorgate. We have two teams ready to go whenever everything is in place."

"Let me get this straight," Taylor then said. "one team is literally going to walk through the front door?"

They are," replied Tony with a grin.

"So, why don't both teams do that?" Taylor then asked.

"Our biggest haul is going to come from Moorgate," explained Tony, "so we don't want anything going wrong there. The idea, therefore, is to make Baker Street more like a normal bank raid with the tunnels and noise attached. If the police are to show any attention then it needs to be with Baker Street."

"You're setting up one team to be caught?" Taylor then asked with outrage in his voice.

"Not at all, we're just pulling off that job in a slightly more conventional manner. Yes, there will be more risks, but I still believe it will be worth it."

"And you remain convinced that we stand to make a lot of money from this venture?" enquired Taylor.

"More money than you could ever imagine," replied Tony, the smile ever wider on his face.

Wednesday, 4th August, 1971 – Rhodes Town

Amy was sitting in a small office that was positively crammed with furniture. Across the desk from her, sat Inspector Parmera. Parmera had met Amy off the plane the previous evening and driven to her hotel. He had returned the following morning, at just after nine and driven her to the police office, where they were now both sitting in that small cramped room.

Amy sat on one side of a wide desk with Parmera on the other. He had removed his hand and was now running his fingers through his thick, black hair. His eyes were dark and across his top lip was a luxuriant moustache that must have taken many months of cultivation. There was a confident air about the man, which Amy found quite appealing.

Parmera had been given the double murder investigation as a form of punishment. He had annoyed his boss on another matter, which had led to a cold case being found and offered to the Inspector. Parmera had begun that investigation with little in the way of motivation. However, as soon as the name Hans Varga cropped up, he decided to show a lot more interest.

Parmera had been able to build up a picture of Varga. He had been a man who had used his position of authority to get what he wanted and that seemed to include half the women on the island. Not that anyone reported Varga for abusing his authority; he hadn't forced himself on any of those women.

Parmera had spoken to anyone who could remember the war years. They all remembered Varga, though none of them were aware that the man had returned to the island in 1948. Parmera could find no smoking gun.

He did find, however, a man who had spent many of those war years trying to woo Nana. He had agreed to meet and tell the Inspector his story. It was at that point that Parmera thought MILO should get involved.

At a little after eleven o'clock, Agathon Chloros shuffled into the front office and announced his arrival in rather subdued terms. He was a small, squat man with a round face and unshaven chin. His hair was dark and curly and he wore trousers and a jacket that might have fitted a man a size or two bigger than he was. He was in his fifties and worked locally as a painter (of portraits rather than walls).

He was shown to an interview room and Parmera and Amy informed of his arrival. They made their way through, taking coffee with them, including one for their guest. When Chloros saw Amy, he physically brightened, sitting up in his seat and holding in a stomach that was in danger of spilling over the belt on his trousers. He thanked them for the coffee and then sat back, waiting to see where the interview might go.

Chloros spoke a little English, but where he had to lapse back into his native tongue, Parmera would quickly translate. Similarly, where Chloros failed to understand Amy, Parmera would fill the gaps. Parmera briefly explained that they were there to hear more about Nana and her brother, Constantine. He then invited Chloros to tell his story.

"Constantine was always a bit strange. It was his sister, Nana, however, who interested all the boys in town. She was beautiful and we all wanted to marry her. However, she would never have gone out with a local boy, she was too in love with her German."

"Hans Varga?" Amy asked, by way of clarification.

Chloros nodded. "Varga used to visit the house a lot. It was clear that Nana loved him, though I doubt if he loved her. Typical man; as long as he got the sex he was happy."

Amy got the impression there was an element of envy in Chloros's tone.

"Varga eventually got Nana off the island. She was killed a matter of months later, probably by someone following her from here. Varga was gone by then, of course. His war finished earlier than others."

Parmera had not considered the possibility of someone from Rhodes following Nana and killing her anyway. However, he could see the sense in it; she would have been hated for fraternising with the enemy so blatantly.

"And what about Constantine?" enquired Amy.

"He just disappeared one night, not long after Nana left the island. I don't know if Varga had organised that as well, it was just a matter of one day he was here and the next day, he wasn't."

"And we've never been able to trace him since," Parmera added towards Amy.

Amy nodded. "Did you ever see Varga in Rhodes after the war?" she then asked.

"I didn't," replied Chloros," but I do have something else to tell you, something I didn't know the last time we spoke," he then added, speaking the last few words towards Parmera.

"Go on," the Inspector said.

"I was speaking to a man, the other day, who worked in the local bank during most of the war."

"His name?" said Parmera.

"He wishes to remain anonymous," came the reply.

"Very well," said Parmera, rather grudgingly, although he had already worked out that there would not be that many possibilities as to who the mystery man might be, after all there couldn't have been that many bank employees during the war.

"Anyway, he told me that Varga had an arrangement with the bank manager to store items in the safe. A few months before he left the island, he visited the bank and removed those items."

"Which were?" pressed Parmera.

"No one was very sure, though there was a strong suspicion there might have been diamonds."

When this was translated for Amy's benefit, she now sat up and paid closer attention.

"So, Varga takes diamonds out of the bank and then leaves the island," she said, almost thinking aloud. She then turned to the Inspector. "There was no record of Varga taking anything off the island in forty-five, was there?"

"Not that we know of," replied Parmera. "I don't think he would have risked taking anything to Turkey with him, just in case the authorities there wanted to speak with him. It would have made more sense to leave the items here and come back for them at a later date."

Amy couldn't have agreed more.

"He comes back in forty-eight and has to kill two people to cover his tracks," she said.

Parmera was now nodding. "It would make sense, though we're not going to find any evidence now/"

Chloros had nothing more to say. He appeared to have given Amy a solution to at least one of the questions MILO had set out to answer. Varga had started his business by selling stolen diamonds. No wonder he'd never wanted that to become common knowledge.

After Chloros had left the building, Parmera contacted Varga and both he and Amy, were surprised by the fact Varga was more than happy to see them that afternoon.

*

It had only been a week since Amy had last seen Hans Varga, but already she felt sure he was looking a little worse for the effect of the cancer eating away inside him. He was coughing a little more and his skin was an unhealthy colour. It was clear that his cancer had become a lot more aggressive.

Varga greeted them outside in the courtyard. It was a hot day and they all sat under shade, nursing a cold drink.

"I thought you said you'd leave me alone," Varga said.

Amy responded.

"We have more information, Herr Varga, therefore we have more questions."

Varga sighed deeply.

"Very good, ask your questions."

Amy actually began with a statement, rather than a question.

"I know where you got the money to start your business."

Varga's expression did not change.

"Do you now?" he said.

"You set aside certain items before you left Rhodes in forty-five.

You then came back in forty-eight to claim them. Unfortunately, your wartime contact was no longer in the house and you were forced into killing two, innocent, people before you could make good your escape with a small bag of diamonds. Those diamonds are what funded the early days of the Varga Corporation."

Varga had said nothing. He had sat, with a half-smile on his face, listening to what Amy had to say and occasionally sipping at his drink. Once she had stopped talking, he still did not show any sign of responding immediately. Finally, he put his glass down and sat forward.

"A lovely story, my dear and beautifully told, if I may say so. However, it is somewhat lacking in substance and certainly lacking in evidence. You have nothing to connect me to that house, whether it be during the war or afterwards. Nana is dead and Constantine is in the wind, so they cannot be of any help to you now. In short, you have a theory and nothing more."

"Don't worry, Herr Varga," Amy then said, "we won't be leaving things there. We'll keep digging and we'll find out more about you. There is evidence out there somewhere and I intend finding it."

Varga's smile was now wider, though it was interrupted by a bout of coughing. It seemed to come from deep in his soul and sounded painful to Amy. When it finally passed, Varga spoke.

"I'm dying, my dear, there's nothing you can do to me now, that nature hasn't already done."

Which Amy took as being the closest she would ever come to a confession.

Amy and Parmera finished their drinks, thanked Varga for taking the time to see them and then they went on their way. They agreed, on the way back to the police office, that Varga was their murderer, but there was really no point in proceeding with the investigation as Herr Varga would probably be dead long before they were ready to charge him formally.

Before Amy left the island, she received one last piece of information regarding Hans Varga, only it wasn't about Varga himself. A local man had come forward to tell Parmera that other Germans had visited the island in the aftermath of the war.

One, in particular, had shown an unhealthy interest in Hans Varga, even going as far as asking for information on the double murder as well. He had paid good money for the information he'd been given and had left the island a happy man.

There was no name for this mystery man, but Amy couldn't help but think that it might have been the reason why Franz

Neuer had become the first employee of Varga's new company.

Tuesday 10th August 1971 – Barclays Bank, Moorgate

Gill Potter had put off complying with Barry Gibb's request for as long as possible. She desperately wanted to have nothing more to do with the man. She had even thought about running away, but she'd quickly decided that it she'd done that she'd never have stopped running because, in essence, she'd be running away from herself.

She was sitting at her desk, thinking. She'd done a lot of that lately and it hadn't really got her anywhere. She still had the problem of getting those impressions and she was still no nearer knowing how.

Gill's desk took up around a third of the office space allocated to her. It was a side-room to the Manager's office which, of course, was much bigger and furnished in a far grander style. No self-respecting bank manager could ever greet his clients in a room that did not befit his status and, of course, most bank managers saw themselves as being far more important than they really were.

The Manager was Horace Wrigglesworth. Gill had worked with worse; Wrigglesworth liked things his own way, but in general he was fairly easy-going. He was a tall, balding man who wore thick-lensed spectacles and looked every inch the bank manager. His suits were immaculate and his office permanently tidy. There were days when Gill wondered if the men actually did anything, such was the lack of evidence lying around his desk.

Gill enjoyed her position in the branch. As the Manager's secretary she had an important role; she knew things the other staff didn't and it gave her a sense of importance as she arrived at work each day.

All that, however, was now in danger of disappearing as she was frog-marched out of the building after being arrested for aiding and abetting a bank robber. That seemed to be the only conclusion to her predicament; she could see now way of doing what Gibb had asked, without getting caught in the process.

As she sat at her desk, that morning, she had come up with a plan of sorts. It was pretty vague and yet dangerous. The danger came from the fact she now knew she'd have to involve someone else, there was simply no way she could do it all herself.

She had identified the someone else, it was now just a matter of getting him onboard and hoping he wouldn't blow the whistle on her once she'd explained the trouble she was getting him into.

She felt confident that she was at least starting from a position of knowing the man she'd identified, probably had feelings for her. He'd asked her out once before, but she'd turned him down, worrying that a relationship with a colleague might not be acceptable to the bank and also might make working life messy once it ended.

The man in question was Terry Ferris. He was younger than Gill and the only man in the branch to have ever paid her any attention, outside of work-related matters. He was a good-looking man, quiet and not so cock-sure of himself as some of the other men working around her. She hated pushy men.

There was another reason for Gill choosing Terry as a possible ally. He was one of only four men in the branch, who had access to the vault keys.

Gill knew she would have to make her move soon. She was running out of time and the impressions wouldn't make themselves. She knew she could do the first part herself and she decided that she might as well do that now.

She rummaged in her bag and took out two of the small tins with the plasticine in them. She then put the tins inside a buff-coloured folder and stood up. Her heart was pumping and she felt faint. She took a couple of deep breaths and made her way to the door.

She knew Mister Wrigglesworth was out to lunch, which meant he'd be away for at least an hour and a half. He'd be at the Head Office, on Lombard Street, seated in the staff canteen, enjoying a three-course meal and small glass of wine. He'd be with other bank managers and they'd be boring each other to death with tales of profit and increased customer numbers.

Gill's only problem was that the Chief Clerk, John Torville, often chose to use the Manager's office, while he was out. He claimed it was to give him peace and quiet to clear his work, but everyone knew he just like sitting in the Manager's chair and imagining he had his own branch. That day would no doubt come; just not yet.

Gill made her way through to the Manager's office, glancing back to check if anyone was watching her. The road seemed clear. Once inside the room, she closed the door and hurried over to the small safe in the corner, tucked away under the window, which due to its opaque glass was only good for letting light in; no one could see through it.

Gill opened the safe. It was something she'd done many times before. It was something she needed to be able to do, so no one would have questioned her knowing the combination. Quickly she took the set of spare keys from the safe and opened the two plasticine filled tins. There were two keys for the front door; it was meant to be for extra security. Gill pressed one key into each tin and checked that the impression looked clean enough.

Happy with her work, she then put the tins back inside the folder and returned the keys to the safe, locking it again in the process. Her heart was beginning to settled down a little, though she still needed a few more deep breaths before she made her way out of the room.

She went back to her office and sat down. She took the tins from the folder and put them in her bag. She still had her hand in the bag when her office door opened and in walked Terry.

Gill nearly asked him what he was doing there. Such was the state of her nerves that nearly gave herself away.

"Something wrong?" Terry asked.

Maybe she had given herself away. Gill pulled herself together and managed a smile.

"No, of course not."

"Wriggley over working you, as usual?" Terry then said, a smile now crossing his face.

He moved closer to Gill's desk and perched himself on the corner of it.

"Nothing I can't cope with," Gill replied, beginning to get her emotions fully under control. She moved to change the subject. "Is that for me?"

As she asked the question, she nodded at two files Terry was carrying

"The Boss asked for comments on a couple of my staff so perhaps you could see that he gets this in the afternoon."

"He's busy until around three," said Gill, "but I'll get them through to him after that. Just put them down there," she added, indicating a space on her desk.

Terry stood up and started to move towards the door. He paused and turned back. Panic began to grip Gill once again.

"You know, you really don't look well, Gill. Are you sure everything is alright?"

Gill was touched by the note of concern in Terry's voice. She smiled again, only this time it was genuine, he really did seem to care.

"I'm okay, honestly," she said. "It's just been one of those days."

"In that case," Terry then said, a grin spreading across his face, "let me take you for a drink after work. No pressure, it's just a drink."

Gill couldn't believe her luck. She needed to get him onboard fairly quickly and here he was, opening the door to a possible relationship. It might just be a drink to Terry, but it was the start of the next phase of her plan, for Gill.

"You know, that's not a bad idea," she then said, trying to sound matter-of-fact about it all.

Terry's grin widened even further. He'd been expecting another knock back. It was now his turn to not believe his luck.

"Great," was all he, initially, managed to say. He then went on to suggest a pub he knew in Finsbury Circus and Gill was more than happy to go there.

"I'll see you later then," Terry said and he was actually whistling as he left her office.

Gill sat back and gave her situation some thought. Winning Terry's trust would not be easy, but at least she was now halfway there to trying.

Tuesday 10th August 1971 – Freiheit Offices, Bonn, West Germany

Wolfgang Brandt was preparing for life without Hans Varga. It was now only a matter of time before Herr Varga passed away and the income Freiheit had enjoyed from the Varga Corporation had already stopped. Not that Freiheit was poor; income continued to come in from all the Tongues as well as the other, many, donors who were spread across Europe.

Over the twenty years it had been in existence, Freiheit had made money and invested wisely. As they had slowly and methodically taken control of governments and big businesses across Europe, they had also built healthy bank balances in accounts across the world. Wherever it was safe to bank money, well away from prying eyes, Freiheit was there. They moved in a no questions asked world, where profit was everything.

Brandt was sitting at a desk in an office that was situated a short walk from the Government Buildings in Bonn. It had made sense, in the early days, to have a Freiheit source close to the Government and the decisions it would be making. Obviously, everyone would have preferred the Government to be back in Berlin, but that city was now isolated within East Germany; it was no longer practical to use it as a base for Government, even though West Berlin was still, effectively, in West Germany.

The decision had been taken to set up the West German government in Bonn and Freiheit had followed suit.

Brandt had never liked the idea of Freiheit putting all its eggs in the one Bonn basket. He was a firm believer in spreading their main offices around West Germany, in offering opponents more than one target, so that if one fell the others could keep the organisation going.

He knew about MILO. They were coming for Freiheit, so he now had to work all the harder to protect everything he believed in. The first move had been taken by Herr Varga. All financial matters were dealt with by their Zurich office. They also had their security section in Hamburg, where Ralf Dinger was currently based.

Brandt was a fan of Hamburg. It was a port which, in itself, was handy. It made certain aspects of Freiheit business easier to undertake when there was a port through which to move to and fro.

Brandt wanted to move the administration centre of Freiheit to Hamburg. He had already been there on a scouting mission and had identified the perfect building for them to move into. It was in the heart of the red-light district where there was already enough illegal activity going on that neither the police, nor MILO, would know where to start looking for any newcomers.

It seemed the perfect choice. However, if the administration was to move to Hamburg, then the security section would now need to go elsewhere.

Brandt had considered telephoning Dinger, but had decided it would be better to speak to him face to face. Brandt appreciated what Dinger did for Freiheit, but he'd never really trusted the man. He wanted to look him in the eye as they discussed moving Dinger's team out of Hamburg.

Dinger was waiting in the outer office. He had been there for over half an hour, having arrived early for his appointment. He was drinking coffee and watching a young woman working at the desk across from him. She was very pretty, far too pretty to ever be interested in a man like Dinger.

Dinger had convinced himself, as he'd travelled from Hamburg to Bonn, that he was about to be fired. He could think of no obvious reason as to why he'd be fired, but equally he could think of no other reason for being invited to Bonn by Wolfgang Brandt.

The small box on the woman's desk buzzed. Dinger watched as she pressed a button and spoke into a small microphone. A reply came back, though Dinger could not make out what was said. She looked across at him and smiled. She then stood up.

"Herr Brandt will see you now; if you'd just follow me."

Once inside Brandt's office, Dinger sat down and refused the offer of another coffee. The woman went away, closing the door behind her. Brandt sat down behind his desk and moved a few papers around, as if selecting something of importance.

"I've been giving some thought to the way in which Freiheit should be organised, as we move forward through the Seventies."

As Brandt spoke, Dinger remained motionless, pressed against the back of his chair, legs crossed. He had no intention of saying anything until invited to do so. Brandt continued.

"I want to set-up our main administrative base in Hamburg. I have already identified the building we'll use and would want to begin the renovations as soon as possible. However, in making that move it does present us with a problem. I would not wish administration and security to be in the same city. If MILO come nosing around, the last thing I want is for them to find two sources of Freiheit activity in the same city. To that end, I want you and your team to move to West Berlin."

Dinger had not meant to react, but at the mention of the words *West Berlin* his muscles had twitched enough to alert Brandt.

"You disagree with that idea?" Brandt then asked.

This appeared to be Dinger's invitation to speak. He took a moment to choose his words before finally sharing them with Herr Brandt.

"It might make our job a little more difficult, having to travel through a part of East Germany every time we wanted to do anything in West Germany."

"On the other hand," countered Brandt, "it puts you inside East Germany, which is where we might want to increase our operations one day."

Dinger could see little reason for offering an alternative opinion. The decision had clearly been made and at least he still had a job. In truth, it didn't matter to him where he was based; he could do his job from anywhere just maybe not with same effectiveness.

"Do you also have a building in West Berlin identified for our use, Herr Brandt?" Dinger now asked.

"I don't, as it happens. I thought it would be best if you made that choice; you'll have a better idea of what you're looking for."

"And when do you want this move made?"

"As soon as possible, though don't go rushing things and making mistakes in the process. It will obviously be a few months before the building in Hamburg is ready."

"If we are to be creating new offices, will we be looking to install modern technology?" Dinger then asked.

"We will install the best, Ralf. If Man can go to the Moon then Freiheit can create offices that are the finest in the world."

Brandt almost bristled with pride as he spoke.

"Will we be vacating Bonn altogether?" Dinger now asked.

"We will retain a small office, somewhere for me to work from when I'm here. The bulk of our work, however, will be moved to Hamburg. I will let you have the detail of our new Hamburg base as soon as we've finalised the contracts."

"Very good, Herr Brandt, it would seem prudent, therefore, for me to review all our security arrangements, including those for the Tongues. Do you wish you own security to be increased?"

"No, what you have in place is perfectly acceptable. We can revisit my security once I've been in Hamburg for a little while."

"As you wish," Dinger said. He stood up. "Now, perhaps I should get down to business. There is much to do."

Tuesday, 10th August, 1971 – The Fiddler's Arms, Finsbury Circus

The pub was quiet, which suited Terry and Gill just fine. For some reason, they were both feeling very nervous as if they were doing something wrong in sharing a drink together. They had left the bank separately and met up again, a little further along Moorgate. They had not wanted colleagues to be aware that they were seeing each other outside business hours.

Gill went to find a seat and Terry went to the bar. As he waited to be served he looked across to where Gill was now removing her coat to reveal a different dress from the one she'd been wearing for work. Terry was surprised that Gill had gone to the bother of changing. He had to assume the dress was new, so did that mean she was out to impress him?

He purchased a gin and tonic and a pint of mild and bitter. He then made his way over to where Gill was now sitting. He noticed she was nervously fiddling with the hem of her skirt, perhaps now thinking it was too short.

"I like the dress," Terry commented as he sat down.

Gill smiled. "Thanks. I didn't think my office dress was smart enough."

"I didn't think to change," Terry added.

"No need," said Gill, accepting her drink from him. "Cheers."

The last word was followed by them clinking their glasses together. They took a first drink and laid their glasses down on a table that was desperately in need of a clean.

A silence followed, as if neither of them really knew what to say next. Terry was there in the hope that a romance might blossom. Gill was there to gain his support in doing something highly illegal.

Eventually Terry spoke.

"You don't really want to be here, do you?"

It was not what Gill had wanted to hear. She was obviously sending out the wrong signals and the words stung her more than she might have expected.

She moved a little closer to Terry. "Of course, I want to be here. I wouldn't have accepted your invitation otherwise."

Gill managed a smile and Terry brightened visibly.

"But there is something wrong?" he then said.

"I've just had a few things to deal with recently."

"Like that bloke you've been going out with?" Terry then said and for the second time Gill was stung by what she was hearing. She hadn't expected Terry to know about Barry Gibb.

"Who's been telling you about him?" Gill enquired, trying not to sound too defensive.

"Just a bit of chat in the staffroom; sorry if I wasn't supposed to mention it."

Gill let a few seconds of silence pass before speaking again.

"No, it's no big deal really."

"But, I take it, the relationship is over?" Terry said.

"It is."

Terry took Gill's hand.

"Does that mean there might be room for me now?" he enquired with a grin.

This was going better than Gill could ever have imagined. Terry really was keen on her. Maybe he would make the perfect ally after all.

Gill now grinned as well.

"There might be," she said.

They both drank some more from their glasses and a sense of relaxation began to flow through both of them. The first hurdle towards a possible relationship had been negotiated. It could only be uphill all the way from here.

Friday 13th August 1971 (Evening) – Le Sac Leather Goods, Baker Street, London

Four men stood in the middle of the floor. Around them were the leather goods that had been in the shop when they had first rented the place. However, they had no need for such things, they had rented the property for one reason only and that was to provide access to the bank situated two doors along.

Between them and the bank lay the Chicken Inn restaurant and being a Friday night, all the tables were occupied with diners who were none the wiser as to what would soon be going on beneath the floor where they were seated.

Tony Rutherford stood with Vince Hammond. There were two other men, each stripped to the waist and ready to begin. All they needed was the go-ahead.

"How long do you think this will take?" Rutherford said.

Hammond thought about the question for a moment, his mind doing a quick calculation. Eventually he gave his answer.

"I'd say a month at most."

"So, you're pretty sure the job can still be done around the middle of September?" Tony Rutherford now added.

"All being well, yes, but if we hit problems along the way, then that estimation could be miles out."

"Okay," Tony said," we'll work on the premise that the job can be carried out by the end of September. Moorgate will only get the green light once this job's good to go."

"Surely we're not ready to go with Moorgate. anyway?" Hammond asked.

"Not far off now. Still waiting on the keys. I've already got the details we'll need on which safe-deposit boxes to hit. We're going to be rich, bloody rich," Tony then said, a grin spreading across his face.

Hammond looked pleased to hear that. He looked at his watch, then turned to the other two men.

"Okay lads, get ready. Next door will be closing up soon and then we can get started."

Everyone in the room could practically smell the money, which was waiting for them two doors down.

"I'll leave you to it, then," said Tony, lighting up a cigarette.

Hammond seemed relieved that Rutherford was going; he had never been a fan of being supervised, particularly by someone who didn't know what he was doing. Tony

Rutherford might have been good for ideas, but when it came to the manual work he met with more success by leaving it up to others.

Tony went to the door and checked for passers-by. It seemed quite quiet, so he opened the door and slipped out. He made his way to his white, E-type jaguar and climbed behind the wheel. He fired up the engine and edged it into the line of traffic. He felt happy and wanted to celebrate. Time to visit his favourite Club and enjoy a few drinks.

But first he'd have to leave the car somewhere safe.

Saturday, 14th August, 1971 – Terry Ferris's flat, Leytonstone, London

Terry and Gill had been out together the previous night. They had enjoyed a nice dinner, then moved on to a pub where a band had been playing. As the music played, they'd worked their way through a number of drinks. By the end of the night, Gill was slightly the worse for wear and Terry had decided to take her back to his place, where he felt he could look after her better.

Terry's flat was close to Leytonstone Station. It was quite small. Living room, bedroom, and galley kitchen. The shared toilet and bathroom were on the landing. There were three other flats in the building, each with two tenants. Everyone got on well.

By the time Terry had got Gill back to the flat she had decided he was being naughty. She kept asking what he had in mind, even though he kept telling her he had nothing in mind, other than seeing she would be okay.

Terry had steered Gill into the bedroom and she'd passed out on the bed. He'd taken her dress off, not wanting it to get creased, especially as she'd need to wear it the following day as well.

Terry had sat in the chair, which was situated in the corner of the bedroom and pulled a blanket over himself. He wanted to remain in the room, just in case Gill did anything stupid in her inebriated state. He'd heard too many stories about people choking on their own vomit.

He hadn't slept well. He awoke at just after eight feeling sore all over and still in need of a good sleep. He got up and crossed to the bed. Gill was lying on her back with the covers thrown off. He watched her sleeping for a few moments. It was one of the nicest things he'd done in a long time.

He left Gill sleeping and pulled on a dressing gown. He went out on to the landing and visited the toilet first. It was separate from the bathroom. He then went through to the bathroom and ran himself a bath. By the time he returned to the flat, Gill was awake, though still in bed.

She was feeling very fragile.

"Coffee?" Terry said to her from the door.

"How did I get here?" she replied.

Terry explained what had happened.

"Did you take my dress off?"

"Didn't want it to get creased."

"Thank you."

"Don't mention it. Now, do you want that coffee?"

"Yes, please. Strong and black."

"Do you want it here?" Terry then asked.

"No, I'll get up. What did you do with my dress?"

"It's over the back of that chair," replied Terry, nodding towards the corner of the room.

"Thank you," Gill said again and Terry left.

As Terry laid two mugs of coffee on the table, Gill appeared from the bedroom. She looked almost white faced and Terry felt sure she'd not get through the day without being sick. She made her way slowly to the table and sat down.

"Did I enjoy myself last night?" she then asked.

"You seemed to be having a good time. You just didn't know when to stop drinking."

"I can be like that sometimes. Sorry."

Terry smiled. "No need to apologise."

"There just seems something wrong with that fact that the first time you see me in my underwear, I happen to be unconscious. Not very romantic, was it?"

"I was worried about you," said Terry. "At least I could keep an eye on you by taking you back to my place."

"Well, thank you. I'd come over there and give you a thank you kiss, but I don't feel too well."

Terry smiled. "And I don't want you throwing up all over me."

"Where is the toilet?" Gill then said.

"Out on the landing."

Gill went straight to the door. "Time to visit I think," she said and hurried out of the room.

It was half an hour before she came back. She was looking a slightly healthier colour and admitted to having been sick. She'd washed in the bathroom and used a towel she'd found there. She still had it with her.

"I'd best wash that before I put it back," Terry said, taking the towel from Gill and adding to a pile of garments already awaiting a wash.

"How are you feeling now?" Terry enquired.

"Bit more human."

"Do you want to go out?"

"Fresh air sounds good."

"Do you want to eat anything?"

"Fresh air sounds good," was all that Gill was prepared to admit, at least for the moment.

*

They spent the day out and about. Gill hadn't felt like eating until after seven in the evening. They had eaten at a restaurant Terry really liked. Gil had kept it light. Terry hadn't. Gill passed on the alcohol; Terry had a couple of pints.

They had then gone back to Terry's flat where one thing had led to another. By eleven o'clock they were in bed, though neither of them had any thought of going to sleep.

Sunday, 15th August, 1971 – Terry Ferris's flat, Leytonstone, London

Sunday was the day when Terry learned just how much trouble Gill was in.

It was a glorious day. The sun shone the whole time and the air felt hot. They had gone for a walk, part of it on the edge of Epping Forest, where they enjoyed the dappled sunshine through the trees and abundant greenery.

They had found a quiet spot and sat down. Gill had then told her story and Terry had listened with growing horror. Gill concluded her story by asking Terry to help her, though she did also say that she'd understand if he said no.

Terry had taken her hand, looked deep into her eyes and said he'd do anything for her. The sense of relief that flowed through Gill's body manifested itself in a desire to kiss Terry. As they surfaced for air, Terry was grinning.

"I need to say I'll help you more often," he said and Gill playfully gave him a slap on the arm.

Terry got serious once again.

"Even if they get the keys, I can't see how that helps them."

"It gets them into the bank and the vault," said Gill.

"Well, I know that," added Terry, "but they can't be intent on hitting all the safe-deposit-boxes; they'd have to prioritise and you can't help with that."

"He never asked me about the safe-deposit boxes."

"Then someone else must be helping him with that, which means you're not the only member of staff who is being used."

Gill actually felt greater relief on hearing Terry say that. Terry changed the subject slightly. "Do you know, for a fact, that those items, designed to blacken your name, actually exist?"

"He showed me a couple of things; they seemed genuine enough."

"Then they've gone to a lot of trouble to plan this raid, which means the returns must be worth the risk. I hadn't realised we had anything of great value in the vault. God, we even nearly ran out of money the other week; we had to send a couple of staff to Fleet Street to get us enough to see us through the day."

They had then discussed what needed to be done. Somehow, Terry had to get copies of the vault keys and do so without drawing attention to himself.

That, in itself, would not be easy, seeing as only four men ever had the keys in the first place. He was taking a far greater risk than Gill, but he was happy to do it.

They returned to the flat in the late afternoon. Terry cooked food for their evening meal and they thought about going out again, only to find other things to occupy their time. By the time sleep overtook them, both Terry and Gill knew their feelings for each other were deepening by the minute.

Life might be getting risky, but it was also getting a whole lot more enjoyable.

Monday, 16th August, 1971 – Terry Ferris's flat, Leytonstone and Barclays Bank, Moorgate

They were both up in plenty time to get ready for work. They washed at the kitchen sink, then dressed and had breakfast. As they sat at the table, finishing a cup of coffee, Terry spoke.

"I've been thinking about this guy, Barry Gibb."

"And?" said Gill.

"And I think I should be the one who contacts him once we have the impressions."

"Why?"

"Firstly, it lets him know that someone else is aware of what he is doing and secondly, it protects you from further harm. As it is, he might be planning to get you out of the road permanently, once you'd given him his impressions."

"But he already has me over a barrel," Gill said.

"He *says* he has, but all that could be bluff, for all you know."

Gill hadn't considered that possibility.

"And another thing," Terry then said, "I don't think five thousand pounds if enough. You're being asked to commit a crime, one that will give this Barry Gibb the chance to make a small fortune. No, I reckon he can stump up a little more and not miss it."

Gill looked scared.

"Don't push him too hard, Terry, you don't know what he's capable of."

"Without the keys he has no bank raid," Terry said. "I think he'll negotiate."

"And how are you going tom get impressions of the vault keys?" Gill then enquired.

"At this precise moment," Terry replied, "I haven't the first idea."

Monday, 23rd August, 1971 – Barclays Bank, Moorgate

John Torville was on annual leave.

Terry Ferris has his vault key and was standing, alongside Horace Wrigglesworth, watching as the caretakers took the cashier's trolleys out of the vault and wheeled them to the lift. which would take them up to the counter. The lift was only big enough for one trolley and nothing else. The staff had to take the stair.

Terry's mind was in overdrive. He had to get his hands on the manager's key and yet still had no clear plan as to how he would do that. He had a half-notion, nothing more.

He had told Gill to keep well out of his way. If he got caught, he didn't want her affected.

Management always retained the keys. Terry qualified as supervisor of their machine room. Wrigglesworth and Torville usually held the keys and the only other man who sometimes got involved, was Alf Cairney. Alf had been at the branch for thirty years. He had failed his banking exams, year in, year out and was now treated with sympathy more than anything else.

He had been nominated as a possible keyholder simply because of his long service. Alf was a lovely man, but a useless employee.

Terry felt sure he could use Alf in some way.

With all the trolleys now out of the vault, the door was closed, though not locked. During the day, the vault was left unlocked to allow easier access for those staff who needed items stored there.

The outer door to the vault was locked, though the key was readily available. Terry would be able to copy that at any time.

Terry went back to his desk. He had a week to come up with a plan.

Time was definitely running out.

Monday, 23rd August, 1971 – MILO HQ, Central London

Sarah had put a lot of work into researching Gunther Weiss. It was another name that cropped up before and during the war, but not after it. Weiss appeared to have been present at more than one atrocity. He seemed, to Sarah, as being the usual psychopath that the SS liked to recruit. He had given orders for so many innocent people to be killed without a second thought. How could any human mind get so warped?

Sarah completed her report on Weiss. He was a man she now desperately wanted to find. His place was on the end of a rope, not walking about enjoying the fresh air of freedom.

There was always the possibility that Weiss was already dead. Twenty-six years had elapsed since the end of the war; anything could have happened in that time.

Sarah had definitely connected Weiss to Jurgen Maier. They had worked together in Berlin as well as crossing paths in parts of Eastern Europe.

Another name she'd come across, was Wolfgang Brandt. He appeared on two of her lists. He was ex-SS, though with no obvious blemishes to his name. He was also on her list of rich Germans; though she could find no apparent reason for him being so wealthy.

Another name with a question mark against it.

Sarah's research had come up with yet another name worthy of that question mark. Julius Podolski had moved in the same circles as Gunther Weiss. They had both been involved in the murder of an entire village. Weiss had gone off the radar shortly after that particular atrocity, but Podolski had surfaced, a few months later, as part of the team working on the V2 rocket project. Sarah was able to find out that Podolski had a physics degree, he'd acquired before the war.

The last piece of information Sarah could uncover about Podolski was of particular interest.

She ran her thoughts passed Amy, on her return from Rhodes and they both agreed that, in all probability, Podolski was now in America.

At the end of the war the Americans had moved quickly to round up as many of the scientists who had worked on the V2 rockets. America saw rockets as part of the future; though at that stage they saw them as weapons and nothing more.

Large numbers were moved to America. Sarah and Amy were convinced that Podolski had been one of them. Amy contacted one of her colleagues, at Langley, and brought him up to speed on Julius Podolski.

He said he'd look into the man and get back to Amy of he found anything of use.

Monday, 23rd August, 1971 – CIA Headquarters, Langley, Virginia

Derbert Liston sat at his desk in what was called his office. It was little more than a cupboard, stuck at the end of a corridor that led to a fire escape door that was only ever opened during fire drills. The wing, in which the MILO work was conducted, had once been the dumping ground for paper and materials awaiting destruction. Eventually, a few offices had been cleared and those staff now assigned to MILO work were able to move in.

Other sections of the CIA saw little importance in any of the work being done for MILO. Many Americans have little time for issues arising in their own country, so the idea that they should have CIA staff working on issues that were, essentially, only of interest or concern in Europe was beyond many people's comprehension. It had been said to Derbert's face that European issues should be left to Europeans to deal with; America had no place meddling in other people's affairs.

To which Derbert would reply: *What about Vietnam- we've meddled enough there?*

That usually led to the whingers walking away and having nothing more to say about MILO and the work being done.

Derbert was a large man, who filled much of his cupboard-sized office, allowing little room for furniture. He was also black, which meant he was already, to many of his colleagues, viewed as a second-class citizen. Most of his colleagues did not see Derbert going that far in the CIA. In fact, to many, he had gone as far as he ever would.

There had been times when even Derbert had thought he was destined to remain in a backwater job in a backwater wing of Langley, but at other times he'd felt every bit as important as anyone else in the building. This was one of those times. He had names to work with and information to uncover.

Derbert knew that Abner McQueen thought a lot of him and was always full of praise for the work he did. Feeling part of something meant a lot to Derbert. It was often difficult to feel part of anything outside of the building. Too many white Americans still found it impossible to share space with someone who had a different skin tone. Over a hundred years on from the Civil War and racial tension in America was still there.

Derbert looked down at the names he'd been given by Amy.

Julius Podolski seemed to have the strongest link to the United States, so Derbert decided to begin there.

It was common knowledge that German scientists had moved to America at the end of the war, and were now working on the Space Race. The need for rockets had moved on from mere weaponry, they were now needed to put Man into Space and hopefully, keep him there.

Derbert passed the names of Weiss and Podolski to the computer room, asking for anything they might have on both men.

Most of the information, gathered at Langley, had been with the threat of Communism in mind. The 1950s, in particular, had been a time when every American believed that Reds were living under their beds. Intelligence gathering had been conducted, mainly with Russia in mind but, in truth, the CIA had gathered information on everyone and anyone.

Derbert also put in a request for the files on the men who had been moved to America and set to work on producing rockets that could be aimed at Russia. He expected quite a few files and he wasn't disappointed.

He had also asked the ladies in the staff cafeteria to fill a thermos flask with coffee for him. He now sat at his desk, coffee to the right, cigarettes to the left and a mound of paper set to fear him, lying in the middle. It was mid-afternoon and time to get down to business.

He opened a notebook, laid down a pen and started reading.

The first thing that struck him about the scientists' files was that there was very little information in any of them. All the files that Derbert looked at were also devoid of any State Department involvement; meaning that, essentially, they had all been allowed to enter the United States of America without the usual background checks that everyone else would have had to go through.

He picked up a file with the name Bud Kramer written on the front. Inside there were three sheets of paper. The top sheet told Derbert that Bud's real name was actually Bernd Krammer but he had chosen to change it so as to appear to be pro-American. Underneath Bud's name on the front of the file someone had written, in red ink, 'non-criminal.'

The second sheet of paper covered Bud's war-time record. Seven years of activity were covered by two sentences.

"1938 to 1943 – Involved in Rocket Development and Production."

"1943 to 1945 – Involved in the development and production of V2 rockets."

Sheet three then informed Derbert that Bud had been flown to America in July, nineteen forty-five where he was to be re-united with other scientists who had been involved in producing rockets for Nazi Germany.

Derbert also noted that not one of the scientists was reported to have been a member of the Nazi Party. Derbert found it impossible to believe that anyone involved in major work for the Third Reich would have been allowed to carry out that work had they not been loyal members of the Party. He deduced, therefore, that the files had been sanitised and were probably, no longer reliable as a valid source of information.

Derbert sat back in his chair and reached for his coffee. What else might have been taken out of these files? What else had the American Government chosen to ignore in the interests of making them the leading country in rocket propulsion? Sure, they were just keeping ahead of the Russians, but did that give them the right to ignore the deeds of others?

Perhaps it was wrong for Derbert to now question those who took decisions at the end of the war, which were now totally wrong when judged by history. But then was it right to judge decisions made in different times. Maybe he'd needed to be there to fully understand why those decisions had been made in the first place?

He lit a cigarette and smoked it thoughtfully. Whatever the reasons behind those decisions they had, effectively, taken away much of the information Derbert was now seeking. If all the files had been cleared of anything contentious then he stood to learn nothing in ploughing through a mound of files.

He laid his half-smoked cigarette on the ashtray and sat forward. He couldn't allow what he was doing to get him down. He had to continue working his way through the files and hope something turned up.

It was into the evening before he struck lucky.

In one file he found a piece of paper that had not been in any of the others. Derbert assumed it was a piece of paper that should have been removed, but someone had missed it. The information on the piece of paper was pure dynamite.

It contained details of the man going through a formal interrogation whilst still in West Germany. At the end of the report, it clearly stated that the man was not only a Nazi, but should also be treated as being very dangerous. It was recommended that he be placed in a detention centre. Derbert checked the dates on the other elements of the file and deduced that the man never saw the inside of a detention centre. In fact, three weeks after he'd been interviewed in West Germany, he was in America.

Derbert dug a bit deeper and was able to uncover general information on the operation to bring German scientists to the United States.

Operation Paperclip, as it had come to be called, had been responsible for ensuring that everyone entering the United States arrived with a clean slate. America needed the expertise of all those scientists and yet it could not be seen to condone the activities of the Nazi Party. The answer was simple; remove all mention of them ever being connected to the Nazi Party.

In nineteen forty-six questions had been asked about how many of the scientists might have been war criminals. A very large carpet was immediately produced and everything swiftly swept under it. Their skills were imperative to the United States rocket programme and it almost became un-American to ask any questions about the scientists, either personal or work-related.

The evening progressed and Derbert delved further into the material he had in front of him. His coffee was finished and he had one cigarette left. He knew he should head for home, but a part of him wanted to know more. As he read, a thought struck him. From the files he'd read, Derbert could find no evidence that any of the men were actually scientists. In their rush to create a team who could build rockets, America may have allowed anyone to enter their country.

Derbert now focussed his attention on Julius Podolski. He had a file under his name, but that was through his SS connections and had nothing to do with rocket science. The last entry on Podolski's war record had him back in Germany in 1944. He had been wounded and allocated a desk job. There was also a small, black and white photograph attached to the inside of the file. Derbert removed it, hoping he might be able to check it against photographs of the scientists later.

Derbert now knew that if Podolski was amongst the scientists who came to America in the aftermath of the war, then he'd arrived under an assumed name.

Derbert looked at his watch. It was late; time to go home. He packed up, put on his coat and headed out of the building.

Tuesday, 24th August, 1971 – CIA Headquarters, Langley, West Virginia

When Derbert arrived back at his desk the following morning he was horrified by the sight that met him. He'd forgotten the mess he'd left. He took one look at the mess and decided he needed to be elsewhere for a while.

He'd been thinking about things and had decided to pay a visit to someone in Langley who would have memories of Operation Paperclip. The name that popped into his head had been that of Phil Lezznavic. Phil was definitely one of the elder statesmen of the Agency, with only a matter of months left before he could retire.

The CIA Headquarters is a rabbit-warren of a building and Derbert felt like he had walked miles before he reached the office he'd been looking for. Phil Lezznavic shared his work space with Wilf Sackett, another agent who had been put out to grass ahead of his ultimate retirement. They both sat opposite each other, almost passing the same piece of paper back and forth and waiting for the day when they could walk out the door and not come back. They hadn't been given access to anything useful in months.

Derbert had collected coffees on the way and was welcomed with open arms as he entered Phil and Wilf's working space. He sat down on the only other chair in the room and handed over two of the coffees.

The room was quite small, though still bigger than Derbert's cupboard. The desks were devoid of work, unlike Derbert's and there was just the one phone, aged and looking in a state of disrepair. Pinned to the wall, roughly equidistant between the two men, was a large photograph of a half-naked woman. Phil noticed Derbert's eyes taking in the large breasts that were on show.

"It's all that keeps us going some days," quipped Phil.

"I'd like to say it brings back memories," Wilf added, "but I never had a broad like that in my life."

They all laughed. Wilf and Phil then thanked Derbert for the coffees and asked what had brought him to their corner of the building.

"I'm doing work for Amy Clinton," Derbert began.

"Nice kid," said Phil.

Derbert nodded his agreement to that statement and then moved on,

"Basically, gentlemen, I need your memories."

"Better catch them while they're still here, I suppose," quipped Phil.

"Do either of you have any memory of Operation Paperclip?" Derbert then enquired.

"Sure, I remember," said Phil. "Not one of our finest hours."

"To say the fucking least," added Wilf, drinking his coffee.

"From what I can see," Derbert then said, "we let a lot of scientists into the country and didn't really bother vetting them first."

Phil drank his coffee, before responding.

"We certainly did and we didn't give a shit what they had been up to prior to coming here as long as they could start work on putting America ahead of the world on rocket propulsion. I mean we weren't thinking about Space back then, we simply wanted weapons that were more powerful than anything the Russians could come up with."

"Do you think tracks were deliberately covered?" said Derbert.

"Too right, they were," came the reply from Phil. "We couldn't afford anyone finding out that some of those guys could have been murderous bastards, so we made them all squeaky clean. In doing so, even we forgot who were the bad guys amongst them."

"Could we have let non-scientists in with them?" Derbert now asked.

Wilf guffawed.

"We could have let Adolf fucking Hitler in, as long as he looked good in a white coat."

Phil continued.

"We didn't really care about who was coming into America at that time. We were in a pissing contest with the Russians. We were all lined up in front of the wall with our dicks out. Those German scientists gave us elevation in our aim, if you get my meaning. They had years of experience, which put us ahead of the Russians right away."

Derbert drank his coffee and considered his next question.

"Once those men were given American citizenship, did we monitor their activities in any way?"

"Wouldn't have thought so," replied Phil. "To be honest, Derbert, if there were any bad pennies amongst them, they would have been in the minority. The guys I ever saw were genuine scientists who only wanted to make amends for the things their country had done under Hitler."

"Do we even know what happened to everyone who came to this country at that time?"

"Their work record will be on file. They must have paid taxes and the like, so you could trace them through that."

"Yeah," Derbert added," but I'm talking about men who had no interest in rockets, only in saving their own skin. I'm talking about war criminals who just wanted to put as many miles as they could between themselves and justice."

Both Wilf and Phil looked horrified. Wilf spoke first.

"Jesus, Derbert, if any of those mad bastards enjoyed freedom because of the generosity of our Government then we really fucked up."

Derbert moved his coffee cup around.

"I'm just saying it's a possibility," said Derbert. "I've only found one file with anything meaningful in it and I can only assume that was a mistake. Anyway, in that file someone categorically rates the scientist as being a dangerous Nazi who should have spent some time in a detention centre. Instead of a detention centre, we bring him straight to America. How many more could have been like that?"

"Put like that, no one will ever know," said Phil.

"Do you have any particular bad apples in mind?" Wilf then asked.

"I have one name I'm checking out," said Derbert, "though I'm pretty sure it's an assumed name, so it ain't gonna get me very far "

Phil thought for a moment and then spoke again.

"I know someone who might be of help to you. He's an old CIA buddy called Jimmy Bush. Jimmy saw problems everywhere. He was known around the office as Jimmy Paranoid. From what you've just told us, I think Jimmy was right to trust no one."

"Can you arrange a meeting?" Derbert then said.

"I sure can; and can I be there as well?"

"Feel free. Phone me when you have a time and place arranged," Derbert then said as he finished his coffee and went off to do battle with his desk once more.

Later the same day – O'Reilly's Bar, Downtown Washington

Derbert arrived at the meeting place a little ahead of the agreed time. The bar was already busy and a number of eyes turned towards the door as Derbert walked in. He looked around the sea of faces, looking for Phil. He saw no one, so instead made his way to the counter where he ordered a Jack Daniels. He was in the process of offering the barmaid money when he noticed an arm being waved from one of the booths to his right. It was Phil.

Derbert made his way over and Phil stood up to welcome him and also introduce Jimmy Bush. Bush was a white-haired man with deep lines on his face. He looked like he'd lived a hard life. When Jimmy spoke, it was with the voice of a man who had spent all of his life smoking the strongest cigarettes he could get his hands on.

He started to say something else, but the words were lost in a bout of coughing that seemed to come from the soles of his feet. Derbert had never heard such a cough; it was definitely the sound of a dying man. Eventually, the coughing passed and Jimmy was able to speak again.

"Phil here tells me you're finally looking into those German scientists we flew here after the war," Bush began.

"One of my colleagues has her suspicions," added Derbert.

"We spent four years fighting the bastards and then we happily flew hundreds of them to America so that they could build rockets for us. We brought them in to America without ever checking any of them in any detail. Basically, if their underwear was clean, they got in."

"But you never really trusted any of them, did you?" Derbert then asked.

A moment or two was required to pass as Bush was once more gripped by a coughing fit that ended with him holding a handkerchief to his mouth and a few droplets of blood were visible. Eventually he settled down again, leaning forward as if about to impart information that only fellow conspirators should hear.

"Not really. I was a bit of a naughty boy, Derbert. If I was ever told to get rid of things I usually didn't. I always had a nose for trouble and when it came to those jokers the old nose would twitch like blazes. I kept as much as I could. I knew, one day, someone would start looking a little deeper."

Bush took a drink from his glass and then continued speaking.

"Just because they got us to the Moon, doesn't make them fucking saints all of a sudden."

"Could we have let war criminals in with the scientists?" Derbert then asked.

"Look Derbert, our approach to those guys was simple. If it walks like a duck and quacks like a duck, then it's a fucking duck. In this case, the duck just happened to wear a white coat as well."

Derbert took a drink, then asked his next question.

"Have you ever heard of an organisation called Freiheit?"

Bush thought for a moment. "I've never *heard* the word in conversation, but I'm pretty sure I did *see* it mentioned occasionally."

"In what context?" said Derbert.

"No context, it would just turn up in a random way, which is why we all ignored it."

"Are we talking about general reports, or something in particular?" Derbert then asked.

"Just general stuff, I really can't remember."

"So, nothing specific?" pressed Derbert.

"Not that I can remember, no. What is this Freiheit then?"

"Ex-SS," replied Derbert.

"Ah, mad bastards inc," quipped Bush and as he started to laugh, another bout of coughing gripped him, to the extent that others in the bar were now looking in his direction. As if sensing he was the centre of attraction, Bush spun round and shouted towards them:

"What's the matter, have you never seen a man dying before?"

Everyone now looked away. There was a murmur of what Derbert took to be embarrassment and then it all went quiet again. Bush turned back.

"Do you think this Freiheit might have connections to the rocket scientists?" Bush asked.

"I have no idea," admitted Derbert. "I'm guessing they'd have been in the States before Freiheit got underway, so the two probably aren't connected."

Jimmy Bush finished his drink and took a notebook from his pocket. "Maybe you should have a look through this," he said, handing the book to Derbert.

Derbert took the book and flicked through a few pages. The writing inside was small, but very neat. There were a number of dates and other, more lengthy entries. It all seemed very interesting.

"I took all that from the various items I was supposed to get rid of," explained Bush. "You ought to find the word Freiheit, here or there, but as I said, it didn't mean anything to me; it was just a word.

"Can I keep this?" asked Derbert, holding the book up.

"It's no use to me now," said Bush. "Don't expect I'll be breathing for much longer anyway and as they say, you can't take it with you."

Derbert again asked if the others wanted another drink and again they refused. Ten minutes later, they were all walking out of the bar and Derbert got the impression that the regulars were not sorry to see a black man leaving.

Wednesday 25th August, 1971 – CIA Headquarters, Langley, Virginia

The Wednesday morning had been filled with sunshine and heat in the air. Derbert had wakened early, enjoyed a light breakfast and then driven to work, feeling quite upbeat about what Jimmy Bush had both said and given him, the night before.

He took another coffee to his desk and cleared away some of the mess he'd left from the day before. He then took out Bush's notebook and started working through it, taking notes of his own as he went along.

There were notes relevant to the time when Operation Paperclip had been in full swing. There was no mention of Julius Podolski, but another name did crop up on more than one occasion, which had Derbert searching for the file and checking the photograph within it.

It was a match to Podolski. So, Podolski had arrived in America as Dieter Hoeness. However, the story did not end there. Once on American soil, he had been given yet another name, that of Toby Reinhardt.

At last, Derbert had found a name he recognised. Toby Reinhardt was one of the major players at NASA and someone who had made a name for himself in helping to put men on the Moon.

Derbert should have been elated, but somehow he couldn't help feeling that this actually complicated matters, rather than simplified them. He picked up the phone again and contacted the Computer Room. He now wanted all that they had on Dieter Hoeness and Toby Reinhardt. He was told they'd get back to him as soon as possible.

The Hoeness file had next to nothing in it, which was becoming the norm as far as Derbert could see. However, the fact that Hoeness had been given a new identity the moment he'd stepped on American soil, did have Derbert wondering if the authorities had known they had a war criminal on their hands and had chosen to cover it up for the sake of the specialist knowledge he was bringing with him.

Less than twenty minutes went by before the door to Derbert's cupboard office opened and a man walked in, closing the door behind him. Derbert could not put a name to the man, but he had seen many of his type walking the corridors of Langley. There was an air of self-confidence bordering on the arrogant and an expression that told those around him not to mess with him. He looked like a man accustomed to giving orders rather than taking them.

He sat down. Derbert reckoned the man's suit had cost more than Derbert would make in a couple of months. Whoever he was, he was from way up the pecking order and that expression told Derbert that he meant business.

Derbert sat back. There was now only one thought in his head:

What could that business be?

Silence hung in the room for a few seconds, so Derbert decided to make the first move.

"Do you mind telling me who you are?"

The man said nothing, but a smile did cross his face, showing some excellent dental work in the process. The precision military haircut bothered Derbert a little. He even began to wonder if this man had been sent to hurt him in some way.

But why, was the obvious question to follow that notion?

"It really doesn't matter who I am, Mister Liston, this call is more about your job, rather than mine."

Derbert was even more confused.

The majority of people at Langley didn't even know Derbert Liston worked there, let alone be the slightest bit interested in anything he might be doing.

"Why would anyone be interested in what I'm doing?" Derbert then asked.

"Why the sudden interest in Operation Paperclip?" the man then asked.

Ah, thought Derbert, *now we're getting to the point.*

"I was checking out a couple of names and one of them is heavily connected to Operation Paperclip. I'm really just following the evidence."

"This name you were checking, who was it?"

"Well, it started as Julius Podolski, then it became Dieter Hoeness, but now it seems to be Toby Reinhardt. A man of many names, which usually means they have something major to hide."

"You do know who Toby Reinhardt is?" the man then said.

"Yes, he works for NASA."

"And since we put a man on the Moon, a bit of a hero in the United States."

"A bit of a hero with a tarnished past," added Derbert. "However, let me guess, you're now here to tell me to drop all interest in Reinhardt and to go back to shuffling paper, like I usually do."

The man's expression grew more serious.

"Don't try being smart with me, son, or you'll find yourself looking for another job."

"So, you don't want me to stop showing an interest in Reinhardt?" Derbert then said and the other man's expression darkened even more.

"I told you not to be smart with me. With regard to Reinhardt, you can back off because there is nothing to find. The man has been a model citizen, since he came to this country after the war and I see no reason for digging up the past now.

Whoever he was, before he came to this country, he's certainly not that man now."

Derbert wasn't so sure that war criminals ever deserved to be let off the hook. They all needed to pay for the what they did in the war, there was no room for sympathy; it wasn't as if they'd afforded any of that to others.

"I'm doing this work for London," Derbert then said, hoping it might take some of the flak off himself.

"Then tell them what I am telling you," the man insisted. "There is nothing to be gained from investigating Toby Reinhardt."

Derbert thought for a moment. "Do you have a problem with anyone else, just to stop me wasting my time on them as well?"

The man continued to look annoyed. "I really don't like your attitude," he then said. Derbert did not respond. The man continued. "No, I don't have a problem with anyone else."

He then stood up and turned to leave. He opened the door then paused.

"Just do as I say, Mister Liston, and don't try being clever. Okay?"

"Message received and understood," he replied and then watched the man leave and close the door behind him.

Derbert then turned his attention to writing his report for Amy. He had no intention of holding back on what he found already, but he thought it best not to dig any deeper. He would let Amy know about Reinhardt and also about the threatening visitor. He would also speak to Abner about his visitor. Whatever the man's reasons, he had no need threatening Derbert in that manner.

After all, they were all supposed to be on the same side.

Friday, 27th August, 1971 – MILO HQ, Central London

The official bag arrived from Washington that morning, filled with the usual items that passed between the UK and the USA.

 Knowing Podolski's new identity was a major step forward, but Sir Tavish was not at all happy that anyone in his team, London or Langley, should be leaned on for doing their job. He decided to phone Abner and discuss the matter.

The other item from Derbert, which had allowed London to move forward, was confirmation that Gunther Weiss and Franz Neuer were one and the same person. Photographic evidence, from within the CIA files had been enough and Sir Tavish now gave the order for Neuer to be arrested and tried for his wartime crimes.

"Knowing that Neuer is really Gunther Weiss, puts another war criminal inside the Varga Corporation," Ben said to Sir Tavish as they sat in the latter's office later that morning. "Surely, we're starting to build a picture, sir, proving we were right to go after Varga in the first place."

Sir Tavish did not look convinced.

"I think it would be fair to say that many German companies, which were formed after the war, are going to have a few criminals in their midst. It doesn't necessarily mean they've accepted them through choice."

"I suppose not," conceded Ben.

"And we still haven't connected anyone directly to Freiheit," Sir Tavish added. "Hanging war criminals is one thing, but bringing down Freiheit is what we're really here to do and that seems a long way off."

"What do we do about Wolfgang Brandt?" Ben then asked.

Sir Tavish gave the question some thought, then answered.

"We have next to nothing on the man. However, he does have a lifestyle that's better than mine and I'd dearly like to know how he finances that. See if he'll meet with you and if so, take Amy and have a chat with the man.

"Very good, sir," said Ben, standing up and leaving the room.

Friday, 27th August, 1971 – Barclays Bank, Moorgate

Terry Ferris had a problem.

It was the last day in which he stood any chance of getting his hands on all the vault keys. It was also the Bank Holiday weekend, the branch would be closed on Monday, which would give him a chance to meet with Barry Gibb.

The timing was right, the plan still a bit short of substance. He had one set of keys, all he needed now was the manager's set as well. Easier said than done.

All week, as they'd opened and closed the vault, he'd looked at the other set of keys and wondered how best to get them. If he wanted those keys then he needed to get the manager out of the way first.

But how?

Terry had gone for lunch. He'd gone to his usual café and sat in his usual seat. A young woman sat opposite him at the same table; she wasn't a regular as far as Terry could tell. He might have paid more attention to her in the days prior to going out with Gill. Now he had his girl, he wasn't interested in anyone else.

As he ate his fish and chips, he mulled over his problem. There had to be a solution, but now he only had a few hours in which to find it. He drank tea from a mug and pushed a mouthful of fish and mushy peas into his mouth. As he did so, a thought struck him.

What if old Wrigglesworth took ill?

If the manager had had to go home, then his keys would pass to Alf. Alf was due to be on leave the following week, which would mean he'd have to leave those keys with someone else, rather than have to bring them in on the Tuesday morning.

Terry could suggest that Alf leave the other keys with him. That would then give him plenty time to take the impressions before getting Gill to lock them away in the manager's safe.

The idea seemed sound. All he had to do now, was find a way of making Wrigglesworth ill. Again, easier said than done.

He finished his food and drank the last of his tea. By the time he was ready to leave the café, his plan was complete. He had remembered seeing a television drama in which someone was made I ill by drinking coffee laced with eyedrops. Terry hoped that, in real life, eyedrops in your coffee wouldn't prove fatal.

He bought them on the way back to the branch. He went to his own desk, just to let the staff see he was back from lunch and then he made his way to Gill's office, taking another folder with him to make the visit look official.

"I need your help," he said, as soon as he entered Gill's office. Terry quickly explained his plan and though Gill didn't like the idea of deliberately making anyone ill, she could see that they were running out of alternatives.

When Gill took Wrigglesworth his afternoon coffee, there as a little extra in it.

*

It did not take long to work.

Horace Wrigglesworth was violently sick within a matter of minutes. He had only just made it to the toilet and was now almost reluctant to leave again. As, effectively, second-in-command, Terry had gone to see what could be done. He found a white-faced and shaking manager who was convinced that he wasn't through with vomiting. He would have to go home.

Terry nearly grinned with joy, on hearing that.

One of the staff lived in the general direction of the manager and they agreed to take him home. It meant their Bank Holiday weekend started a little quicker; they just hoped that Wrigglesworth didn't throw up over their car, or they'd be spending that holiday weekend mopping up.

Wrigglesworth left his keys with Alf and it was agreed that Alf would then leave them in the safe for Tuesday morning. Terry felt sure he could persuade Alf to do things his way, when the time came.

Everything went smoothly after Wrigglesworth was out of the way. The cashiers balanced at the first time of asking and the machine room also balanced everything almost immediately. It meant an early finish for everyone. Most of the staff had already left when Terry and Alf, along with one of the caretakers, put the cashiers' trolleys away and locked all the doors. Alf was then about to go and see Gill, when Terry suggested he started his leave early and Terry would see Gill. Alf did not need much persuading. He had his coat on and was halfway to the front door, before Terry reached Gill's office.

The impressions were taken and Wrigglesworth's keys locked in the safe. Both Terry and Gill were smiling broadly as they left the building that afternoon. The caretaker in the front door just assumed they were looking forward to a long weekend.

Monday, 30th August, 1971 – The Albany Tavern, Great Portland Street, London, W1

The pubs were all busy; it was a glorious Bank Holiday Monday and most people wanted to spend it as far away from home as they could get. Terry had got to the meeting place early. He was nervous and wanted a couple of drinks to calm the nerves. He was about to meet the man calling himself

Barry Gibb. It would be their first face to face meeting and Terry wasn't sure how it would go. Gill had wanted to be there, but Terry had suggested it would go better if she wasn't. Barry Gibb didn't know what to expect from Terry and that small advantage might yet be of help to his negotiations.

Terry had phoned the number Gill had for Gibb on the previous Saturday. He had kept the call short, simply suggested a pub as a meeting place and said he'd be there at one o'clock. As it was, Terry had been there since just after midday.

He had sat watching all the men coming through the front door and wondering which one would be Gibb. Gill had given him a brief description, so he felt he knew who he was looking for.

He had it all thought out in his head, he just wasn't sure the reality would pass quite so smoothly. Terry went to the bar and ordered his third pint. The alcohol was beginning to have an effect and he could feel his blood pressure dropping and his anxiety settling down.

He was served by a barmaid wearing a Deep Purple tee shirt. Terry thought the group had never looked so good as it did, stretched across her ample bosom.

He returned to his seat, all the time trying to keep some space around him as the place started to fill up. Eventually, a man came into the bar. Terry was sure it was Gibb. He watched him look around the bar, seeking out the one clue Terry had given him by way of identity. He'd be wearing a black polo neck and purple loons. As luck would have it, no one else in the bar that day had gone for the same look.

Gibb bought a pint and came over. He eyed Terry with suspicion as he sat down.

"When did you come into the equation?" Tony asked, his tone already hostile.

"I don't think that really matters, does it?" Terry replied, trying to sound quite hard himself.

"Do you have what I asked for?" was Tony's next question.

"I told you on the phone I did," said Terry.

"So, where is it?" Tony said, making a dramatic gesture of looking around the table.

"It's not that easy," said Terry. "You clear Gill's name and I give you the impressions. Without one, you don't get the other."

Terry stared at Tony; still hopeful he was coming across more like a Mafia Don than a bank employee. Tony stared back, still not sure who he was dealing with. He was obviously a friend of Gill's, but in what capacity?

"There's nothing I can do today," Tony eventually said. "The banks are shut."

"They'll be open again tomorrow," Terry then said. "Be here at five-thirty and we can exchange items."

Tony considered the matter for a moment. He knew he had no other option, but to go along with what was being said. He really wanted to pull this annoying man across the table and rip his head off. Unfortunately, he needed those impressions. Maybe he'd rip his head off later.

"Okay, we'll meet again tomorrow."

"Good. Oh, and there's one more thing."

Tony took a drink of his beer and then put the mug down.

"And what would that be?" he said.

"Five thousand isn't enough," Terry said, "Gill may need to put distance between herself and the law; that'll take more than five thousand."

"You little........," Tony started to say, but quickly got his emotions under control again. "How much do you want?"

"Ten thousand sounds better," Terry replied.

"Ten grand, you must be........," Tony again started, but once more stopped himself. There really was no point in arguing. It was a stupid amount of money for what he was getting in return, however as a percentage of what they would get from robbing both banks, it was peanuts.

"Okay," he said. "I'll have the account topped up."

"And you'll bring all the paperwork Gill will need to access that account?" Terry said, by way of confirmation.

"Yes, I'll bring that along with the contents of the safe-deposit box."

"And don't go keeping copies," Terry added.

Tony laughed. "Why the fuck would I do that? Look, mate, you're welcome to Gill Potter, I only needed her for the keys. She never meant anything to me. You give me those impressions and I'll give you everything on Gill."

"And the ten thousand," said Terry, "don't forget that."

Tony downed the last of his beer.

"I won't. See you here tomorrow."

And with that Tony Rutherford left the bar and Terry Ferris breathed again for the first time in what seemed like a while.

*

The following day, Tony and Terry met for five minutes. Items were exchanged and comments made, along the lines of hoping they'd never see each other again.

Tony had left without even having a drink. Gill had then appeared from the Ladies' toilet and joined Terry for what she hoped would be a celebratory drink.

"How was he?" asked Gill.

"Angry."

"Did you get everything?"

"He tells me it's all here. I've had a quick look and I think you're safe now."

"What about copies?"

"He says there aren't any and quite frankly, I believe him. Gill, he has no use for either of us, now he has what he wanted."

Gill visibly breathed a sigh of relief.

And you got the money?" Gill then asked.

Terry grinned.

"He paid us all the money I asked for."

Gill looked a little confused.

"Which was how much?"

Terry opened the hold-all, which Tony had brought with him and let Gill see the contents. It was full of money. Gill's eyes lit up.

"How much?" was all she could say.

"Ten thousand pounds," laughed Terry. "We are rich, Gill, we are so fucking rich."

Even though it was a public place, they kissed passionately.

PART FIVE

Wednesday, 1st September, 1971 – Wolfgang Brandt's home, Puerto de Soller, Majorca

Ben and Amy were in Wolfgang Brandt's sitting room, looking out of the picture window down across the harbour. The view was spectacular.

"How the hell does he afford all this?" Amy said, keeping her voice low.

"Maybe we'll get an answer to that question over the next few minutes," replied Ben.

At that moment, the door opened and two men walked into the room. The leading man looked to be in his thirties, dressed in a smart suit with polished shoes. He looked well-groomed and every inch a lawyer. The second man was a lot older, though still with an aristocratic air about him. He was dressed casually in open-necked shirt and slacks.

Ben wondered why Brandt felt the need to have a lawyer present. After all, if any questions were asked that Brandt didn't want to answer, then he just had to say so. MILO had no legal reason to ask him anything.

Brandt smiled, though mainly in Amy's direction. He offered a handshake to them both, which they rather felt compelled to accept. Ben introduced himself and then Amy. Brandt introduced the other man as being Ramon Gonzales, a local lawyer who dealt with all Brandt's personal legal business. Gonzales nodded his head in the direction of their visitors and then took a seat beside Brandt, on a long sofa.

"May I offer you coffee, or something else?" Brandt then said, his English almost perfect.

"No thank you," said Ben, "we don't intend taking up much of your time."

Brandt seemed pleased to hear that. Ben continued.

"Your name has cropped up in one of our investigations, Herr Brandt, and it's led to one or two questions we hope you won't mind answering."

"I'm sure that will depend on what the questions are," added Brandt with another slight smile. Gonzales, meanwhile, bristled a little, keen to defend his client at every turn.

"How much do you still think about the war?" Ben then asked.

It had not been the question that Brandt might have expected. He almost rocked back in his chair; such was his surprise in what he'd just heard.

"I don't think about it at all."

"Not even about the people you met?"

"Especially the people I met. It was wartime, I only met them because of the circumstances of the moment. There was never any need to remember them."

"So, the name Gunther Weiss won't mean anything to you?" Ben then said. Both Ben and Amy were studying Brandt even more closely as the question was asked. There was little reaction.

"The name means nothing to me," Brandt then said, "though I'm guessing that if you are here, there is every likelihood that you've managed to connect us. Who is he?"

If Brandt had known Weiss then it was fine piece of acting. Maybe after a lifetime of lies, new lies just come all the easier.

"He is someone we know you crossed paths with on more than one occasion, both before and during the war," Ben then said.

Brandt smiled again. "I'm sure I crossed paths with many people between nineteen thirty-three and nineteen forty-five, but I couldn't even begin to put a name to most of them. How about you, Mister Ward, can you name everyone in your office, for example?"

"How about Franz Neuer?" Amy now asked.

Brandt turned to look at her, his eyes travelling down her body and back up again. Even accustomed, as she was, to men looking at her, having Brandt's eyes on her unsettled her far more than normal.

"Now, that name I do recognise. I believe Herr Neuer works for the Varga Corporation, a company I have occasional dealings with."

"What kind of dealings?" Ben added.

"*Business* dealings, Mister Ward and therefore nothing to do with you," replied Brandt.

"So, move on," added Gonzales.

Ben smiled. He was ready to tell Brandt something that he hoped would illicit a reaction. Earlier that day, Ben had received information that Gunther Weiss had been arrested and was now being held in a police cell in Stuttgart, awaiting transport to The Hague, where he was to stand trial for war crimes.

As Ben told Brandt about Weiss, he and Amy were looking once more for any obvious reaction to the news. There was a slight twitch at the corner of Brandt's right eye but, generally, he took the news without any sign of it meaning anything to him.

"I'm sorry to hear that, even after all this time, my fellow officers are still being hounded by do-gooders who fail to realise we were only following orders," Brandt then said.

The usual cop-out, thought Ben. He was about to say something else when the door opened and a man came in. He moved over to where Brandt was sitting and whispered something in his ear. As he listened, Brandt glanced across at Ben, making Ben wonder if this might be Brandt getting conformation of what had happened to Weiss.

The messenger went away again and Brandt stood up. "I'm afraid that was bad news, so I would now like time on my own to process it. Mister Gonzales will show you out."

Brandt left the room and even Gonzales looked surprised at the speed with which his mood had changed. Gonzales stood up and led the way to the front door. Ben and Amy went out and the door was closed behind them again.

By the time they were out of the house, Brandt was already on the phone to Dinger. He told Dinger that Neuer had been arrested and where he was being held.

"Make sure Franz has no chance to say anything damaging to our cause," Brandt said.

"I will see to it at once, Herr Brandt," Dinger replied.

Brandt put the phone down and poured himself a drink. The MILO visit had worried him more than he might have imagined. He also knew, that in contacting Dinger with the news about Neuer, he was pointing the finger at himself in terms of MILO knowing how the news got out.

When Dinger completed his mission, MILO would know who had sent him.

It was time to instigate some changes. Time for Brandt to take a back seat and hand over the baton of power to someone else. As he sat drinking, his mind was clear. He knew exactly what to do next and who to involve.

Thursday, 2nd September, 1971 – Stuttgart Police Headquarters

The door to Holding Cell Three opened and a police officer walked in.

"Your lawyer is here to see you," he said gruffly and stepped back to let the man behind him pass.

Neuer smiled at seeing who it was coming in to the room. The police officer then said that they would have twenty minutes and no longer to discuss matters. He then closed the door. Even though he was chained to the table, Neuer still managed to stand up.

"Ralf, you had no need to come yourself," he said as he held his hand out towards Ralf Dinger.

Dinger ignored the offer of a handshake as he reached the table and sat down. "I thought it best if I came to see you in person rather than have a third-party passing information between us."

"I take it you've come to get me out," Neuer then said.

Dinger looked at him, his expression never having looked more serious.

"No one can get you out of this, Herr Neuer," he then said. "You *did* do what they'll say you did and for that, you have to pay for the crimes you committed."

Neuer's face fell. This was not the news he expected to hear from Dinger. From the moment he'd been arrested, he had felt it would only be a matter of time before someone came to free him.

"But surely something could be done?" Neuer said.

"I'm sure that something *could*," agreed Dinger, "but the sad truth, Herr Neuer, is that it won't. Freiheit has to be protected at all costs, so we cannot afford anything to come out at your trial that we might not be able to deal with. In short, Herr Neuer, you can't go to trial."

It took a minute for those last words to sink in, then Neuer began to shift nervously in his chair.

"What are you saying, Ralf?" he then enquired.

Dinger opened the briefcase he had brought with him. The same briefcase he had watched the police check so thoroughly before he was allowed to see Neuer. The same briefcase that had a slight tear in the lining, which Dinger now opened a little further. Taped to the inside of the lid was a capsule, which Dinger now removed and handed to Neuer.

"This is the only way out," he then said.

Neuer focussed on the capsule. He knew exactly what it was; it had been something he had carried around with him for those first few years after the war. Had the Nazi hunters caught up with him he would have taken the honourable way out. But that was over twenty years ago. He no longer wanted to take the honourable way out.

There just had to be another option.

"And if I won't take your bitter pill?" he said.

Dinger's expression hardened.

"If you are not pronounced dead within the next twenty-four hours, then I shall return to personally shove it down your throat. This is not for debate, Herr Neuer, this is an order. You will obey."

Neuer could see the truth in Dinger's eyes. Dinger would carry out his threat because he was a man who followed orders without question. Neuer now knew he had only two options left. Either he took his own life, or Dinger would murder him. Even if he survived all that the courts would then sentence him to death.

There really was no way out,

Neuer took the capsule from Dinger and nodded his head. Dinger relaxed a little as he closed the briefcase.

"Excellent," he then said and stood up. "Within twenty-four hours, Herr Neuer, or I will be back."

And with that Dinger called for the cell door to be opened and, without looking back, he went on his way. Neuer sat for a moment. He kept the capsule well hidden. He would choose his time; only he would decide when to bring the final curtain down.

Friday, 3rd September, 1971 – MILO HQ, Central London.

"What?!!"

One word, but delivered with so much venom. Sir Tavish could not believe what he was being told. They had finally captured a man who was not only a war criminal but also, in every likelihood, a member of Freiheit.

And he was dead. Committed suicide in his cell.

"How the blue blazes did he get his hands on a cyanide capsule?" was Sir Tavish's obvious next question.

No one could be sure, his only visitor had been his lawyer and he and his belongings had been well searched before he'd seen Neuer,

"Obviously, not well enough," Sir Tavish had added, his anger rising to levels where he thought steam might actually be visible from his ears.

The news of Neuer's death had come little more than half an hour from Sir Tavish being told that Hans Varga had died, finally succumbing to the cancer eating away at his inside. Two major leads now gone; two men whose past would now be forever protected. There was no point in continuing with an investigation with both men now safe from prosecution.

*

At roughly the same time as Sir Tavish was receiving the call about Neuer, Wolfgang Brandt was receiving a call from his own sources. The news was the same, only this time it was met with greater joy. What had been a lead to MILO was no more than a loose end to Freiheit. A loose end that had now been tied off. Gunther Weiss was now at peace and there was nothing that anyone could do to spoil that.

Thursday 09th September 1971 – The Dog and Duck Pub, Bateman Street, London, W1

Tony Rutherford met with Vince Hammond at lunchtime. They bought a drink and found a quiet corner to talk. Hammond had hit upon a problem that needed a decision from Tony.

"I've been thinking," Hammond began.

"I thought you were looking pained," quipped Tony, but his effort at wit was duly ignored.

"I think we're going to need a Peterman," Hammond then said.

"What the hell for, you never mentioned any need to blow safes before?"

"It's a safety net, nothing more," explained Hammond. "I'm not planning on needing one, but if we dig all the way into that bank and then find we have to blow some doors, I want a man sitting there ready and waiting, I don't want to be putting out a call and then having to sit around waiting, in the hope someone turns up."

"Do you have someone in mind?" asked Tony.

Hammond sipped his beer. "The best man for this job has to be Seamus O'Lafferty."

"He's IRA isn't he?" Rutherford asked with disgust.

"He has done work for the IRA," admitted Hammond, "but they were just contracts, same as anything else he might do."

"Killing civilians is not my idea of *just a contract*," Rutherford added.

"I don't think Seamus has ever killed anyone," Hammond said." Anyway, we don't have the time to debate the morals of this job; if we need to blow the vault then we'll need the right man."

Rutherford pondered on the problem for a few seconds. "Very well. Get in touch with Seamus and find out his price. Let me know what that is and I'll transfer the necessary funds."

"Excellent."

"But apart from that, everything else is going well?" Rutherford then added by way of needing reassurance.

"We're still on schedule to do the job this weekend, assuming we can get a hold of Seamus today."

Friday 10th September 1971 – Abner McQueen's Office, CIA HQ, Langley, Virginia

Abner McQueen and Sir Tavish were already in agreement about what to do about Derbert's mystery visitor. The plan was
simple, flush him out and deal with him. Abner told Sir Tavish it would be a pleasure.

Abner had also met with Derbert and a plan discussed. Firstly, Derbert's office had been bugged, with wires running to the room next door. A tape recorder was attached to the bugging device, so that anything said could be recorded for posterity. Once the two rooms had been set up, Derbert was instructed to put the plan into operation. He contacted the Computer Room and asked them to get him information concerning Toby Reinhardt. Having lit the blue touch paper, Derbert then sat back and waited.

He did not need to wait long. Less than half an hour later, the door opened and the mystery man returned. Derbert casually let his right hand drop and he pushed a small button that had been installed under his desk.

"I'm really disappointed with you, Derbert," the man said, approaching Derbert's desk "I really thought you had the prospect of a good career in this organisation, but you can't expect to be backed for promotion if you won't listen to simple instructions."

"I told you I was working for London and they wanted more information," Derbert said. "In my corner of this building Sir Tavish Viewforth actually carries more weight than you do."

The stranger nearly exploded. "You work for the CIA, Derbert, which means you abide by CIA rules and the CIA hierarchy. Do I make myself clear?"

The stranger picked up Derbert's phone.

"At this precise moment, Derbert, your future ain't looking too bright. I'm going to have to suspend you."

Derbert did not look so concerned as the stranger might have expected.

"Actually," he said, "I thought my future was just beginning to look up."

"Not from where I'm standing," said the stranger.

"Ah, yes," said Derbert, "but from where you are standing, you can't see who's behind you."

Derbert was now smiling, which was not what the stranger might have expected. He tried to bluff it out.

"Not the old, he's behind you routine?"

Derbert continued to smile.

"A comment with true meaning when there *really* is someone behind you; he's standing at the door."

The mystery man at first looked as if he still did not believe what Derbert was saying, but there was a certain something in Derbert's expression that made him slowly turn his head. The door behind him was, indeed, open and standing in the doorway, watching and hearing all that was going on, was Abner McQueen.

The mystery man stood up straight again, his countenance lightening immeasurably and an attempt at a smile playing around his lips.

"Abner," he said, "what brings you here?"

Abner McQueen knew immediately who he was facing. He had known the minute he heard the voice coming through the speaker. This was Roger Templeman, Director of Overseas Operations and a man who was several pay grades above most people working at Langley. He was certainly in a role that should have had nothing to do with petty issues like the work that Derbert might have been doing.

"You bring me here, Roger."

Templeman tried to look surprised. "But I'm just here having a quiet word with Derbert. It's nothing that need bother you."

"But Derbert's a member of my staff, Roger and as such everything that happens to him, involves me at some point."

Templeman was still trying to bring that smile to the surface, but somehow it just wouldn't cooperate.

"Still, this was just a minor point between Derbert and myself, it need not involve you at all, Abner."

"Now, Roger, you don't expect me to believe that a man in your position would get involved in *anything* minor, let alone work being done in a MILO cupboard,"

"Derbert just happened to come across something that I felt should involve me. It's dealt with now."

Abner now smiled.

"I have it all on tape, Roger," he then said.

Templeman's expression turned to one of both concern and concentration. He had a problem that needed to be nipped in the bud, before it became terminal.

"Look, Abner, Derbert had been asking questions about someone that the American Government now feels should be left alone. It's been a long time since the war and everyone deserves a second chance."

"So, as so many Nazis said in the war, you were just following instructions, is that how it is, Roger?"

"Yeah, got it in one, Abner. I was just following instructions."

"Might I ask who gave you those instructions?" Abner then enquired.

"Ah, now that is information outside of your pay grade," Templeman replied. He was trying to make it sound like a joke, but the concern for his predicament was still evident in his tone.

At that moment, Abner took a piece of paper from his pocket and handed it to Templeman. At first he looked like he might ignore the gesture, but eventually he took the paper and started to read what was written on it.

The handwriting was clearly that of Richard M. Helms, the Director of Central Intelligence. He was everyone's boss. The message was written in neat and tidy writing and perfectly clear in its meaning. Helms was handing authority to Abner McQueen in all matters relating to Toby Reinhardt.

"Now, I think it's time we had a chat, Mister Templeman," Abner then said, "if you'd just follow me."

It was a short journey. They only went to the next room along the corridor and as Templeman entered the colour drained from his face. The room was furnished with a long table and four chairs. Two men in dark suits were already there, one hovering by a large tape recorder, the other by the door.

Abner sat down and invited Templeman to do the same. The man by the tape recorder also sat down, the man by the door remained standing.

"Is it all right if I smoke?"

"No," was Abner's blunt reply. "We have things to discuss, Director," he then said, finally giving the man the courtesy of using his title.

Templeman put away the pack of cigarettes he'd started to remove from his pocket.

"This must be serious," he said, glancing across at the tape recorder again.

"Why are you so interested in protecting Toby Reinhardt?" Abner then asked.

"Is that all this is about?" replied Templeman, forcing a smile. "As I tried to explain to Derbert, Reinhardt has done a lot of excellent work for this country and I see no reason in dragging up the past. He's a changed man, Abner, take my word for it."

"I think we all know, Director, that Reinhardt is really Julius Podolski who just happens to be on the list of wanted war criminals. I think we both also know that Podolski has enjoyed the protection of our Government for the last twenty-five years. I think it's time that protection stopped and yet, here you are, doing all that you can to protect him. I feel I have to ask why, Director?"

"As I said, Abner, he's not the man he was during the war."

It was a lame reply and Abner knew it. Abner sat forward in his chair, placing his weight on his arms.

"Look, Director, Adolf Hitler could have become everyone's pal after the war, but he'd still have been strung up for what he did during the war. Those crimes never go away and no one deserves a get out of jail card, just because they know how to build rockets."

"It's in no one's interest to drag that man through the courts," Templeman insisted.

Abner nodded to the man sitting beside the tape recorder. He flicked a switch and the massive tapes began turning. The full conversation, which Templeman had had with Derbert, was played. As Templeman listened he thought. He was in a corner and needed to get out.

"That seems rather heavy-handed, Director," Abner said as the recording ended. "In fact, I'd go as far as to say you were threatening Derbert, which seems very strange to me. You could have simply issued an order; we'd have ignored it of course, but it was still your prerogative to issue it. And yet you come all the way round to our bit of the building to lean on an employee who is just doing his job. Just following orders, as I think you put it. Now, I ask again, why would you do that?"

Templeman was still thinking, but nothing of any use would come to mind.

"He works for NASA," was the only answer he could give.

Abner laughed.

"And that trumps him being a war criminal?"

Even Templeman knew the inadequacy of his answer, he was just buying time in the hope something better would come to him. Abner spoke next.

"You'll need to do better than that, Mister Templeman. Why are you, of all people, doing everything he can to protect Julius Podolski?"

Templeman decided to go on the offensive, to effectively pull rank and see if that made any difference.

"I don't like your tone, Abner, you need to remember who you are speaking to."

"Oh, I know exactly who I am speaking to, Director and that's what makes all this ten times worse. You should be in your ivory tower playing politics, not skulking around the corridors threatening staff. For you to get involved in something so petty, there just has to be a reason that you're not prepared to tell us. I want you to take a polygraph test."

It was now Templeman's turn to laugh.

"Come now, Abner, you know how unreliable those damn things are. A test will tell you nothing."

"Maybe," agreed Abner, "but you'll take one anyway."

Templeman looked, almost pleadingly, at Abner.

"You're really serious about this, aren't you?"

"Never more so. I look forward to the results."

And with that Abner stood up and left the room.

*

Half an hour later Templeman was wired up to a polygraph machine and a thin man with gold rimmed spectacles and hair hanging to his shoulders was sitting ready to study the results of the answers he was about to be given.

McQueen had provided a list of questions he wanted asked. Unbeknown to Templeman, Abner McQueen was actually watching and listening to the proceedings from the room next door. What appeared to be a mirror on the wall was now a two-way viewing system. Sitting beside Abner was Richard Helms himself. He had decided to take a personal interest in anything that Templeman might have to say for himself. Clearly, if the Director of Overseas Operations was involved in anything criminal, then action would have to be taken immediately. The two men nursed freshly made coffees, as they watched the proceedings unfold in the other room.

The first seven or eight questions simply set the scene. The answers to those questions were already known and the man with the spectacles made a few notes as the needles made their marks on the paper. Templeman seemed relaxed enough, after all he had watched others go through this many times and he knew the procedure.

The next batch of questions probed a little further in to the work that Templeman was involved in and then began to touch on Podolski. The needles moved across the paper and more notes were made. Templeman still seemed calm and in control of his answers.

Question twenty-one was the one that McQueen was waiting for with particular interest. He put his cup down ahead of the question being asked and he watched Templeman's face even more intently. The man with the spectacles asked question number twenty-one.

"Do you know anything about an organisation known as Freiheit?"

The man with the spectacles had no idea what the question meant. It wasn't his job to know why he was asking the questions he asked, it was simply his role to analyse the responses. In this case, however, it would not have taken an expert to realise that the question had been of greater significance to Templeman than the others.

The needles almost leapt off the paper and had smoke actually risen from the machine, no one would have been surprised. Templeman's air of relaxed control fell apart as his eyes looked almost pleadingly at his interrogator. A line of sweat broke out on his brow and though he eventually answered 'no' to the question everyone knew that he was lying.

"Jesus," exclaimed Helms. "What the hell was in that question?"

"The word Freiheit, sir," replied Abner, "and that's not good."

"But what the Hell could Freiheit have to do with Roger?" Helms then asked.

"That, sir, is what I'm about to find out."

*

Twenty minutes later, Abner and Templeman were back in the room with the tape recorder, their two minders once more in the room with them. Abner had another coffee, Templeman had asked for a cup of water. He was even allowed to smoke this time. Abner asked his first question.

"What exactly does Freiheit mean to you?"

"Nothing much," Templeman replied, puffing hard on his cigarette.

"Oh, come on, Director, the polygraph machine nearly blew up when the word was mentioned. You know about Freiheit because you're involved with them, in some way."

Templeman sat in silence for a little while longer. He sipped at his water and seemed to be giving the situation a lot of thought. The silence began to annoy McQueen so he spoke again.

"Look, Director, the next few minutes will be critical to your future. Depending on the level at which you are involved with Freiheit, you will either be totally finished with the CIA or, at best, retain a lower job until your retirement. One carries an element of respectability, the other ends in shame. How do you think your wife will respond to such a dramatic fall from grace?"

Templeman continued to think. Eventually he stubbed out the last of his cigarette and sat back in his chair with his water. He looked up at McQueen and finally spoke.

"All right, I'll tell you what I can about Freiheit, but I promise it's not what you think."

"And what am I thinking?" McQueen then asked.

"You seem to see this as being sinister, perhaps even illegal. Well, it's not."

"It all looks suspicious at best and highly illegal at worst. Put my mind at rest, Director and tell me all about the connection between yourself and Freiheit?"

Templeman put his water down on the desk and lit another cigarette. Just before he began to speak, Abner nodded to the man by the tape recorder once more and the tapes started turning again. Every word Roger Templeman said was going to be recorded; there would be no opportunity to deny anything at some later stage.

"When I was still in my last job, I was approached by a man at a party. I'd had a few drinks and was happy to talk to anyone. Anyway, as it happened, the stranger did most of the talking. He played to my ego, spent time bumming me up, making me think I was something special. He said I ought to be in higher-paid job, one with more responsibility. He said he could help me get that job. I laughingly said that would be great and then promptly forgot all about it."

"And then you got your current job?" prompted Abner.

Templeman inhaled deeply and let the smoke escape through his nose. He nodded.

"Yeah, I got my current job."

"And?" said Abner.

"And around three months after I took up the post, the same stranger appeared while I was at an official function. He told me how he'd arranged for me to get the job and how he had proof of wrong-doing, which didn't show me in a very good light."

"So, they started blackmailing you?" enquired Abner.

"That's just it, Abner, they didn't. I never heard from them again, until about two weeks ago. The same man spoke to me in the rest room, when I was out for a meal with my wife. I don't know how he knew I'd be there, but he did. He said he wanted a favour and when he told me what it was, I honestly saw no harm in doing what he asked."

"Which was to make sure nothing happened to Podolski?" said Abner.

"Got it in one. I mean, it wasn't as if he was asking me to sell secrets to the Russians, or anything."

"That's not how Freiheit works, Director," Abner then explained. "They place people in positions of authority and then wait for the day when that person can be of most use to the Freiheit cause."

"But protecting Podolski couldn't benefit anyone, apart from Podolski himself," said Templeman.

"It was a test, Director," Abner then said. "Give you a low-level task and see if you'll do it. Once you've agreed to that they've even more evidence to show how rotten you are. The next request might not be so low-level."

Templeman looked shocked.

"I'd never do anything to damage the reputation of the United States."

"However, let's say for argument's sake, that you were to replace Mister Helms someday. Just think how useful that would be to an organisation like Freiheit."

"But I'd never......," Templeman began to say.

Abner interrupted. "You might not have had any option; they'd have had you over a barrel by that time."

Templeman looked even more horrified.

"Jesus," he said softly to himself, "I just never thought."

"Not many people do," said Abner, "especially when they have an ego the size of yours."

Templeman looked like he was about to rise to the insult, but the moment passed almost as quickly as it had arrived. He was a broken man, there was no fight left in him. He finished on cigarette and lit another. His face now betrayed fear. He looked up at Abner again.

"Get protection to my family and I'll tell you what I know."

"Do you think you're in danger?" said Abner.

"I was told that if I spoke to anyone about my career success, then they'd come after my family. They could have people everywhere, for all I know and that might mean they know I'm here talking to you."

Highly unlikely, thought Abner, but he was willing to accept that Templeman's fear was genuine. He told the man at the door to arrange for a team to go to Director Templeman's house and have his family moved to a safe location.

The man left the room and Templeman voiced his thanks towards Abner.

"We'll speak again later," Abner then said and he, too, left the room.

Saturday 11th September, 1971 – Barclays Bank, 1-3 Moorgate, London, EC1

It was Saturday evening and Moorgate was completely devoid of life. It was common knowledge that the City of London was a ghost town at the weekend. Thousands of people arrived by various forms of transport from Monday through to Friday and then they all went home for the weekend. Apart from the occasional member of staff doing a spot of overtime there was no reason for anyone to be in the City after five o'clock on a Friday.

At ten minutes to eight a short, stocky man, wearing a three-piece, pin-striped suit arrived outside the Barclays branch at the Bank Station end of Moorgate. He used his keys to let himself in to the bank and then switched off the alarm system. He had everything he needed to enter and then leave the bank without attracting any attention whatsoever. He did not put the lights on within the branch, but instead used a torch to guide him down the length of the cashier points to the door at the end. He opened it and entered the staffing area of the bank. He checked his watch and then sat down to wait.

At a quarter past eight a van pulled up outside and three men got out. They went to the front door and knocked. The man inside opened the door and let them in. The van then drove a short distance where it was parked. The driver remained in the car, his eyes surveying the length of Moorgate in case anyone showed an interest in what was going on at the Bank.

Inside, the four men made their way down to the vaults where the leader used his keys to open all the doors. Once inside, they went to the bank's safe-deposit boxes and selected those numbers that had been provided. Each chosen box was emptied and the contents placed in a bag along with the number of the safe-deposit box. They already had a list of who owned which box. All boxes had been ticked in advance.

The men worked at their own pace, knowing that no one even knew they were there.

Across London, in the Lloyds Bank on Baker Street, things were not going quite so quietly. The gang had broken through into the bank and were in the process of removing both money and safe-deposit contents. Unlike Moorgate, there had been ample opportunity for someone to get wind of what they were doing. They'd been digging, which made noise and even their attendance at the bankrupt leather shop could have attracted attention.

There was always a concern that the police might come asking questions, out of curiosity more than anything else. The men at Baker Street worked more quickly; they wanted to get the job done and get out of there as soon as they could.

In working quickly, however, they were more likely to make mistakes.

And that's exactly what they did.

They had eyes outside the bank and those eyes were in constant contact with the gang through a two-way radio. The eyes got bored. He was fed-up sitting on a rooftop watching and waiting for possible police activity.

He kept calling the gang, just for a chat more than anything else. He kept being told to shut up and get off the line. A Radio Ham picked up on their signal. He'd phoned the police immediately and told them he thought a bank raid was going down at that very minute.

No one believed him. Nothing was done. A little later he had phoned Scotland Yard directly and finally found someone prepared to take action.

All banks, within a ten-mile radius of the Radio Ham's signal, were visited by either cars, or police officers on the beat. It meant that both Baker Street and Moorgate were visited. Both banks were found to be secure, with no sign of life inside. The police moved on, happy that all was well.

Inside both banks, the gangs now finished their work and left the premises. One gang forced to head back through a tunnel, the other simply walking out through the front door.

An hour later, Gerald Taylor received a call from Tony Rutherford.

"Total success, we have everything," was all that Rutherford said.

It was great news and Taylor came off the phone in a better mood than when he'd answered it. His evening had not gone well. His wife, Helen, had been in a mood, almost spoiling for an argument. She had gone off to bed early. He had wanted to join her, but knew that Tony would be calling.

Taylor opened a bottle of wine, picked up a couple of glasses and made his way upstairs. He was hoping that Helen would still be awake and that a glass of wine might put her in a slightly more romantic mood.

His hopes were dashed. She was fast asleep and he was left with no other option than to go back downstairs and celebrate on his own.

PART SIX

Tuesday, 14th September, 1971 – The Home Office, London

Sir Tavish had been asked to wait in the outer office. He had been given a cup of tea and a couple of biscuits and was now waiting patiently for the Home Secretary to become available. Sir Tavish had been summoned to the Home Office at six o'clock that morning and it was now nearly nine. Having missed valuable sleeping time and his usual, proper breakfast, Sir Tavish was less than happy at being kept waiting, but knew better than to complain to anyone.

At a little after a quarter to ten the door to Sir Tavish's right opened and a man dressed in a dark, pin-striped suit, appeared. He looked a nervous individual who gave the impression that he was accustomed to being someone else's doormat. He made his way over to Sir Tavish and offered him a weak handshake accompanied by a rather forced smile. When he spoke, there was even a slimy tone to his voice. Sir Tavish took an instant dislike to the man.

"I am Theo Butler, Principal Private Secretary to the Minister. So sorry to have kept you waiting for this long, Sir Tavish, the Home Secretary had urgent correspondence to deal with. However, he is free now and looking forward to seeing you."

Butler led and Sir Tavish followed/

They went through to the plush environment of the Home Secretary's Office. The current Home Secretary was Reginald Maudling. He sat behind his desk looking very glum. He glanced up and looked at Sir Tavish through heavy framed spectacles. His hair was thinning at the front with the rest covered in a glossy layer of Brylcreem. Reginald Maudling was fifty-four years of age and yet the strains of holding various Government positions had left him looking older.

"Have a seat, Sir Tavish," the Home Secretary said looking back down at a pile of papers lying in front of him. Theo Butler sat down as well. A few more moments of silence passed as the Home Secretary continued to read the top sheet of a pile of papers. Sir Tavish fumed inside, but said nothing. Reginald Maudling finally looked up.

"As if I haven't got enough on my bloody plate with Ireland, we now have this to deal with," he said and slapped the papers in front of him with anger. Sir Tavish was keen to know what was annoying the Home Secretary but he chose to let the Minister tell him in his own time. Eventually Maudling got to the point of their meeting.

"I thought long and hard about who I would ask to deal with this particular problem. I have been in touch with MI5 as there may yet be national security implications, but eventually I decided to contact you, Sir Tavish and have MILO take control of the situation. I believe you are investigating the Varga Corporation, is that correct?"

"We were, Home Secretary," replied Sir Tavish, "but it hasn't really been going anywhere."

"However, it has thrown up the possibility that someone within the Varga Corporation may have funded the Great Train Robbery," Maudling then said, by way of making a statement, rather than asking a question.

"We believe their then Chief Executive may have had something to do with it, yes," conceded Sir Tavish. He was still puzzled about why he was there and now went as far as asking the Home Secretary that very question.

Maudling sat back in his chair. He did not really like Sir Tavish Viewforth, finding the man abrasive and disrespectful. However, the fact remained that he was good at his job and if Reginald Maudling needed anything at that moment, it was someone who could do his job well. The Home Secretary eventually spoke again.

"I presume you will have been informed of the bank raids that took place on Saturday night?"

"Raids?" Viewforth repeated with obvious surprise. "I was only told about one back raid, which took place on Baker Street."

"Robbers also emptied the vaults at the Moorgate Branch of Barclays Bank."

"So why wasn't that announced at the same time?"

"Because, I decided to keep a lid on it," said Maudling.

"Why would you decide to do that, Home Secretary?"

It was Theo Butler who actually answered.

"At the moment, Sir Tavish, outside of a very small number of people, no one knows that Moorgate has been raided."

Sir Tavish was genuinely surprised.

"Someone must have noticed the vault was empty," he said, looking from Butler to the Home Secretary and back again. It was Butler who spoke again.

"That's just it, Sir Tavish, the robbers didn't take any money from Moorgate, only the contents of certain safe-deposit boxes."

"Ah," said Sir Tavish, "now I begin to understand."

"They emptied safe-deposit boxes at Baker Street as well," added Butler, "but they also took the cash from there, which was why staff knew they'd been raided."

"Not to mention the hole in the floor of the vault, eh?" added Sir Tavish, rather enjoying the fact that the Home Secretary was squirming a little in his chair.

"Indeed," was all that Maudling would add.

"How many safe-deposit boxes were emptied?" Sir Tavish then asked.

"Two hundred in total, though it appears the thieves selected their boxes carefully, especially at Moorgate."

"Inside information?" enquired Sir Tavish.

"Almost certainly, but considering the gang at Moorgate must have had the keys, the alarm code and God knows what all else, it would appear the whole staff could have been involved in aiding and abetting," said the Home Secretary. "The police will have a devil of a job pinning it on any one individual."

Sir Tavish considered the matter for a moment and then asked another question.

"And no one reported anything whilst these raids were happening?"

Maudling shuffled in his seat. Sir Tavish felt sure that the Home Secretary's discomfort had just got that little bit worse.

"That is, perhaps, the most annoying part in all this. There was a report of a raid taking place at Baker Street."

"And the police did not respond?" Sir Tavish asked with a tone of surprise.

"A Radio Ham reported hearing men talking but the police did not believe him. He first phoned the local police at a quarter past eleven but they did nothing. He then phoned Scotland Yard at one in the morning and they took action immediately. Unfortunately, that only led to the police visiting both locations and deciding nothing was amiss. Talk about incompetence."

"Are you telling me that the Radio Ham was actually able to listen to the robbers?" Sir Tavish asked with amazement in his tone.

"That is exactly what I am telling you," added the Home Secretary. "The man not only listened to the robbers he had time to record them. They were apparently talking to a look-out situated outside the bank."

"And the police went to both Moorgate and Baker Street yet found nothing suspicious?"

"That appears to be the sum and substance of it all, yes," replied Maudling with growing anger.

"Do we have a full list of the owners whose safe-deposit boxes were affected?"

"Perhaps not a *full* list as many people do not like to make these things public. Obviously, we may never know the full contents of the boxes but knowing that they were owned by Government Ministers, members of the Royal Family and many other, extremely wealthy individuals, we can assume that what was in those boxes was of great value to the owners. It is for that reason that I have asked you here. Much of what needs to be investigated goes above the rank of local police officers."

"So, the thieves are likely to make more from blackmail and extortion than they did from the cash they stole?" surmised Sir Tavish.

"I think we can take that as a given fact, Sir Tavish," the Home Secretary agreed.

Another aspect of Sir Tavish doing his job well was him having a sense for those occasions when he wasn't being told everything. This was one of those occasions when he could sense, very strongly, that something else was bothering the Home Secretary and he now sat and patiently waited to be told what that might be.

Maudling eventually sat forward in his chair with a rather disgruntled expression on his face.

"There's more."

Sir Tavish smiled. "I thought there might be."

"We know that in at least one of the safe-deposit boxes in Moorgate there were certain photographs of a senior Government Minister that could potentially do as much damage to Mr Heath's government as the Profumo Affair did for Harold MacMillan. These things always seem to come to light during the time of a Conservative Government."

"A clear example of how the thieves stand to make more from the contents of the safe deposit boxes?" said Sir Tavish.

"They could either blackmail the individuals, or offer to sell the material back to them," said the Home Secretary, "Either way, they stand to make a lot of money out of it. I certainly wouldn't want to put a figure on it."

Sir Tavish thought for a moment. "You said you were trying to keep a lid on the Moorgate robbery, what did you mean by that?"

"Only the people in this room, a handful of police officers and a couple of bank staff know that Moorgate has been raided. I want to keep it that way, at least for the moment."

"But surely the bank staff must know something is wrong?"

"Apparently not," said Butler, "the thieves were very tidy."

Sir Tavish nearly laughed out loud at the thought of a gang of thieves taking the time to tidy up after themselves.

"Have the box owners been notified?" Sir Tavish then asked.

The Home Secretary squirmed a little more. "The police are working their way through the list. Obviously, the main priority is to ensure the Press don't get word of this."

"Surely, the main priority should be telling the box owners that they've been robbed. The last thing you should want is that they find out through the robbers contacting them. That would make the crime worse."

"You are right, of course," Maudling agreed, though rather grudgingly.

"And what about the bank staff who must have helped the crooks; are the police going after them?" Sir Tavish now said.

The Home Secretary looked even more irritated.

"Quite frankly, I don't give a damn about them. I am more concerned about highly sensitive material now being in the hands of common criminals."

"Oh, there's nothing common about whoever pulled off these jobs," Sir Tavish commented. "They were well funded, well planned and apart from the cock-up with the radio at Baker Street, well-drilled in what they had to do. This was a highly professional job, Home Secretary, which almost smacks of a military connection."

"The point about it being well funded, takes me back to why I asked you here in the first place," Maudling then said. "See if you can find any connection between the Varga Corporation and the money behind this job. I know it's a longshot, but we have to start somewhere."

"Very good, Home Secretary," Sir Tavish said and stood up to leave the room.

"Work closely with the police and keep MI5 updated."

Sir Tavish wouldn't be that upset at working with the police, but the bit about keeping MI5 informed might not happen quite as the Home Secretary would have liked.

As he left the Home Office that day, Sir Tavish was happy in the knowledge that MILO had been invited to sit at the big table, but less enamoured by the idea that it was highly unlikely that the robbers would ever be brought to justice.

However, for the moment, he would just rejoice in how embarrassed the Home Secretary had been by what had happened and how much more the man would squirm if any of it was made public.

Thursday, 16th September 1971 – MILO HQ, London

Detective Superintendent Matthew Holding was shown in to a room and left for a few moments. Eventually he was joined by Ben and Amy. They were carrying coffees for all three. They sat down and Ben flipped open a notebook, ready to write down anything that might be of interest to them.

"How is the investigation in to the Baker Street raid going?" Ben then asked after the introductions had been completed and the coffee gratefully accepted by Holding.

"Not well. We have no leads on who took part in the raid and currently no idea as to what might have happened to the stuff that was stolen. They were certainly calm; they didn't even take everything from the boxes they opened."

"You mean they left things behind?" said Ben.

"Yes. It seems it may have been out of some form of moral conscience," said Holding. "There were boxes filled with child pornography, for example. We'll be paying the owners of those boxes a visit, needless to say."

"So, if they left potential dynamite like that behind just what the hell did they take?" asked Amy.

"Your guess is as good as mine," replied Holding, with honesty.

"Obviously people use safe-deposit boxes for a variety of reasons and not all of them are legal. They often keep items of a very personal nature there as well, so I'm guessing we'll never be told what many of those items were."

"What have you done so far?" Ben then said.

"We've been trying to trace the money for a start. We have a fair idea of what we are looking for so if it surfaces anywhere we ought to know. We also have an open invitation out to all the safe-deposit box holders to come forward and tell us what they've lost. I'm not expecting a rush of information."

"Are you getting anywhere on who might have provided the inside information?" Amy then asked.

"Not really. To be fair most of the inside information was relevant to Moorgate and that's your problem, not ours. As far as Baker Street was concerned, it was more old-fashioned. They dug a tunnel, blew a hole and that was that."

"What about the Radio Ham?" Ben now asked.

"He's genuine. The man was trying to help and we pretty much ignored him. Even when we did try to take action we still managed to cock things up. Never mind, he's having his five minutes of fame out of it as every newspaper in London wants to interview him."

"Tell me about the Baker Street raid," Ben said.

Holding talked through what he knew. They'd tunnelled from the leather shop, blown a small hole in the floor of the vault and helped themselves.

"Why didn't the explosives set off the sensors in the bank?" Ben enquired.

"The floor sensors had been switched off. Mind you, the explosives had been well placed to do minimal damage. They had a professional on-board, there can be no doubt about that."

"That should be a lead," Ben said hopefully. "There can't be many up to a job like that."

"We have a few names in mind, but they're all connected to the IRA and we don't stand much chance of finding them."

"Maybe the IRA pulled off the job," said Amy.

"I wouldn't have thought so," said Holding. "They've got banks of their own; why bother coming to the mainland?"

"Going back to the robbers and their two-way radio," Ben then said. "Why the need for them to be in constant contact with the guy outside?"

"What do you mean?" said Holding.

"The guy outside is there to warn the gang if anyone was approaching the bank. Apart from the police making that one visit, no one did approach the bank, so why the need for the constant chat?"

"Chummy on the roof was getting bored. They did tell him to shut up, but he didn't."

"It doesn't fit though, does it?" Ben continued. "You have this well planned, highly professional job and yet you put some rank amateur on look-out duties. It was almost as if they wanted to be caught."

"Well, that's just daft," said Holding with a laugh.

"No gang sets out to be caught," he added quickly.

"Maybe they were meant to be a distraction though," Ben then said. "Had the police picked up on the Radio Ham's message a bit quicker they could have been all over Baker Street like a rash. That, in turn, would have attracted the media and suddenly, all eyes are on one specific part of London. Meanwhile, in Moorgate another gang are quietly emptying any safe-deposit box they choose and driving off with the contents. Maybe Baker Street was always a diversion and because your lads cocked it up, they actually walked away with the contents of both vaults."

It was certainly a possibility, but not one that fired Holding with any enthusiasm in terms of ever solving the crime. If it were *that* professional then they'd all be back behind the skirting board again. No leads; no lines of inquiry. Nothing.

He left MILO's Headquarters a very depressed man.

**Friday, 17th September, 1971 – Gerald Taylor's Freiheit
Office, Central London**

Tony Rutherford sat in Gerald Taylor's Freiheit office. They
were both relaxed, Tony telling jokes and Gerald finding them
funny, even though half of them weren't. They were drinking
coffee and Tony was smoking.

"So, it all went well?" Gerald eventually said.

"Like clockwork."

"What did we get away with?" asked Taylor.

Tony grinned. "What *didn't* we get away with? I'm telling you,
it's pure dynamite. We'll have individuals begging us to return
their stuff and telling us to name our price in the process. Very
few will be going to the police, that's for sure."

"The police will still ask their questions," commented Taylor.

"I'm telling you; no one will be talking. They'll want it all swept
away as fast as possible."

"I heard the police turned up at both locations?" Taylor then
said.

"Turned up, rattled the front doors and then buggered off
again. Bloody useless, the whole lot of them."

"Just as well, for us," added Taylor. "Any idea how much we
got away with?"

"Just shy of a million and a half in cash. The contents of the
safe-deposit boxes will more than triple that figure. We can
state our price, people *will* pay."

"What kind of person owned those boxes?" said Taylor.

"Government Ministers, top businessmen and the odd
member of the Royal Family."

To Gerald Taylor, *all* members of the Royal Family were odd.
He just didn't get the monarchy, in any shape or form. Taylor
laughed out loud.

"The bloody Establishment will be having kittens."

"All the way to the Prime Minister. He may not have owned one of the boxes, but he knows plenty who did."

"What now?" said Taylor.

"Now we start contacting individuals and discussing exactly how much they are prepared to pay to get their items back."

"Excellent. Keep me posted on developments."

Friday 17th, September, 1971 – Barclays Bank, Moorgate

Ben and Mike arrived at the Moorgate Branch of Barclays Bank and asked to see the Manager. They did not show any identification, but did say that an appointment had been arranged and that they were expected. Gill had been called first and she had shown the two men through to Wrigglesworth's office. Gill got the impression Wrigglesworth was not looking forward to speaking to his visitors. Might they be police? Gill guessed they were high-ranking police officers, if that was what they were.

Did that mean the raid had taken place and if so, why hadn't the staff been told? Gill was very perplexed as she went back to her desk.

Back in the Manager's office, Ben and Mike were now seated and a very nervous Horace Wrigglesworth sat waiting for the questions to begin. Where once had been a proud man, who held himself erect and exuded self-confidence, there was now just a shell. He was not only struggling with the fact his bank had been robbed, but also the number of staff who must have given the robbers information. Wrigglesworth felt like a man betrayed.

Wrigglesworth explained how they had first discovered all was not well in the vault, The Chief Clerk had gone down to get a box for one of their customers, only to find that the box was no longer locked. It was also empty. The Chief Clerk had then asked the customer to come back the following day, citing a problem with the lock on the vault door. He had then gone to the Manager and told him what he's found.

The two men had gone back down to the vault and checked the other boxes. It was then that they realised the magnitude of what had happened and the police had been phoned.

"Could we speak with your Chief Clerk?" Ben then asked.

"Of course," said Wrigglesworth, pressing a button on his intercom. He asked Gill to get John Torville to come through.

A moment later, the door opened and Torville entered. He confirmed what Wrigglesworth had already said. Ben then asked how many keyholders they had. Torville said that he and the Manager had keys to the front door and the vault room. The caretakers had keys to the front door and there was as spare set of all the keys in the Manager's, for use in an emergency."

"Does anyone else have access to those keys?" Mike asked.

"Terry Ferris covers for either of us, when we're on leave," Wrigglesworth explained.

"And Alf Cairney is called in when absolutely necessary," added Torville.

"How about the code for your alarm?" Ben then asked.

"That comes from Head Office every Monday morning," said Wrigglesworth. "We have a new number every week and it was decided it could be even more secure to get that number from the computer. Someone punches in the question and out comes a numerical answer. That's our alarm code for the week."

"And who knows what that code is?" said Mike.

"We do, along with the caretakers. They're the ones responsible for opening in the morning and closing at night," said Torville.

"Would Terry Ferris, or Alf Cairney, know the code?" said Ben.

"There's no need for them to know it," replied Wrigglesworth.

"Let's go back to the keys," Ben now said. "Has there been any reason for either Ferris or Cairney to have a set of keys recently?"

"I was on holiday about three weeks ago," said Torville. "Terry would have had my keys that week."

Mike made a note of the dates Torville had been off. He was just looking up from his notebook when Wrigglesworth spoke again.

"Come to think of it, I went home sick on the Friday afternoon of that week. It was the Bank Holiday weekend, which is why I can be so exact. Anyway, I took a funny turn in the afternoon and was violently sick. I was driven home and Alf Cairney took my keys. I got them in my safe when I got back on the Tuesday."

"Are both those gentlemen on duty today?" said Ben.

"They are."

"Then, may we speak to them?"

"Of course, who would you like to see first?"

"Let's make it alphabetical order, shall we?" replied Ben.

Wrigglesworth pressed the intercom again and asked Gill to get Alf. He also warned her that he'd like to see Terry, once he was finished with Alf.

Before going to get Alf, Gill called through to Terry. What she said to him would have sounded perfectly normal to prying ears for only Terry knew it was a pre-arranged code. It basically said:

Get the hell out of there.

When Alf went through to Wrigglesworth's office, he was his usual helpful self. Yes, he'd had the Manager's keys, but only to lock the vault doors. He had then left those keys with Terry.

"I was on leave the following week," he explained, "and didn't want to have to come into work, just to deliver the keys."

"So, for a period of time, Terry Ferris had both sets of keys?" Ben then said.

"I suppose so," said Alf.

Ben hadn't needed to ask. Wrigglesworth already had his finger on the intercom button.

"Gill, will you ask Terry to come through?"

"Of course, Mister Wrigglesworth."

Alf was excused and the others now waited for Terry to come through. Time went by until, eventually, the door opened and Gill came in.

"I'm really sorry, Mister Wrigglesworth, but Terry appears to be out of the office at the moment."

The Manager looked at his watch. "Is it a tea-break?"

"I really don't know," replied Gill, trying to sound as vague as possible.

"I think we'd better find, Mister Ferris," Ben then said, standing up. "Could you give us a note of his address?"

"Of course," said Wrigglesworth, looking across at Gill. "Gill, would you get Terry's address for these gentlemen?"

"Certainly, Mister Wrigglesworth," replied Gill, trying hard to hide the fear and anxiety rising inside her. She went back to her office, but took her time finding and writing down Terry's address. She knew he'd not be going back there, but she still wanted to buy him more time to initiate their getaway plan.

Gill gave Terry's address to Mike and watched the two men leave the office. She then packed her bag with personal items before finding little jobs to fill her time until she could leave for lunch at her normal time. There was no sadness in her heart as she walked out the front door, knowing there was little chance of her ever returning.

All that was now in Gill's mind was to put as many miles as possible between herself and possible arrest.

Friday 17th September, 1971 – Heinz Franke's home, Bonn

The hotel was within walking distance of Heinz Franke's home. Brandt had decided to enjoy the fresh air in the afternoon, walking the streets with no particular route in mind. Brandt wasn't that familiar with Bonn and worried that if he went too far from the hotel, he may not find his way back. It was eventually the weather that chased him back to the hotel as dark clouds formed overhead and rain started to fall.

Although it had initially been at his request, Brandt was in Bonn at the invitation of Heinz Franke. Brandt had wanted an opportunity to speak with Franke and it had made more sense for Brandt to go to Bonn, than for Franke to make time to go to Majorca.

Dinner was to be at eight and after they had eaten, Brandt then intended having a long conversation with Franke. Decisions had to be taken and plans, for the future of Freiheit, made.

The dinner was not a Freiheit affair, although Brandt knew that a few of his trusted colleagues would be there. He knew it would be a wives' affair and that any business discussions would have to occur at opportune moments. Brandt hoped that he and Franke might find somewhere a little quieter to discuss the more pertinent matters.

Dinner began at eight. There were forty people around the table, which all but filled a huge room at the back of the house. Needless to say, it was a huge house, one befitting of a man on the rise in German politics. However, he was a man whose career was only on the up, thanks to the influence of Freiheit, He, in turn, had always acknowledged that assistance by making regular, large payments to the cause. He had also always made it known that if they wanted him to do more, then they only had to ask.

Brandt was there that night to ask.

Brandt had been positioned with Gerd Seeler and his wife to his right and Heinz Franke and his wife on the left. Franke was currently deputy to the Defence Minister, Helmut Schmidt. Many people were quietly confident that Schmidt might one day be Chancellor, which would open the door for Franke to be given a position of importance in that Government.

Franke was now forty-three years of age. He had been sixteen, going on seventeen, when the war had ended and had spent the last eight months of the war wearing a uniform but not really knowing why.

Franke had seen the country of his youth destroyed by war. He had seen the poverty and starvation that had followed. He had heard the horror stories of what the Red Army had done to the women of Germany in retribution for events acted out earlier in the war. He had then heard the horror stories about the extermination of the Jews and the manner in which the Reich had tried to obliterate them all.

Until he had gone to university Franke had been ashamed to call himself German. History would forever damn Germany for what happened during Hitler's leadership. Hitler would be forever cast as the Devil incarnate and the many good things that he had achieved would never be acknowledged.

However, whilst furthering his education, Franke had met up with a group of radical students who had ideas that went well beyond the boundaries of mainstream politics. Whilst not exactly being dissidents, they were certainly averse to much of what was being discussed in world politics. They were a group of young men who hated living in a country split by Communist rulers and they would constantly vow to put things right. Many of those vows were made on nights of drunken debauchery, however and few of them were to ever take their radical thoughts any further.

Heinz Franke was not someone, however, who took his political ideals lightly. He wanted a unified Germany and he wanted to find ways and means of achieving that goal.

At the age of twenty-five he went in to politics though at a very low level. As time went by, he began to attract the attention of more senior politicians, who could see a bright future for Herr Franke. Freiheit was notified of this bright new star and began to pay closer attention to the Franke's rise through the ranks.

Eventually, Franke was approached by a member of Freiheit and he agreed to become an active part of the movement. In return, Freiheit began to clear the path ahead of Herr Franke, to make it a little easier for him to continue moving onwards and upwards.

During the time he had been climbing the political ladder, he had met his wife, Anna. They had been married for ten years and had two boys. They lived in luxury and wanted for nothing. Anna had no idea that her husband had received so much help in his political journey. Had she known that he was now keen

to give something back to an organisation run by ex-SS then she would have been horrified.

The Frankes were a handsome couple and Brandt felt sure that one day they would be the face of Germany. If Franke could become Chancellor one day then the world would be his oyster. He and his wife would be seen at all the meetings of world leaders. They could easily become the Kennedys of the Seventies.

The first course was brought to the table. Brandt waited until all the food had been served before continuing with the conversation he had started with Franke over the aperitif.

"Have you given any thought to the content of my letter?" Brandt asked as he shook a little salt on to his soup.

The letter in question had been one of three that Brandt had written in the fortnight leading up to the dinner. This particular letter had offered Franke a place on the Grand Committee of Freiheit.

"I have."

"And?"

Franke glanced at his wife who was oblivious to what her husband was saying as she had engaged in conversation with a woman to her right.

"I am interested. Any opportunity to further serve my country must be accepted. I believe that we will only have a strong Germany through Freiheit being strong."

"That is good news, Herr Franke," said Brandt, "however, I have a slightly different request than that intimated in my letters."

Franke looked at Brandt with an expression of both confusion and interest. He said nothing, but simply waited for Brandt to continue.

"I want you to become the Grand Master of Freiheit," Brandt eventually said.

Franke now looked surprised.

"But that is your role, Wolfgang?" he then said.

"*Was* my role. I fear my position had been compromised and it is time to hand over the baton."

"I am honoured to be asked," said Franke, "but I really don't think I'd be able to devote enough time to Freiheit to actually be its leader."

"Which is why I want to appoint Fritz as a kind of deputy," said Brandt. "You would make the decisions and Fritz would see that they were carried out. He would be your eyes and ears, but you would be the brains."

Franke looked across the table towards a silver haired man with steely-blue eyes and a military bearing.

Fritz Wagner was fifty-five and had fought in the war as part of the great SS war machine. However, unlike many of his compatriots he had committed no crimes along the way. He had come out of the war relatively unscathed and had set about building a new life for himself. This had proved a lot easier for Fritz Wagner than it would have done for others, mainly due to the fact he had come from money in the first place. His family were of rich, Prussian stock.

The only skeleton hanging in Wagner's cupboard was that he had a preference for younger women, rarely being seen with anyone nearer to his own age. He was accompanied that night by a woman who could have been his grand-daughter.

"Is that the famous personal assistant?" Franke then asked; his eyes now falling on the woman sitting to the left of Wagner.

"It is indeed; pretty, isn't she?" added Brandt.

"Very pretty. Word is that Wagner and the girl are *close*, would that be true?"

Brandt smiled. "I don't believe you could get any closer."

"In that case, he is a very lucky man indeed," commented Franke looking across at the woman again.

"Anyway, I did not mention Herr Wagner to discuss his sexual prowess, I simply wanted an opinion on whether, or not, you thought he would make a good addition to our Freiheit hierarchy?"

"Oh, I should think that Fritz would be ideal. He has family money; he has a successful business and he has knowledge of the camaraderie that you all felt during the war. Unfortunately, that is the part I cannot share with you."

"Perhaps not, Herr Franke, but you bring us everything else and more importantly, you bring us youth and a guaranteed future for Freiheit. The last thing my generation wants is for this organisation to die with us."

"I'm sure Freiheit will never die, Wolfgang and, please, call me Heinz."

Brandt smiled. "Very good, Heinz. Perhaps, we can find time to talk later."

"I'm sure that will be possible," said Franke, turning away to talk to his wife.

*

A little later, Franke had managed to arrange a few moments alone with Brandt, Seeler and Fritz Wagner. They had used the excuse of cigars and brandy, but really they wished to talk about Freiheit and no one else was ever to know that.

The main purpose of the short meeting was to announce to Gerd Seeler that the Grand Master was changing and in doing so would inherit an assistant. Fritz was most definitely not a deputy, that would imply authority he wasn't being given.

Franke also took the opportunity to say a few words as to how he saw Freiheit developing over the coming years. He referred to a troubled world, where there always seemed to be conflicts somewhere. The Americans in Vietnam was still the most high- profile of those.

Franke spoke of Freiheit's control of Europe strengthening. By continuing to hide in the background, Freiheit would go from strength to strength and no one would be any the wiser.

Franke then asked for suggestions regarding a replacement for Neuer in Bonn. Seeler had an idea and was instructed to sound the man out, with a view to him joining the Grand Committee,

The man in question was Emmerich Kassmeyer, a sixty-year-old, ex-SS officer, known to Seeler for many years and already active within Freiheit, working as an advisor to the current West German government. Franke had heard of the man without ever actually meeting him, however, everyone was happy to endorse any nominations made by Gerd Seeler.

One problem, which Heinz Franke did raise, was the total lack of any Freiheit activity in the East. The wall not only kept conquered residents in, but also Western influences out. He announced that he wanted to change that; he wanted Freiheit to at least try to have an impact on the East and the best place to start would, surely, be East Germany. If they could find a foothold in the East German government then that would at least be a start.

Friday,17th September, 1971 -The National Liberal Club, Central London

Roddy McIntosh, Member of Parliament for Highland, sat in The National Liberal Club and nursed what was his third brandy of the day. He had lit a cigarette but wasn't really smoking it. He had too much on his mind. He looked around the Club at the other Members and wondered if any of them had the same kind of worries on their mind.

McIntosh had been the owner of one of the safe-deposit boxes raided in Barclays Bank, Moorgate. Like most other safe-deposit box owners, he had kept things in that bank vault that he wished no one else to know about. In fact, if the contents of that box became public knowledge then Roddy McIntosh was finished, not only as a politician, but in every other way possible.

Roddy looked at his watch; it was just after ten at night. He had had a light dinner, on arrival at the Club, but was now content to sit and get slightly drunk. He was waiting for his guest to arrive, a guest who he hoped might yet get him out of the predicament he found himself in. He finished his drink and was looking to attract one of the white-jacketed employees, when the door opened and his guest was shown to his table.

Roddy stood up and shook hands with the man who had just arrived. It was Ben Ward. They sat down and when the white-jacketed man, with a tray and smile, arrived he was given an order for one whisky and another brandy for Roddy.

"Thank you for coming, Ben" McIntosh then said.

"Your message sounded quite urgent," said Ben. "Are you in trouble?"

"I believe you're investigating the bank raids."

"Are you affected by that?" asked Ben, not willing to be drawn on anything, just at the moment.

"I had a safe-deposit box in Moorgate."

"Ah," was all that Ben could add.

"I received a letter yesterday, which informed me that the contents of my safe-deposit box will remain secret, at least for the moment. The bastards want money from me, Ben, money I simply don't have."

"That's more a police matter, Roddy," added Ben.

Their drinks arrived and Roddy fell silent as they were laid down in front of them. Once again, Roddy noted the nice smile he got from the man who had brought those drinks. Once they were alone again, Roddy continued.

"You don't seriously expect me to go to the police over this?" Roddy said, horror in his tone. "No one can ever know about what's been stolen."

Ben drank from his glass, then spoke. "Look, Roddy, no one can help you without knowing the full facts and that includes what we're looking for. How can I get back something I don't know anything about?"

Roddy McIntosh drank his brandy. For all the alcohol he'd put away, there was still not an ounce of Dutch Courage forming inside him. Much as he knew Ben was right in what he'd said, the shame was still too great. However, he knew he'd have to tell him something, if there was to be any hope of him offering his help.

"I'm not proud of how I have lived my life, Ben, but the things that have caused me most personal angst have been the things I have done in private and it is those private matters that I seek to protect. Suffice to say that I had certain photographs in the box along with one or two personal items, which I had been given by a dear friend; a dear, *male* friend, if you get my meaning?"

Ben nodded his head. "I believe I am getting the picture, Roddy. Clearly your wife would be both surprised and annoyed to find out that her husband has been living a double life."

McIntosh's expression of horror deepened.

"It would destroy her; not to mention the effect it would have on our children. Look, Ben, I didn't set out to be the way that I am, but equally I can't change anything either."

"Is your male friend also in the public domain?" Ben then asked, sipping at his drink.

McIntosh lit another cigarette, only this time he inhaled deeply, before letting the smoke drift out through his nose.

"Yes and to make matters worse he's a bloody Tory," Roddy then said by way of trying to lighten the situation.

Although Ben smiled at the weak attempt at humour, he could clearly see that his friend was deeply worried.

"In that case, Roddy, I can only say how sorry I am for you," Ben now said.

He then continued. "You may have noticed that the raid on Moorgate has never been mentioned in any of the papers?"

"Yes, I did think that was rather strange."

"The lid has been quickly and efficiently slammed shut on that little job, my friend. MILO is the only organisation investigating the Moorgate robbery. Now, as no one is supposed to know that there even was a raid, you can imagine how difficult it is for anyone to gather evidence. They can't ask the usual questions; they can't interview the usual people. In short, they can't do very much at all."

"But that's outrageous, Ben. A crime has been committed so someone needs to get on and make some arrests."

"Roddy, you are not alone in regretting the loss of what was in those safe-deposit boxes. From what we've been told there are Government Ministers as worried as you are, as well as a few members of the Royal Family who probably now wish they'd kept their personal belongings in a box under the bed. Bad enough that another member of the family should find it, but having it out in the public domain has to be a thousand times worse."

McIntosh took another mouthful of brandy.

He was already looking around for a re-fill. "My God, it sounds a whole lot worse than even I had thought!"

The panic in his tone was rising and the fact no one was rushing to provide him with that re-fill didn't help.

"It is," agreed Ben. "The Home Secretary is shitting bricks over the fact this happened on his watch and he'll, no doubt, be opening avenues of negotiation to get as much back without anyone being any the wiser of what was stolen in the first place."

"How the hell will he achieve that?" Roddy then said, waving once more for his glass to be filled again.

"By paying a lot of money; it's the only way those robbers will return anything. It's all about money, plain and simple."

"But that's just it, Ben, I don't have the kind of money these people are asking for. Everyone thinks if you're an MP then you must be rich, but that's just not the case. I could afford a little, but not what they are asking."

Finally, Roddy was able to order another drink. As he waited, rather impatiently, for it to be brought to him, he drank a little more of what still remained in his glass.

"How were you supposed to pay these robbers?" Ben then asked.

"Instructions to follow later."

"Then you have to let them know that you can't afford what they are asking. Make a counter offer and see what happens."

Roddy McIntosh noticed a full glass on its way, so he drained the last of what was in his glass and laid it down on the table with a little more noise than had been intended. The alcohol was beginning to affect his actions. As he turned to look at Ben again, there was an increasing fear in his eyes.

"I don't think I can stop these men from going public. Unless they contact me, I don't know how to contact them and there seems little chance of them believing my plea of poverty."

A thought struck Ben.

"Roddy, are you already paying blackmail money?"

Roddy nodded, but said nothing. He was already drinking from the glass, which had just arrived.

"Have these payments being going on for a while?"

Roddy nodded again and continued drinking. How often did people search for the answers to their problems at the bottom of a bottle?

"I was set up one night and a photograph was taken of me meeting with a man in a toilet in Central London. My feelings for my wife only go skin deep, Ben, my real passion is for men and there's nothing I can do about that. I know everyone sees that as being wrong, but it's just the way I am."

Ben thought for a moment.

When he eventually spoke, it was not what Roddy McIntosh would have wanted to hear.

"I'll be honest with you, Roddy, there's not a great deal that I can do. We have no idea who these robbers are and the chances of us getting anything back are beyond remote at the moment. All I can promise is, that if I get my hands on your property, I'll try to keep it away from prying eyes. Beyond that, I suggest you either find the money they are asking for, or find a way of living with the consequences."

Roddy sat in silence. He stared at the wall and seemed lost in his own little world. He then thanked Ben for at least lending an ear. Ben stood up to leave, he was due at Camilla's flat and was already late. Roddy said he'd have another drink and then be on his way. They shook hands and Ben left.

Roddy sat thinking. He knew he had limited options, but one option seemed to stand head and shoulders above the others.

After two more brandies, he knew exactly what he was going to do.

Saturday 18th September 1971 – Just after Midnight – Embankment Underground Station

Roddy McIntosh had sat in the National Liberal Club until eleven o'clock. By the time he had gone for his coat and left the building, he was feeling quite inebriated, which was exactly how he had wanted to feel. He had thanked those at the door and left a hefty tip for the staff on the cloakroom. Outside, he had found the late-night air to be warm and the sky overhead, to be clear. The pavements were quiet, though a number of taxis went by, in various directions.

By the time he left the Club, he knew exactly what he had to do next. He could not let his own shame tarnish the lives of his wife and children; they deserved better than that. Prior to leaving the Club, he had written a short note, acquired an envelope and stamp from the Club reception and addressed it to his wife. He had asked one of the doormen to post it for him, but to make sure they posted it that night, they were not to wait for any reason.

With everything now in place, Roddy walked to the underground station at Embankment. He bought a ticket covering a journey of one stop and made his way to the platform. As he waited for the train to arrive he kept thinking back over his life. There had been good times and there had been bad times, but the overriding factor has been his sexuality. His entire life had been a lie and the bigger that lie became, the more difficult it became for him to protect his own privacy.

He took a photograph from his wallet and looked down at it. His wife and children smiled back at him, content with the life he had given them if not, at least in his wife's case, the love they might have expected. He had done his best; he could do no more now.

The sound of the approaching train reached Roddy's ears, closely followed by the wind it created as it travelled through the tunnel. Then it appeared, it's brakes already squealing as they were applied and the speeding train was urged to slow to a stop before reaching the end of the platform.

Roddy knew what he had to do now.

Those waiting on the platform started to move forward, Roddy moved faster.

The driver saw movement out of the corner of his eye, but assumed that the movement would stop long before he reached that point of the platform.

It didn't.

Roddy McIntosh had made his decision.

Monday 20th September, 1971 – Gerald Taylor's Office, Oxford Street, London

Tony Rutherford was shown in to Taylor's office at a little after nine that morning. He was looking a little upset as he sat down and Taylor sensed that something was wrong.

"What's happened?" Taylor then asked.

"We've had our first casualty of the robbery."

Taylor looked vague. "What do you mean?"

"Roddy McIntosh, Member of Parliament for Highland, threw himself in front a train at Embankment Station on Saturday night."

"What did we have on him?"

"Homosexual photographs. The other man is a Member of Parliament as well, though not so high-powered as McIntosh."

"So, we lost one, there have to be others to take his place," Taylor suggested.

"No shortage of other options and that really isn't what's bothering me," Rutherford then said.

"What's the problem then?" prompted Taylor.

"This," replied Rutherford taking a sheet of paper from his pocket and unfolding it. He handed it across to Taylor who scanned it with his eyes and then looked up, bewilderment written all over his face.

"It's in Russian."

"Well, I know it's in Russian. Strange then that we find it in a box owned by Jeremy Spencer, MP, who just happens to be a Junior Minister working with Jim Callaghan in the Shadow Home Office. Mr Spencer has many friends in the world of politics and has already been touted, by none other than Jim Callaghan himself, as being a possible Prime Minister in the future."

Taylor now studied the paper a little more closely even though he didn't understand a word of it.

"I've had it translated," Tony then said, "and it seems clear that Spencer is receiving information and money from Russian contacts while, presumably, passing information in the other direction."

"Holy shit," Taylor muttered under his breath.

"Did you know anything about him?" Rutherford then asked.

"I've never heard of him, if I'm being honest," said Taylor, "but if, as you say, he's a rising star in British politics, then the last thing you'd want to find in his possession, was anything relating to the Russians."

"That's just what I was thinking," agreed Rutherford. "The question now is, what do we do with this information?"

Taylor thought for a moment.

"There is only one course of action we *can* take, Tony. This man needs to be hung by his balls somewhere for all to see. Find a way of getting what we have to the authorities; they can have that arrest on us."

"If you're sure," said Tony.

"Quite sure."

Tony stood up. "Then it's as good as done."

Monday, 20th September, 1971 – Barclays Bank, Moorgate, Central London

Ben and Mike found themselves back at the Moorgate Branch of Barclays Bank. They had received a call from Wrigglesworth that he wanted to speak with them. The weekend had been rather unproductive in the sense that Terry Ferris was now, officially, deemed as missing. There had been no sign of him at his flat and his bank account hadn't been touched for days. Word had been passed to all police forces, airports and ferry terminals in the hope that someone would see him somewhere.

Once seated in Wrigglesworth's office, the Manager began telling Ben and Mike why he'd asked to see them.

"I think another of my staff might be missing. My secretary, Gill, never came back after lunch on Friday and she didn't turn up at work today. I asked around the staff and there are some who suspected Terry and Gill were in a relationship. I might add that the bank strongly disapproves of relationships between staff for the very reason that they might find it easier to indulge in criminal activity."

"Presumably, Gill had access to all your work?" Ben then asked.

"Well, yes, but she would not have known anything about the safe-deposit boxes; that's something she never deals with."

"But she and Terry could have got copies of all the keys," Ben said.

Wrigglesworth looked even more betrayed.

"Yes, I suppose she could have helped Terry."

"Okay," Ben then said," this is what we'll do. Let it be known that we are investigating an internal fraud and that Terry and Gill are our number one suspects. At least then we'll be able to speak to some of the staff and maybe build a better picture of what Terry and Gill are really like."

Mike went to use one of the phones. He contacted HQ and asked for them to add Gill Potter's name to the information already out on Terry Ferris.

"I think we can assume they are travelling together," he'd added. "I'll get a description of Gill to you, as soon as we have one," he'd then added and put the phone down.

By the time Mike got back to Wrigglesworth's office, Ben had details of where Gill lived. They agreed to visit the flat once they'd spoken to some of the staff. Ben started in the section where Terry was the Supervisor.

He spoke to all the girls. They'd really liked Terry and couldn't believe he'd ever steal from the bank. Most of those Ben spoke to had come to the conclusion that there was something going on between Gill and Terry. It was just the way they acted when they were together. They all added that they didn't think it had been going on that long, however.

Feeling they had learned all they were going to, from the bank staff, Ben and Mike then left the building and headed off to Gill Potter's flat.

Wednesday, 22nd September, 1971 – Interview Room, Central London Police Station

It was ten o'clock at night. Sitting in a rather grubby room, with a cigarette in one hand and a chipped cup, with coffee in it, in the other was a woman. From her appearance it was clear how she made her living. Her choice of attire involved showing off as much of her body as possible and the thick layer of make-up on her face, did little to enhance her looks.

Her hair was dark and tied up and her eyes betrayed the fear she felt inside.

The woman was Vera Stringer, known to all her customers as Doll. She had been on the street for ten years and now knew that with this bust, she was going to prison for a long time, unless she did something and quickly.

That something had been to ask to see Chief Inspector Atherton. She knew he'd have to be contacted and could only hope that he would come. He'd know that if she was asking for him, she would have information that might be of use to him. Of course, he had always come running in the past and Vera could only hope that he would do so on this occasion.

Time was passing and there had been little sign of Atherton coming. He had, however, asked for her to be given a coffee, which Vera took as an indication that he *was* on his way.

As it happened, it was nearer eleven before Atherton walked through the door and told the officer, waiting with Vera, that he could wait outside now. Atherton was carrying two coffees, one of which he now gave to Vera. She was on her tenth cigarette. Atherton joined her by lighting a cigarette of his own. He then sat back and looked at Vera for a moment.

He eventually spoke.

"I told you that if you got busted one more time, you'd be going to prison, didn't I Vera?"

Vera looked, almost pleadingly, back at Atherton.

"I don't want to go to prison, Mister Atherton."

"Then stop opening your legs to the highest bidder," Atherton responded, rather bluntly.

"A girl's got to make a living, the best that she can."

"Then learn to type," said Atherton. "Anyway, I was led to believe that you had information for me."

"I have," said Vera, "but you'll only hear it after you clear the way for me to walk out of here, after we're finished with our little chat."

Atherton allowed a little smoke to drift from his nose and sighed deeply.

"I'm no longer sure that I can, Vera," he then said. "I've got you out of situations like this in the past, but you've been arrested too many times. The cumulative effect is that you'll have to go to prison."

The fear in Vera's eyes intensified.

"What I have for you this time is big, Mister Atherton, really big. I think you'll want to hear it."

Atherton drank the coffee and grimaced; it was awful. He thought for a minute. What he had just said to her was perfectly true but, of course, he could still intervene; still ask the young officer who had arrested her to forget about what had happened that night. Yes, Atherton *could* do all that, but did he really want to, that was the question.

He'd known Vera for a few years now. In all that time he had never used his position to force himself on her, nor had he ever been anything other than thoughtful towards her constant predicament. Vera lived off the street because that was all she knew. Selling her body had been the only means of income known to her and even Atherton knew that a prison sentence was unlikely to change that. In fact, there was every chance that a prison sentence might make Vera's life even harder.

He decided to hear what she had to say, even though he made no promises in advance. Vera then told her story.

"One of my clients is a Member of Parliament and likes a bit of rough on the side. He pays me well and always takes me somewhere nice to do the business. He's a quiet sort, reckons actions speak louder than words, if you get my meaning. Anyway, I met with him at the weekend and he was more nervous than usual, far more talkative and paid for even more of my time than normal. Seemed he really wanted someone to talk to and I was probably seen as a safe bet not to pass on anything he said. Well. we did the business, even though it was fairly uninspiring; I don't think his mind was really on it, if truth be known."

"Vera," Atherton said sternly, "will you please get to the point."

"Oh, sorry, Mister Atherton," said Vera, lighting yet another cigarette and sipping at her coffee. "The fact of the matter is that my MP client had just had stuff nicked from his bank. Important stuff, if he was to be believed and he was properly shitting himself at the fact that stuff was now in the hands of criminals. He was terrified that they'd go public with it as he didn't feel he'd be able to pay them blackmail money."

"Did he say what kind of information had been stolen?" Atherton then asked, beginning to think that Vera really did have something big for him this time.

"Not exactly. He did, however, talk about being helped in his career and now having to pay for it. Said some bloke had offered to open doors for him in his career. He seemed really worried."

"What did he mean by someone opening doors?"

"Well, I've no idea, but I thought you might," countered Vera.

Atherton thought about what she had just said. *Having to pay for it* could mean financially, or it could also mean payback in another form. The idea of a Member of Parliament owing anyone anything was dangerous at best.

"Did he say anything else?" Atherton then asked.

"He didn't put much into words, but I could tell he was worried, perhaps even scared of what might come out. I mean he didn't want us to do any of the usual stuff, his mind just wasn't on it."

"Okay," Atherton then said, "what's the name of this client?"

Vera seemed unwilling to answer the question at first. Atherton quickly explained that, without a name, she would have no chance of escaping jail. She did not think for much longer.

"Clarence Duvall."

Clarence Duvall was a junior minister in the Government. He worked in the Treasury and one of his main duties was to work as an advisor to the Chancellor.

Atherton thought a little more. It wasn't much, but it intrigued him nonetheless. He decided to put in a word for Vera. She would potentially be more use to him out on the street, than locked away in a prison cell.

He went away to speak with the arresting officer.

Thursday, 23rd September, 1971 – Sir Tavish's Office, MILO HQ

Atherton had done a little homework on Clarence Duvall. He had moved through the ranks at an alarming rate and Atherton began to wonder just how much help had been offered along the way. His first concern was for Duvall passing secrets to some foreign power and he suggested, to his boss, that they pass on what they had to MI5. Atherton's boss had suggested MILO instead. Atherton had no idea why, but had arranged to meet with Sir Tavish Viewforth anyway.

Atherton had called on MILO Headquarters and been given a ten-minute slot with Sir Tavish. He passed on all that Vera had said, plus what little extra he'd learned from his research on Duvall. He further stated that Duvall might now be a spy and passing secrets to the Russians.

From what he'd been told, Sir Tavish did not believe that that was the case. He did believe, however, that they might just have been given a current operative with Freiheit.

Sir Tavish had hurried back to his desk and called for Ben to come through. He brought Ben up to speed and then sent him off to investigate Duvall, with a view to knowing more about the safe-deposit box and the help that might have been offered,

Once he felt the time was right to do so, Ben was then to bring Duvall in for interview.

Thursday, 23rd September, 1971 – Bonn, West Germany

Lunch had been arranged by Gerd Seeler. His guest, Emmerich Kassmeyer, arrived at just after one, keen to hear what Gerd had to say to him. Little had been said in advance, though Gerd had said it would be in Emmerich's best interests to be there.

The restaurant was not far from the Government Buildings and was often frequented by politicians and their staff. Gerd had bribed the Head Waiter to give them the best situated table and by that he meant the one furthest from the ears and eyes of others. The Head Waiter had duly delivered and made sure that his prettiest waitress served the men who would be sitting at that table. As it was, neither man really noticed the waitress, they were too busy talking.

Kassmeyer was delighted to be offered the post in Bonn. He was already based there, but would now have access to the office vacated by Neuer. Being the Tongue of Germany would be a great honour.

"One more thing," Seeler had said as the meal came to an end.

"The new Grand Master wants us to spread our wings into Eastern Europe, beginning with East Germany. Fritz Wagner has been given the rather unenviable task of finding someone who can get us that foothold in the East. It might be a feather in your own cap, if you could help him, in any way."

"Suggest a person who could open doors in the East, do you mean?"

"Exactly."

Kassmeyer thought for a moment. "I might have a few ideas."

"Excellent. I'll leave that with you and when you have a suggestion to make, phone this number."
Seeler slid a piece of paper across the table and Kassmeyer picked it up. The bill was then paid and the two men went on their way.

Friday, 24th September, 1971 – MILO HQ, Central London

Ben had been doing his homework on Clarence Duvall. He was now busy telling Amy and Mike what he now knew.
"Member of Parliament for the last five years. Clarence Duvall is thirty-five years old and at present is a junior minister in the Treasury. His rise has been fairly meteoric and it does bear all the hallmarks of a Freiheit intervention. He's apparently been talking too freely to a prostitute he meets with regularly. He's been talking about payback for help received and also having something very important stolen from him."
"Safe-deposit box?" said Mike.
Ben nodded.
"So, what now?" added Amy.
"We speak with Mister Duvall," said Ben. "There's really not much on him, though he does have membership for a casino that he hardly ever visits."
"An MP who likes a flutter now and again is hardly earth-shattering," commented Mike.
"True, but people with memberships to casinos tend to never be out of the place," said Ben.
"Which casino is it?" asked Amy.
Ben checked his notes. "The Chips Are Down in Soho."
"When do we speak with Mister Duvall?" was Amy's next question.
"We'll enjoy the weekend first, then I'll arrange something."
Amy left the room. Mike put his jacket on.
"See you later," he then said, as he made his way to the door.

"Don't be late," added Ben. "Camilla panics if guests are late."
Mike grinned. "We won't be late, don't worry."

Friday, 24th September, 1971 – Camilla's Flat, Central London

Ben and Camilla were busy in the kitchen. Camilla was checking the food, while Ben opened a bottle of wine to allow it to breathe.

Ben had been spending more time at Camilla's flat, mainly because it afforded them more space than his own. She had the extra bedroom for a start.

Having the extra space would come in handy that night, as it would allow their guests to sleep over.

They were having dinner with Mike and Maria. The initial idea had been to book a restaurant and go out, but Camilla had thought it made more sense for them to eat at her place. That way they could chat more openly and maybe make it easier for Maria to feel part of the group.

They had met her before, but this would be the first time they'd get a chance to really speak with her, to really get to know her. Ben and Mike were under strict instructions not to talk shop all night.

Mike and Maria weren't exactly living together, but Mike had taken to spending more and more time with her at the safe house. He had spoken to Sir Tavish about having Maria moved and he now intended speaking to her and suggesting she move in with him, if only until she sorted herself out. Mike hoped he would get a favourable response to his question.

It turned out to be a lovely evening, stretching into the early morning, by which time Camilla and Maria had gone off to bed, leaving Mike and Ben to their last drink and the conclusion to a debate that had started earlier in the evening and which Ben had wished to go back to, before they called it a night.

Mike had suggested he wanted to pack in his job and find something a little less dangerous to do. Ben was hoping to change his mind. However, Mike had given the subject a great deal of thought and was adamant his days with MILO were now numbered.

"I really love Maria," Mike said. "I know I haven't known her long, but my feelings for her were almost instantaneous. I'm pretty sure she feels the same way about me."

"I get the love thing," said Ben, "but is that any reason to give up a job your good at and also one which won't always involve being out in the field. Even now, I feel sure that Sir Tavish could find you something else."

"I don't want anything else within MILO," countered Mike. "I enjoy being in the field, I just don't want to put Maria through the turmoil of worrying about me when I was away doing God knows what. I know we don't wander about firing guns at everyone, but there is a strong element of danger to what we do and it simply wouldn't be fair on Maria."

"What about Camilla?" Ben had then said. "Am I some kind of heel for not thinking about her, when I go off to work every day?"

"You've obviously found a way to deal with it and I envy you that, but even you must admit that Camilla will be worried for you, until you come back at the end of every day."

Ben knew that Camilla worried and that did upset him. However, he was an ambitious man, doing a job that he really loved and he didn't want to give it up. Was that being selfish? He had had discussions with Camilla, since he'd told her what he did and he knew that she was saying certain things more to please him than to actually explain how she felt.

By the time that last drink had been finished and the two men went off to bed, they had come to an agreement. Ben was now supportive of Mike's decision, but had absolutely no plans to follow suit. He would, however, be a lot more thoughtful of Camilla's situation from now on.

Monday, 27th September, 1971 – The White House, Washington, USA

Abner had never been to the White House before. He had always been outranked on those occasions where CIA briefings had been required by either the President, or his team. Even on this occasion, Helms would have pulled rank, only he didn't know what Abner knew and it would take every ounce of evidence against the man now calling himself Toby Reinhardt to get the President to agree to further action being taken.

Abner was taken through the usual round of security checks and then left waiting in a room that was bigger than his apartment. On the walls were paintings of people who meant nothing to Abner but who, presumably, meant something to the White House. He had been given a coffee, by a cheerful young man who wore that permanent smug expression of someone who could tell the world that they worked in the White House. *No job could be any better than that,* thought Abner.

Eventually, after waiting an hour and a half, Abner was shown, by the same cheerful young man, through to the Oval Office, where the President was sitting on a sofa, coffee in hand and a look on his face which conveyed to Abner a sense that all was far from well. Clearly, the long wait had been because the President had been dealing with something and clearly, that something would probably be far more important than what Abner had come to discuss.

Which meant that the half hour he had been promised would now turn out to be five minutes and the decision he had come to get would not be given.

Abner had never been a fan of Richard Nixon. He had never voted for him and never felt that the man was fully equipped to hold the office of President. There was always a shifty expression on Nixon's face, an expression that would always prevent anyone from fully trusting him. He had the look of a man who was always up to no good, even when he wasn't. Everyone remembered Nixon's performance during his televised debate with Kennedy. Kennedy, the youthful, smiling candidate, wearing a suit that looked good on a black and white television. Nixon, the older, shiftier looking opponent who sweated a lot in front of the cameras and looked ill-at-ease in answering every question.

On that night alone, JFK swung the Presidency in his direction.

But then, years later, Nixon finally got his chance to be President and still he looked shifty and indecisive most of the time.

As he offered Abner a seat, Nixon did manage a smile. He then offered Abner a coffee, which he declined. The next thing he did was look at his watch. Abner now knew, for sure, that his time in the Oval Office would be limited to just a few minutes. He was about to speak when a door opened and a man walked in apologising, as he did so, for being delayed. Abner recognised him at once as being John Ehrlichman, Assistant to the President for Domestic Affairs. Ehrlichman was forty-six years old, wore a serious countenance most of the time and had a hairline that was receding quicker than he might have preferred. He was known to be very close to the President and Nixon put a lot of faith in Ehrlichman's advice.

"Just happy you could find the time to join us," said the President.

Ehrlichman smiled and sat down. Both he and Nixon now turned and looked at Abner. It was Ehrlichman who spoke next.

"We've had a look at the papers you sent across, Abner and we have a few concerns."

Abner had been expecting such a reaction, that was why he had requested a personal interview with the President, so that he could further argue his corner.

"Are you prepared to share those concerns?" Abner then enquired.

Nixon drank the last of his coffee and put the cup down on a table in front of him. He then sat back in his seat and crossed his legs. He looked first at Ehrlichman and then across at Abner. The smile that now formed on his face looked insincere and almost out of place.

"We don't think you should do anything more regarding Toby Reinhardt."

Abner noted the use of the word *we*. Was the President actually making this decision, or was he merely going along with the wishes of others?

"Because?" said Abner, trying hard to hold back the anger that was beginning to rise inside.

"There are a few reasons," Ehrlichman then said, "but the main one is we don't want the United States of America to be embarrassed by your actions."

"And why would charging Toby Reinhardt with war crimes embarrass the United States in anyway whatsoever?" was Abner's next question.

"Just think about it, Abner," Ehrlichman responded in a tone that really said *oh, come now, Abner, even you wouldn't do something as daft as that.*

"I have thought about it, Mister Ehrlichman," said Abner. "I've thought about nothing else, these last few weeks and I am firmly of the opinion that Reinhardt, or Podolski as we should now be calling him, should be charged with war crimes and put before a jury as soon as possible."

Ehrlichman sat back in his seat and looked at the President before responding to Abner.

"Abner, *if* we were to allow Reinhardt to face trial then we would also be allowing the man's past to become public knowledge. That would, in turn, let the world know that the United States of America probably knew what kind of man we were letting into our country, back in forty-six. Now, I don't know about you, but I don't like the idea of the world throwing accusations at us, all these years later; accusations that the President would then have to deal with."

"But we *did* know who we were letting in," insisted Abner, "and we did nothing about it then. Now is our chance to atone for that error."

Ehrlichman gave Abner a sympathetic smile and in that moment, Abner knew he was going to get nowhere with his argument.

"Assuming that we *did* know who Reinhardt really was and chose to say nothing, then don't you think that just makes us look all the worse if we now come forward and admit our mistake?"

Abner's anger was nearer the surface, but he still managed to control it.

"It would be a whole lot worse to let a war criminal die in his bed of old age, rather than at the end of rope."

Nixon now sat forward.

"I hear what you say," he said, "but John is correct, we simply can't admit that we got it so wrong all those years ago."

"Plus, the fact that Reinhardt is so important to NASA now, let's not forget that Mister President," added Abner, his anger beginning to spill over. He realised, as soon as he'd said it, that those last few words were a trifle disrespectful to the position of President, but he was getting a might pissed off at the way he was being treated.

Nixon took Abner's words on the chin and showed little reaction. The fake smile returned.

"I don't deny that Toby is very important to our work in space exploration, but that has nothing to do with my decision. I make it purely to protect the United States of America from undue criticism from the world at large."

Abner could see that he was beaten. The President had made his decision and nothing would change that now. Julius Podolski would continue to be protected and there was nothing Abner could do about that, at least for the moment. As far as the White House was concerned Podolski would be filed in the sub-dormant, to not see the light of day again until Richard Nixon was no longer President.

Abner knew it was pointless to continue the discussion. He thanked the President for his time, but said nothing more to Ehrlichman. Abner stood up and left the room. A security man was waiting for him outside, so that he could be accompanied back to the exit.

Abner seethed the whole way.

He wanted to do something, but knew that if he did, he would be putting his own position in jeopardy. However, that did not stop his mind mulling over the problem as he climbed into the car, waiting for him, and made his way back to the office.

Thursday 30th September, 1971 – MILO Safe House, Greater London

Ben and Mike had decided to take Clarence Duvall somewhere quiet to interview him about his possible connections to Freiheit. They had had to wait until after ten o'clock that evening due to the fact Duvall had been a guest speaker at a charity dinner and Ben had thought it prudent to let the event pass before taking Duvall away for a chat.

Duvall had responded in exactly the way Ben and Mike would have expected. First there was the surprise in being informed that men from an intelligence agency would wish to speak with him, then there was the *you do know who I am* moment, when people in authority have that misguided moment when they actually believe they ought to be above the law. Once he realised he wasn't going to prevent being interviewed, he'd then asked to have a lawyer present. His request was denied, as was a further request to make a phone call. Instead, Clarence Duvall was led to a car and driven away.

Twenty minutes later they arrived at a large house, set back from the road and situated among a number of other large houses, no doubt occupied by people with large salaries. The car stopped at the front door and by the time the door had been opened and Duvall allowed to get out, the front door had been opened by a third man, who now stood in the light from the hallway.

Ben led Duvall into the house and down a flight of stairs. They went into a room with no windows and a musty smell. The furniture was basic; just a table and three chairs. The light bulb was naked and bright and the floor had a thin dusting of sawdust on it. Duvall was told to sit down on a chair positioned on the opposite side of the table.

He saw little reason in arguing, so he sat down.

At that moment, the door opened and Mike came into the room.

He was carrying three mugs of steaming coffee. Nothing was said as he and Ben sat down.

Duvall took one of the coffees and leaned across the table, cupping the mug between his hands and staring down at the contents. He had wanted to rant and rave, wanted to demand his rights and threaten to have Sir Tavish's balls on a plate for putting him through such a degrading experience. He had wanted to say all that, but had thought better of it. After all, no one knew where he was. They could leave him here for long enough and he'd never be found. No, if MILO wanted to play silly beggars then they held all the trump cards.

Best to drink his coffee and await what they had to say.

"You have a safe-deposit box at the Moorgate Branch of Barclays Bank," Ben began. It was a statement more than a question and Duvall had not realised, at first, that he had been meant to respond. The silence hung in the air for a while before he eventually did.

"You obviously know that I do."

"There's nothing in it any more, is there?" Ben now said. This time it was a question and one that he knew Duvall would not wish to answer.

More silence. Eventually another answer.

"I'm guessing you already know that as well."

Ben didn't actually *know* Duvall's safe-deposit box was empty, but after what Vera had told Atherton, it was a fair assumption. Duvall had now confirmed that assumption, so Ben felt he was on safer ground as he moved forward with the interview.

"We know that the contents were stolen, Mister Duvall and we also know that you're greatly concerned about those contents possibly falling into the wrong hands."

"Well, of course I'm concerned. Those items were deeply personal to me."

"Has anyone offered to sell them back to you?" Mike now asked.

"Not as yet."

"But it will take some form of payment to get those items back, won't it?"

Duvall was now thinking more about how these men knew about his safe-deposit box being emptied. The bank shouldn't have given out that information and no one else knew.

At least, that was his first thought. His second thought, which followed very close behind, offered him a solution.

Vera. Bloody Vera.

"Mister Duvall?" prompted Mike, thinking an answer was not forthcoming.

"Yes; yes, I suppose it will."

"And, of course, we're dealing with criminals, aren't we, Mister Duvall?" Ben now said. "We're dealing with men who care little for where those payments come from. They'll be happy to be paid for the contents of those boxes and they'll not mind who makes the payment."

Duvall started to look more than a little worried.

"What do you mean?" he then said.

Ben smiled and glanced at Mike. He, in turn, smiled back but it was a conspiratorial smile, the kind that passes between two people who know something that others don't. They were worrying smiles from Clarence Duvall's viewpoint.

"We've manged to make contact with someone in the gang, Mister Duvall," Ben now said. Of course, it wasn't true, but Duvall was not to know that. "We've offered a sum of money to have your items returned, only they are to be returned to us, instead of you."

Duvall's eyes opened in horror. "But, you can't do that!" he almost shouted.

"Oh, but we can," said Ben, as calm as ever. "You see, we believe it is in the interests of our nation's security to know what was in that safe-deposit box. We don't think you are a traitor, as such, but we do believe you've been consorting with the enemy."

Duvall's expression changed from horror to confusion.

"Now, I *really* don't know what you're talking about," he then said.

"You've been quite successful in your career, haven't you?" Mike then asked.

Duvall's eyes flicked in Mike's direction, the look of confusion deepening.

"I suppose so, but what has that......?" Duvall began to say.

Ben interrupted.

"You've had help along the way, haven't you?"

Duvall now knew that all this had come from his loose talk towards Vera. Why did he always have to feel so damned comfortable in her company? Why did he *always* end up saying too much to her?

"I've had a few breaks, yes."

"Let me guess," Ben then said, "you were approached by someone saying they could be good for your career; telling you that they could help you get places, perhaps even be Prime Minister one day. You wouldn't have to do anything, just sit back and enjoy a successful career. How am I doing?"

Duvall's face paled significantly and Ben knew that he had hit the nail firmly on the head.

He did not wait for Duvall to say anything, but continued himself.

"The people who approached you, Mister Duvall, work for an organisation called Freiheit and I'm willing to bet that, amongst the items stolen from your safe-deposit box, was an item that ties you to that organisation. An item that would destroy your budding career, were it to become public knowledge."

Duvall drank some coffee and appeared to be buying some time, before responding.. Eventually, he spoke.

"Yes," was all he said.

"How was the contact made?" Mike now enquired.

Duvall told them the whole story, but insisted he had done nothing wrong in the sense that he'd given away no Government secrets, nor had he done anything else for them. So far, it had been one-way.

"The only thing I have to do is make my payment every month," Duvall added. "They joked that it was by way of a subscription."

"What kind of payment?" Ben now asked.

"I was given membership to a casino in Soho. I was told that I had to go there on the first Monday of every month and deliberately lose one hundred pounds. In return for those payments, they would ensure I had a successful career. They've never asked for anything other than the money, so I saw no wrong in what I was doing."

"And yet you worry about others knowing you have a connection to them," added Ben.

"Well, I worry that others may read the situation wrongly," said Duvall. "As I said, I've done nothing wrong, but others might not think that."

"And you'd be right, Mister Duvall," Mike now said. "We know how Freiheit work. The day would have come when they would have demanded their pound of flesh and you would have been in no position to refuse. They would have had you over a barrel, not only will there be written evidence of your links with Freiheit, but there will also be those payments you've been making. If that became public knowledge then your career would be down the pan along with your personal reputation. You'd be toxic, Mister Duvall; no one would want to know you."

"Oh God," was all Duvall could say. "You don't happen to have a cigarette, do you?" he then asked.

"No, I'm sorry, we don't," said Ben.

Duvall drank his coffee instead.

"What's the name of the casino?" Ben enquired.

"The Chips Are Down in Soho. It's a private club really, you don't get in unless you're a member."

Ben knew the place. There would never have been any need to think that the place could be a front for Freiheit, until now.

Ben thought for a moment. "You said you went there on the first Monday of each month?"

"Yes."

"So, you're due there this Monday coming?"

"Yes."

"Good," Ben said with a smile. "In that case, you'll be there on Monday night and you'll have a couple of guests with you. I take it you can sign in guests?"

"I can," agreed Duvall, "but I've never been there with guests before; they'll get suspicious?"

"Who'll get suspicious?" pressed Mike.

"The Manager for a start; he's a nasty piece of work."

"What's his name?" asked Mike, notebook at the ready.

"Gary Stock."

It wasn't a name that meant anything to either Ben or Mike. They'd do a little more digging on the man later.

"Do you have a set arrangement for when you go to the casino?" Ben now asked.

"Not really. I usually get there around nine and leave about ten. I try to hide the fact I'm trying to lose money but I've always thought that everyone else there might be doing the same.

We might all be subscribers rather than members."

Very likely, thought Ben, *which is why we need to get inside the building.*

"Okay," Ben then said, "myself and another colleague will meet with you on Monday for dinner. We'll let you know the where and when of that dinner date once the necessary arrangements have been made. After dinner, we'll all go to the casino where we will be viewed as acquaintances, rather than friends. Don't worry, we'll give you a back story."

Duvall looked even more worried.

"Oh, I don't think I could do that," he said.

"Why not?" asked Ben.

"I'd be hopeless at undercover work. I get nervous; I'd give the game away; I just know I would."

Ben smiled. "I'm not giving you an option, Mister Duvall. You meet us for dinner and we all go to the casino on Monday evening. How you cope with being undercover is your problem, but if you blow it, we'll make sure you're finished in whatever career you choose to follow."

Duvall had continued to look at Ben for a few seconds after he'd stopped speaking. He was caught between that rock and a hard place. There was no way out. All he could now do was comply with this man's wishes.

Monday 04th October, 1971 – The Chips Are Down Casino, Soho

At a little after nine in the evening, Clarence Duvall arrived at The Chips Are Down casino with two friends, Mac and Katy Kasem from New York. Mac and Katy were, of course, Ben and Amy, looking every inch the wealthy businessman in town with his gorgeous wife and looking to have a good time.

Ben and Duvall were dressed in dinner suits, though Ben had undone his bow tie and it now hung loose around his neck with the top button of his white shirt unbuttoned. As they arrived there was much talk of the dinner they had just enjoyed and how much they were now looking forward to winning some money. They were talking loudly, hopefully conveying the impression that they had been drinking heavily prior to their arrival.

They were stopped at the door by two gorillas in suits who asked to see Duvall's membership card and to remind him that he was required to sign his guests in. While Duvall signed the book, the two gorillas kept staring at Ben and Amy. Ben could well understand why Amy might be attracting their attention as she was dressed in a long, red dress with a plunging neckline. He could not, however, understand why he would be creating such interest unless, of course, this was an establishment used to trusting no one if they were not already known.

Eventually they were allowed to move through to the cloakroom where they left their coats. From there, they proceeded through to the main body of the casino where there were a variety of tables, spread across the entire floor space and each table was already well attended.

"Shall we win some money?" Ben then announced, rather louder than was necessary. Amy had given him a crash course in at least sounding American, though his accent would have been hard to place for any true American.

They went to the pay desk and bought a stack of chips. Ben and Duvall then split up and found a table at which they could start gambling. Amy played the part of the dutiful wife as she stood behind Ben, placing a comforting hand on his shoulder. All the time they continued to keep one eye on their surroundings, hoping that they might see, or hear, something that would be of use to them. Duvall had wanted to lose his usual hundred pounds and then leave immediately after. Ben had told him that that was not what was going to happen. After all, Duvall was supposed to be entertaining his guests and it would, therefore, be those guests who dictated the events of that evening.

To that end, Duvall had no other option, but to spend more time at the tables. He wasn't concentrating, so he knew he'd be losing even more money that night. However, he could do nothing about that, other than try to play the part of a man happy to be in the company of friends.

Before visiting the casino, Ben had done his homework on it. He knew that the venue was owned by a rich Arab, who rarely visited Britain. From all accounts, he chose to sit at home and watch the profits roll in. The manager was indeed Gary Stock, but Ben had not been able to find out much about the man.

As Ben scanned the immediate area, he noticed a squat man, wearing an immaculate dinner suit and blue tinted spectacles, come out of a door with 'Private' written on it. The man stopped beside another gorilla in a suit and asked something of him. Ben noticed that both men seemed to be looking in the direction of Clarence Duvall which, given the plunge of Amy's dress, was a surprise to Ben. The squat man then glanced in Ben's direction. Ben's interest remained on the chips in front of him.

The squat man then turned and went back through the door marked 'Private.'

Ben placed another bet while Amy continued to allow her gaze to wander round the room. She counted a number of cameras, located in various places and all moving independently of each other. It was clear that everyone was under surveillance and Amy was pretty sure that they were being closely watched at that very moment. She squeezed Ben's shoulder and when he looked up at her, she nodded slightly in the direction of one of the cameras. Ben understood immediately what she was telling him.

*

Gary Stock, meantime, was sitting in a small room looking at a bank of three monitors. In front of him was a joystick, which allowed him to move the cameras, located around the casino and zoom in on any one individual, if he chose to do so. The main purpose of the cameras was to spot anyone cheating but, tonight, he was more interested in 'guests' than anything else.

Clarence Duvall had never brought guests with him. In fact, few of their 'members' ever did, after all, most of them were only there to pay their dues, they wouldn't have been there for any other reason. Stock immediately had a deep mistrust of those guests. He already had a member of staff trying to find out what he could about Mac and Katie Kasem.

He turned one camera and focussed it on the Kasems. Stock moved the camera towards the blonde's face. She was a good-looking woman and she definitely *looked* American. He then moved the camera to the man. He was concentrating on placing bets and seemed to be meeting with an element of success. Stock decided he'd let the man win; he had a feeling he wouldn't see him again anyway.

As Stock watched the two 'guests' he began to feel uneasy, even though he probably couldn't have explained why. The fact that Duvall never went there with anyone else was the main source of concern. Why, suddenly, decide to bring guests now? As he watched the screen, Stock reached for a phone and a dialled a number from memory. Almost immediately a man's voice was in his ear.

"Yes?" was all it said.

"There might be a problem," said Stock.

"How big a problem?"

"Not sure. Clarence Duvall is here and he's brought a couple of guests. He's never done that before."

"Who are the guests?"

"They've given their names as Mac and Katie Kasem. I'm having them checked out."

"Do you think they're undercover?"

"They look genuine enough, but I just thought I'd tell you."

"Okay. See what comes back on this Mac and Katie Kasem and depending on what you learn, take the appropriate action."

"Whatever action is necessary?" said Stock.

"Whatever action is necessary," confirmed the voice in his ear.

Stock put the phone down and went back through to where all the tables were still in full swing. The two Americans were still at the roulette table, though Duvall was now trying his luck at Blackjack. Stock went over and had a word in Duvall's ear. They both then started towards the door marked 'Private.'

Ben leapt to his feet and headed across to intercept the two of them. He deliberately lurched around a little, trying to act like a man still suffering from the effects of alcohol.

"Where are you off to now, Clarence, we were just thinking of moving on again."

"Just a small, membership matter. Mr Duvall will be back in no time at all," said Stock as they brushed past Ben and headed through the door. Amy appeared at Ben's side. The look of concern on her face was genuine, she really was worried about what might now happen to Duvall. There seemed little else to do, however, than to go back to the tables and continue playing the part of visitors to London enjoying having a flutter.

Duvall, meanwhile, found himself in a room at the back of the casino with Gary Stock and another man with the word 'evil' tattooed on the knuckles of his right hand.

"So, tell me about your friends?" asked Stock.

Duvall was sweating already, something which Stock had not failed to notice. Duvall looked every bit the man with secrets to hide. It made Stock feel very nervous.

"I guess they're more acquaintances, than friends," Duvall eventually said.

"How long have you known them?"

"Couple of years. We met at a party and now they make a point of ringing me, when they're in town. They take me for dinner and that's usually where our evenings end. However, on this occasion, they found out that I had membership to this casino and insisted they get the chance to win a little money. I really didn't see any harm in taking them along, especially as I was coming here anyway."

Duvall was starting to relax a little. The more he got into the back story, the better he began to feel. He knew that MILO had covered their tracks and that nothing *should* be going wrong. In fact, Duvall now felt confident enough to add a little more. "Plus, there is the little matter of Katie's chest; I mean wouldn't you want to keep those beauties in view a little longer?"

Stock let the comment pass. He thought for a moment.

"Tell me what you know about them." he then said.

"As I said, we've known each other a couple of years but, in all honesty, we've only ever met about four times. Mac owns his own business in New York and Katie's just the trophy wife."

"What's his business?" was Stock's next question.

Duvall took his wallet from an inside jacket pocket and then took from that a small card, which he now handed to Stock. Stock read what was on it. *Mac Kasem, Import and Export.* There followed an address in New York, along with a telephone number.

Stock went over to where a phone was lying and picked up the receiver. He first phoned a number he knew by heart and waited for a reply. The followed a brief discussion with someone about whether, or not, there really was an export/import business being run by Mac Kasem. It turned out that there was. Stock seemed happier to hear that. He then telephoned the number on the card. Stock spoke to a couple of people and seemed satisfied when he came off the phone.

He had just had it confirmed that Mac Kasem did run a business in New York and that was currently on vacation in London. It was also confirmed that his wife, Katie, was with him.

In reality, Mac and Katie Kasem were still in New York, living in a hotel room at MILO's expense. Mac did run a business and Katie was a beautiful blonde. However, they had never been to London, nor had any desire to do so. The call to Mac's office had been answered by two MILO employees, both fully conversant with Ben and Amy's back story.

Everything appeared to have gone smoothly. Stock had come off the phone beginning to believe Duvall's story. There seemed no reason to keep Duvall any longer. He was told he could go. Stock then watched the reaction of the Kasems when Duvall appeared back in the casino. Mac Kasem offered to buy him a drink and it was accepted. The three of them then sat at the bar for half an hour longer, before collecting their coats and leaving.

*

Sitting in a car, across the street from the entrance to the casino, were two men. They had responded to a call from Ben Ward, a call made the moment he had left the casino. Once it felt safe to do so, he wanted the men to enter the casino and have a snoop around. He gave them a brief description of the inner lay-out and then asked them to find anything that might link the casino with Freiheit. The two men had parked at just before midnight. Now it was nearer three and they were still waiting for the lights to go out above the door. People had been leaving for the last hour, but still no one had come out and then locked the door, prior to heading on their way.

At just on three in the morning, the door opened and a woman came out. She was buttoning her short coat and then running her hand through her hair. She looked up and down the street, as if checking for anyone waiting for her and then began walking along the pavement, away from where the two men were still waiting patiently in their car.

Moments later a man came out. He, too, seemed to be checking for anyone watching him, before turning and locking the door. A few seconds later, the lights went out. The men in the car assumed the lights had to be on a timer.

"That must be the boss," one of the men said.

"And she must have been his latest shag," added the other.

"I wish they could have done the business somewhere else," said the first man.

Once the area had remained quiet for a little longer, the two men got out of the car and made their way across to the casino building. They passed the front door and walked to a lane, which disappeared down the side of the building. They found a door at the back, which they forced open with more ease than the owners might have preferred. So much for security.

Once inside the building, they found themselves in a long corridor, with doors coming off on either side. The brawn of the two, had a torch and they slowly made their way along the corridor until they reached a door with the word *Manager* on it. The door was locked but, again with a little persuasion, it was soon open.

The two men were in Stock's office for less than ten minutes. Having locked the door, Stock had not bothered locking the drawers. The men quickly searched all the drawers and found two sheets of paper that were of particular interest. The sheets were laid on the desk and a lamp switched on. Photographs were taken and the sheets returned to the drawer they'd been found in. The men then left the office, locked the door again and made their way out through the back once more.

They returned to the car and then drove to MILO Headquarters where they handed the camera to a member of staff who would be able to arrange for prints to be taken from the film. They were instructed to leave the photographs with Ben Ward, along with a brief note one of the men had written.

Tuesday, 5ᵗʰ October, 1971 – MILO HQ, Central London

The following morning, Ben had studied the photographs from the casino, carefully. They were of two, separate, sheets of paper. One was a document dealing with the lease of the property and the other was a sheet with scribbled writing on it; presumably Gary Stock's writing. The lease document mentioned a company that had five similar properties in other parts of Europe. The owner of the company was that rich Arab, whom Ben had pretty much already proved, didn't exist. His name appeared to be no more than a front for someone else.

But who might that someone else be?

The sheet with the scribbled writing proved to be of far more interest. On it were two names and two telephone numbers. The bottom name meant nothing to Ben, but the top name most certainly did. Gerald Taylor, the current Chief Executive of the Varga Corporation in London. But what could possibly connect him to a casino in Soho?

Seeing Gerald Taylor's name had set Ben's mind going. He now knew that the casino had a connection to both Freiheit and Taylor. However, did that, in itself, connect Taylor directly with Freiheit? Probably not, though it did heighten his curiosity towards Gerald Taylor.

Ben knew he had to find out more and the one person who seemed best placed to help him, was Gary Stock. Questions would have to be asked of Stock, but not in any conventional manner. Ben had an idea, but it meant that Mike would have to do the interview. Stock had already seen Ben at the casino, if there was any acting to do then he was no longer the right candidate.

He did one last check on the mysterious Arab and confirmed what he had already suspected. There was no hard evidence of the man even existing. Someone else had to be hiding behind the name. But who?

Once he had all the information he felt he would need, Ben brought Mike up to speed and told him how he thought the interview should go.

Mike thought it a good idea and looked forward to honing his acting skills. It was time to speak to Gary Stock.

Wednesday, 6th, October, 1971 – Central London

It was three o'clock in the morning.

Gary Stock had been sleeping. It had been a deep sleep, in which he was dreaming of a beautiful woman paying him a lot of attention.

And then the roof had caved in. Not literally, but definitely in every other way.

The door of the bedroom had burst open and a group of men rushed in. Stock woke with a start and could see the shapes coming at him. He couldn't see how many and he had no time to react before they were upon him. A rag was thrust into his mouth and a bag pulled over his head. He was manhandled out of bed and dragged from the house. He could only hope that his 'visitors' had at least taken the time to close the front door behind them, if he survived the next few hours he didn't want to return to a burgled house.

Stock was then bundled into the back of a van and driven for what seemed like ages. When the van stopped, he was dragged from the vehicle and manhandled a short distance, until he got the sense of being indoors. He stumbled down some stairs, for once grateful for the fact he was being held so tightly by at least two men. Finally, he was pushed into a seat and the bag removed from his head.

He blinked furiously as the light flooded into his eyes. For a moment he shut them again, finding the light just too bright. Slowly, he became accustomed to his surroundings and was able to study the room around him.

There was not much to study.

White, bare walls. A stone floor and three chairs. He noticed that, behind him, there was a small window at ceiling height. It would have let in some light during the day, but at the moment it was redundant.

Stock's visual journey around the room ended with the two men who were with him in the room. They looked big, they looked military; they looked dangerous. Gary Stock was gripped with fear, his vocal cords too tight to allow him to say anything.

He sat in silence and stared at his captors.

Stock was trying to work out why he was there. Had he done something wrong? If so, who would deem that something to be so bad as to send heavies round in the middle of the night? He finally decided that it had to be a case of 'wrong spy.' Yes, that was it, they had the wrong man. They'd soon realise that and let him go.

Still nothing was said. After a few moments the door opened and a third man came in. Not that Stock knew who he was, but this was Mike. He was pushing a trolley with squeaky wheels. He parked it beside Stock and removed a cloth from the top, revealing an array of shiny surgical instruments.

The fear gripping Stock tightened all the more. This was definitely not looking good.

Mike now sat down. The other two men moved to stand by the door. They almost stood to attention as they stared at the wall in front of them. Still nothing had been said.

Stock wanted to break the silence but he simply couldn't force the words out. Eventually the man with the trolley spoke and when he did, it was in German. It confused Stock even more but, finally, he at least managed to out something into words.

"I don't speak German," he said, his tone rising with the horror of the predicament he now found himself in. "You'll have to speak English; you have to tell me what this is about."

"Freiheit," Mike then said.

Stock was waiting for more to be said, but he soon realised that one word was all he was going to get.

"Freiheit?" he repeated. "I don't know what you mean."

Mike was watching Stock closely. He was terrified and his reactions seemed genuine. Maybe Freiheit didn't mean anything to him? But what then was Gerald Taylor's connection to the casino? This was now going to be the tricky bit for Mike. He would have to speak in English, but make it sound as if the words were coming from a German.

He doubted if Stock would be paying much attention to his accent anyway.

"Gerald Taylor. What does that name mean to you?"

At last, thought Stock, *something I can talk about.*

"He's just a name to me. I was told to organise a payment to an account, in Taylor's name, every month. The payment is based on the casino takings for that month. Taylor gets ten per cent."

"Why?"

"I don't know. I was just told to make the payments. I don't ask questions; I just do my job."

"Who do you work for?"

"A man calling himself Barry Gibb. I've never believed, for one moment, that that's his real name, but that's the only one he's ever given me. I've never met the man; we only speak on the phone."

"If you've never seen this Barry Gibb, how did you get the job in the first place?" Mike then asked.

"I got the job through an agency. I was given an address and told to be there on a certain date. A woman met me and showed me around the room that was to be my office. I was then phoned by this bloke, calling himself Barry Gibb and told that I would get all my instructions by telephone and that, meantime, I was to get on with managing the casino. My only objective was to make money. You have to believe me. I just run the casino."

Barry Gibb had been the other name on the sheet of paper photographed in Stock's office.

"Does Gerald Taylor own the casino; is that why he gets ten per cent of the profits?" Mike then asked.

"It's some Arab bloke who seems to be the owner; I really don't know where Taylor fits into anything."

"And what about this Barry Gibb?"

"Again, I have no idea who he is. He's really nothing more than a voice on the end of the telephone. If I have any problems, I phone him."

Mike studied Stock for a moment. Either the man was an Oscar nominee, or he really didn't know anything about the ownership of the casino. Mike went back to Freiheit,

"We know that there are a number of people who come to your casino and deliberately lose one hundred pounds, once a month. These people are of the opinion that they are paying for the services of an organisation known as Freiheit, yet you want me to believe that you know nothing about Freiheit."

"I don't," insisted Stock.

Mike stood up and moved the trolley a little closer to Stock. He noticed the man's eyes widening. He was now absolutely terrified and unlikely to be thinking about lying. Only professionals would have the confidence to try lying their way out of such a situation.

"I really don't want to have to use these," Mike then said, his voice made to sound as menacing as possible.

It seemed to do the trick.

"Okay, I know about those losses," Stock finally admitted. "We have a list of ten people who come into the casino every month and lose one hundred pounds. We keep that money aside and someone comes to collect it."

"As cash?"

"Yes."

"Same person every month?"

"No. Hardly ever the same person, in fact."

"So, you don't know what happens to that money?" Mike then said.

"No, I swear, I only do my job. Barry Gibb told me about the arrangement with those ten people and the need to keep the money separate from the rest of the casino takings. I was then to wait for someone to come and collect the cash."

"When does this happen?" was Mike's next question.

"Second Monday of each month the losers come in and the second Wednesday of each month, the money gets collected."

Ben made a mental note. That would be later that same day. The timing couldn't have been better.

"What time is the money collected?"

"Usually, around eleven at night."

"Who collects it?"

"As I said, it's normally someone different every time, though always a girl, funnily enough."

"What age?"

"Teens. I expect they get a backhander for picking up the money."

"Mister Stock. You are in the company of representatives of Freiheit and we believe you are ripping us off," Mike then said, picking up one of the surgical utensils.

Stock looked even more frightened.

"I'm not ripping anyone off," he then said, "you have to believe me."

Those last words were almost shouted. He continued speaking.

"The money is set aside; the girls come and collect it and that is the last I see of it. If anyone is ripping you off then is has to be Gibb, or even those girls."

Mike walked around the room for a moment, as if he were deciding on what to do next. He eventually came around the front of Stock again.

"Okay, we need to check this for ourselves. You should have a collection tonight, is that correct?"

"Yes."

"Then tell no one that we have had this little chat and we will do the rest."

"No worries," said Stock, "my lips are sealed. Permanently."

"But before we let you go," Mike then said, "tell us why you have a note of Gerald Taylor's phone number?"

"Just in case there are any problems with the payments we make to him. I've never needed to phone him; I just have his number."

"Very well," Mike then said, signalling to one of the others. A rag was pushed back into Stock's mouth and the bag pulled over his head. He was then manhandled out to the van and driven home, where they simply opened the back door and threw him out on to the street.

As the van drove off, the men in the car thought there was little chance of Gary Stock telling anyone about his meeting with the men from Freiheit.

Wednesday, 6th October, 1971 – The Chips Are Down Casino

Ben and Mike were outside the casino from ten o'clock. Mike had made contact with Stock again, a little earlier in the evening. He had phoned to say he wanted a signal when the money was collected. It was agreed that when the girl left his office, Stock would phone the men on the front door and one of them would come on to the street and tie his shoelace.

At eleven o'clock a girl, wearing a short coat, short skirt and high heels, came out of a taxi and went into the casino. The taxi did not go away. Time passed and then a gorilla in a suit came on to the pavement and knelt down to fiddle with his shoelaces. Moments later the girl came out and got into the taxi. Ben started the engine and as soon as the taxi pulled away, he started to follow.

They followed the taxi to a block of flats in Crystal Palace where the girl, once more, got out of the taxi, only this time she paid the driver and turned to make her way into the building. Mike leapt from the car and hurried to catch up with her. By the time he reached the ground floor, the girl was already in the lift, so Mike started running up the stairs, checking on each level for a sign of life.

He just made it to the third floor in time to see the girl disappear through a door towards the end of the corridor. Mike hurried along to check the name on the door. It was Gibb. Mike assumed it had to be Barry Gibb. He had to admit, he'd not expected Gibb to exist.

Ben joined Mike, who explained the girl was still inside.

"Let's break up the party then," said Ben and put his shoulder to the door. It gave way without much of a fight. Ben and Mike rushed in and stopped, almost immediately, in their tracks.

The flat was completely empty. There was nothing in the way of furniture, apart from a telephone. The girl was currently on the phone, though she dropped it with the shock of the front door caving in on her.

"What the f........," was all the girl managed to say.

Mike hurried over and took the package from her. He picked up the hanging phone and listened. There was just a dialling tone; whoever the girl had been speaking to had gone and probably taken a major lead with them. They now knew the flat had been compromised; it would never be used again.

"Who are you?" the girl now said.

"No one that need worry you," replied Ben. "What are you doing here?"

"Delivering that," the girl said, nodding at the package in Mike's hand.

"To an empty flat?" said Ben.

"Yeah."

"Do you always deliver packages to empty flats?"

The girl looked at Ben, then to Mike.

"I don't usually deliver packages to anywhere," she then said.

"So, why this one?"

"Money, what else? I was told to come here and use the phone. I was given a number and told to tell the person who answered that the package was here for their collection. I was then to go home."

"How was all this set up?" Mike now asked.

"Some bloke spoke to me in the pub," the girl then said. "Gave me twenty quid to collect a package and take it here. Even paid for the taxi. I don't know who he was or what's in that package. I just did as I was told."

Ben could see that the girl was telling the truth. He could also see that they'd blown any chance of finding out who Barry Gibb really was. There was no way that anyone would be collecting a package from that address now.

"Okay," he eventually said to the girl, "you can go."

The girl hurried from the property and her heels were heard clipping along the corridor, no doubt heading for the lift. Ben turned to Mike.

"I think this is what's called a dead end," he said.

Mike could see no reason to disagree.

PART SEVEN

Friday, 8th October, 1971 – Gerald Taylor's Varga Office – London

The meeting had been arranged for 2pm.

Gerald Taylor had received the request for a visit from MILO the day before. On the same day he had also received a call from Tony Rutherford, telling him that the flat was now compromised and they'd need to find a different way of getting the money from the casino. Tony also said that he was going to retire Barry Gibb; it was proving too dangerous to do anything under that name.

Taylor had also contacted Wolfgang Brandt ahead of MILO calling. It was Brandt's name that should have been on the casino lease; he was the true owner of all the casinos in that chain, which were spread across Europe. They were all taking in money for Freiheit.

Brandt had been concerned to hear how close MILO was getting to the work Taylor was doing. They hadn't connected all the dots, but they at least seemed to know that the dots were there. Brandt gave Taylor permission to give MILO his name, in connection with the casinos. It wouldn't matter now as all Freiheit operations, within the casinos, would cease forthwith. MILO could dig as much as they wanted, they'd find nothing of any consequence.

Brandt was happy to speak with MILO again, should they wish to do so. He had made arrangements to hand over the Freiheit reins, so it was time to take a giant step backwards and leave any worries, concerning Freiheit, to others.

Taylor, therefore, felt well prepared for his meeting with MILO. As a precaution, however, he asked his lawyer to be there, more as a witness than anything else.

Ben and Amy were in Taylor's office by five minutes past two. They were all seated, glasses of water in front of them and a very relaxed looking Taylor sitting back in his chair and looking out the window. The lawyer was an elderly gentleman who looked like he'd been round the legal block a few times and was now whiling away his days waiting for retirement.

Ben began by asking general questions about the British arm of the Varga Corporation but paid little attention to the answers he received. Eventually, he brought the subject around to why they were really there.

"In our investigation, Mister Taylor, we have uncovered payments that appear to be going to you from a casino in Soho. This casino is called The Chips Are Down and we wondered why you were in the habit of receiving payments from there?"

Taylor continued looking out the window. He noticed, out of the corner of his eye, that his lawyer visibly twitched, but managed to hold back from saying anything. Taylor allowed the question to hang in the air a little longer, before swivelling his chair round so that he could look Ben fully in the eye.

"I am what is called in the business world, a silent partner. In return for my initial investment, I receive a percentage of the profits on a monthly basis. It is by way of my retirement fund as I chose not to pay towards that retirement through my Varga job."

"May we ask who your partner, or partners are?" Ben then said.

"Just the one partner," was all that Taylor said. He swivelled his chair again and looked out of the window once more.

"Does he have a name?" Amy then said, her anger clearly showing in her tone.

Taylor turned back, this time fixing his gaze on Amy. He smiled.

"Indeed, he does have a name," he then said. "Would you like to know what it is?"

Amy was hating every minute of this. Taylor was toying with them and she didn't like it. She so wanted to wipe that grin off his face. However, she regained her composure enough to answer Taylor's rather sarcastic question.

"I would be very grateful, Mister Taylor."

"Wolfgang Brandt," Taylor then said. "I believe you've already spoken to him."

So, Herr Brandt is back in the picture, thought Ben. He seemed to be involved in so much and yet couldn't be tied to anything specific.

"Does the name Freiheit mean anything to you, Mister Taylor?" Ben then asked.

Taylor swivelled his chair again, but gave the impression he was mulling over the question, before replying that it didn't.

"And yet money is being paid into the casino in the name of Freiheit," Ben added, all the time trying to detect any change in Taylor's demeanour. Ben could now see why Taylor insisted on looking away from them all the time; it was impossible to see his face clearly.

"Is it?" was the only reply to come back.

"A group of people are under instruction to go to the casino every month and deliberately lose money," Ben explained. "Were you aware of that?"

"No."

"Do you have any input to the running of the casino?" asked Ben.

"No."

Single word answers and all delivered while looking away from Ben and Amy. Even the lawyer looked bored. Ben began to wonder if he might be barking up the wrong tree.

"Are the payments from the casino included in your accounts?" Amy now asked.

That got a reaction. Taylor turned to face them, an expression of anger forming on his face. The lawyer sat forward, as if about to offer an opinion, but he was silenced by Taylor raising a hand.

"Are you accusing me of something?" Taylor then said, his eyes burrowing though Amy's skull. She found this sudden change in mood quite intimidating, but managed not to show it.

"I'm just asking a question, Mister Taylor. I'm sorry if it upsets you."

The wave of anger seemed to pass and Taylor relaxed back into his chair. He even managed a smile.

"It doesn't upset me; I just don't understand the need to ask it in the first place."

"Curiosity, plain and simple," said Amy. "Now, are you going to answer it?"

Taylor smiled again. "Everything I do is properly accounted for."

"I can vouch for that," the lawyer then said. "Now, would you please move on."

Ben would have liked to have moved on, only he had nowhere really to go. There was one area he still felt the need to explore.

"Do you know a man by the name of Barry Gibb?"

"Sings in the Bee Gees," replied Taylor with a grin. "Good voice. Writes some good songs."

Ben let the attempt at humour pass.

"Obviously, I'm referring to another Barry Gibb."

"In that case, I don't know anyone else by that name."

"He runs the casino," Ben then said.

"I thought that was Gary Stock."

"He works for Mister Gibb," explained Ben.

"Does he? News to me," said Taylor.

Ben could see he was getting nowhere. Taylor had appeared too calm from the very beginning of their discussion. He looked like a man with no worries. Ben decided to call it a day. They'd maybe get more on Taylor but, for the moment, they had nothing.

Once outside, Amy let out with a yell.

"What a bastard," she then said.

"Too sure of himself for my liking," said Ben. "Over confidence will be his downfall, just you wait."

"And when he falls I hope I'm there to witness the drop," Amy added.

Monday, 11ᵗʰ October, 1971 – Wolfgang Brandt's house, Puerto de Soller, Majorca

As soon as Ben walked into the room he knew that it would be a complete waste of time.

Brandt was sitting on the sofa, brandy and cigar in hand and with a look of a man without a care in the world. It was like Gerald Taylor all over again. Had there every been something to worry both men, then it was gone now.

The biggest tell was the lack of a lawyer; in fact, the lack of anyone else being there. If Brandt was happy to deal with this himself then he no longer had anything to fear.

Ben and Amy were invited to sit and offered a drink. They both asked for iced water and Brandt summoned his housekeeper to get it for them. Once they were settled, Ben began his line of questioning.

"Since we last spoke, Herr Brandt, we've found out that you own a chain of casinos. Why didn't you tell us that the last time?"

"Because, as I think I said at the time, it was none of your damned business. In fact, it still isn't."

"We think your casinos are linked to an organisation called Freiheit," said Ben, "which makes it our business."

"Freiheit?" repeated Brandt, "never heard of it."

"Freiheit is an organisation, which seeks to benefit itself ahead of everything else," Ben then said.

"Still haven't heard of it," said Brandt, sipping his brandy.

"We know that there's a group of people being told to attend your casino and deliberately lose money. We believe that money is collected for Freiheit."

"Still haven't heard of it," was all that Brandt would say.

"Do you know anyone called Barry Gibb?"

"He's my main man in London. He oversees things regarding the casino."

"Did you employ him?"

"Not directly. He was already doing a similar role for the previous owner and I thought it only right that he continued to work for me."

"What can you tell us about Mister Gibb?" Amy now asked.

"Absolutely nothing."

"You've never met him?" Ben enquired with surprise in his tone.

"I've never met any of my employees, there's never been a need," Brandt said.

"The money I spoke of earlier," Ben then said, "is collected and delivered to a property that is in the name of Mister Gibb. Are you telling us that you know nothing about it?"

"That's exactly what I am telling you and I suggest that if you have any further questions regarding that money, that you take them up with Mister Gibb himself."

"How well do you know Gerald Taylor?" was Ben's next question.

"Quite well. He invested heavily when I started the casino chain. That is why he gets a payment from us every month, it was part of our initial agreement."

"You must have known each other well before Mister Taylor would agree to putting so much money into your casino venture?" Ben then asked.

"We were business acquaintances, nothing more. I made my pitch and he could see a profit in backing me. He wasn't wrong."

"Why, then, does the paperwork quote an Arab as being the owner?" Amy now asked.

"A necessary smokescreen to protect my privacy," Brandt replied. "Publicly, it looks like the Arabs own the casino chain, but you only have to scratch the surface and you'll find my name somewhere."

Ben was aware that MILO had scratched all over the surface and come up with nothing. However, he saw no mileage in asking anymore about the ownership of the casinos. In fact, Ben saw no mileage in asking anything else, full stop. Brandt was too relaxed, even Amy was picking up on that.

They decided to leave. Brandt saw them to the door and politely hoped he'd not see them again. As Ben and Amy made their way down to the harbour they both knew that Wolfgang Brandt would, most certainly, be taken off their Persons of Interest list.

*

Wolfgang Brandt had watched his visitors disappear through the main gate. He was still smiling as he closed the door and went back into the house. He went into his study and picked up the phone. Moments later, he was speaking to Ralf Dinger.

"I've dealt with MILO," he said, "and now it's time for me to retire. Herr Franke and Herr Wagner can take Freiheit forward from here, I want to sit back and enjoy the sunny days now."

"I will contact Herr Wagner from now on," Dinger said.

"Is that a problem?" asked Brandt, sensing Dinger was not happy about something.

"Not at all, Herr Brandt, you know me, I can work with anyone."

The words sounded upbeat, the tone didn't. Not that that bothered Brandt anymore. He had retired now and already it felt good to leave problems to others. He wished Dinger and Freiheit all the best for the future and put the phone down.

Brandt went back to the sitting room and poured himself another brandy. He sat down and looked out of the window, down on to the harbour. It was such a peaceful view, one that he could look at all day and never get bored.

Life had been good; Brandt could only hope that his retirement would be every bit as enjoyable.

Wednesday, 13th October, 1971 – Sir Tavish's Office, MILO HQ, Central London

Ben was sitting with Sir Tavish and both men were more than a little depressed. It had been reported, in that morning's Financial Times, that the casino chain, including The Chips Are Down in Soho, was now on the market and looking for a new owner. It further reported that the owner, an as yet unnamed Arab businessman, had set an asking price that was below the market value for the business. No reason had been given for this, but it had been assumed that he was simply looking for a quick sale. No one, at The Chips Are Down casino, had been available for comment.

To Ben and Sir Tavish it was another door slamming shut on them and a clear indication that, had Brandt been involved in anything useful to MILO, he certainly wasn't now.

In fact, as far as Ben and Sir Tavish were concerned that morning, much of what they had done over the last few weeks and months had all been rendered pretty useless. Their main problem had been turning suspicion into hard fact. Acquiring evidence against an organisation so well organised as

Freiheit was going to be difficult at best. The risk was that every time MILO got close to anything useful, Freiheit would just shut it down and move on to someone, or something, else.

Even the investigation into the bank raids had barely moved. Terry Ferris and Gail Potter were still on the run and MILO had no leads, whatsoever, as to where they might be. With little appetite, from on high, for finding the guilty parties amongst the bank staff, the investigation was meandering along, rather than going anywhere specific. The police were still looking for the robbers themselves, but with few clues and an underworld unwilling to talk they, too, were going nowhere fast.

It seemed to be one unholy bloody mess and no one was that well placed to sort it out. On top of it all, Sir Tavish was due to meet with the Home Secretary again, the following day and he really had nothing new to talk about.

Ben shared Sir Tavish's frustrations. Some of their leads had promised much but delivered little. He would have wanted to tell his boss so much more than he did. It was just a deeply frustrating time for everyone working for MILO.

"At least my time with the Home Secretary will be short," Sir Tavish said. "He'll give my arse a good spanking and send me on my way. That should make his day; I swear he doesn't like me."

"You don't like him much either, sir," added Ben.

"True," was all that Sir Tavish added.

Ben left the room and went back to his desk. Sir Tavish sat back in his chair and thought for a moment.

There were times when he questioned the job he did and wondered if he ever actually made a difference.

This was one of those times.

Thursday 14th October, 1971 – Home Secretary's Office, Central London

Reginald Maudling sat behind his impressive desk and sipped a cup of tea. He looked comfortable in his padded chair and surprisingly, for a Government Minister, seemed at peace with the world. He wasn't exactly smiling, but there was a contentment to his countenance, which Sir Tavish had seldom seen and certainly had not witnessed during his last visit to the Home Office.

"I'm hearing the investigation in to the bank raids has rather stalled?" Maudling said.

Sir Tavish put his tea down on the corner of the desk and picked up his briefcase. He took out a file and placed that beside his tea. He then put the briefcase back on the floor and flipped open the file so as to be able to read the front page of the report contained within.

"I would not agree, Home Secretary that it has stalled as such, though I will admit that we have reached a point where we dare not proceed without further authority from a level such as yours."

Maudling looked mildly interested. "Why do you need my input, Sir Tavish?"

"Our biggest problem, all along, has been with Moorgate. As soon as the decision was taken to hide the fact a raid had even taken place, our hands were tied. We were able to interview the staff regarding Ferris and Potter, but we've never been able to talk about the raid itself."

"Ah, yes, Ferris and Potter," said Maudling with a look of disappointment. "No arrests there, either."

Sir Tavish checked the anger rising in him.

"With respect, Home Secretary, due to the constraints, which I have already mentioned, it was highly unlikely that any arrests would ever have been made."

"Perhaps," was all that Maudling would say.

"Anyway, Home Secretary, I would have thought the last thing you'd want now was for Ferris and Potter to be arrested. A court case would bring out all that happened at Moorgate and you don't want that, do you?"

Maudling drank a little more tea and carefully laid the cup back in its saucer.

"It might be better if we never go down the court road," he then said. "It's a case of the less said, the better, eh?"

Sir Tavish did not agree, but one thing he had learned a long time ago, was that when a Government Minister called for silence on a subject, then it was best to comply. Moorgate was another investigation going nowhere fast, so being given the green light to drop it was actually a relief. Yes, it meant criminals getting away with their crime, but that was of no consequence to Sir Tavish. His conscience was clear; he was only dropping the investigation because he'd been told to.

If anything was to come out later it would be the Home Secretary and not Sir Tavish Viewforth who would be facing the awkward questions.

"You do realise, Home Secretary," Sir Tavish finally continued, "that those people who had items stolen *will* be expecting a full investigation into the crime and yet, here you are, effectively closing it all down."

Maudling picked up his tea cup again and sat back in his chair.

"The police can still go through the motions, there's really no need for MILO to be involved."

"And what about the items you were so concerned about the last time we spoke?" Sir Tavish now enquired.

He already knew the answer, of course. The Home Secretary was relaxed and happy, so his own arse was covered and that was all that really mattered to him. If the Home Secretary's arse was covered, however, it meant that those items, which had caused him such concern, were now safely back with their owners.

Which meant payments had been made and lines of inquiry closed. Government Ministers and members of the Royal Family could once more sleep soundly in their beds.

But what of the Roddy McIntosh's of this world, thought Sir Tavish. *There's no one left to fight for them.*

Maudling eventually answered Sir Tavish's question.

"I admit to being slightly concerned the last time we spoke, Sir Tavish, but I'm pleased to say that most of my concerns were unfounded. Things were never as bad as I had feared."

What utter shit, thought Sir Tavish. He now knew for certain that his own initial thoughts were accurate. Everything that mattered to Her Majesty's Government had now been returned. The whole affair left a bad taste in Sir Tavish's mouth. His already bad mood was about to get worse as the Home Secretary started to speak again.

"I'm hearing that you've been pestering Gerald Taylor. You seem to have some idea that he's connected to Freiheit."

"Taylor receives a monthly payment from a casino in Soho that we now know, for certain, has ties to Freiheit," replied Sir Tavish.

"These monthly payments are for what?" Maudling then said, finally putting down his tea cup.

"Mister Taylor claims they are part of an agreement he had with the owner of the casino, Wolfgang Brandt. Mister Taylor gave Herr Brandt money with which to start his casino business and in return, he arranged for Taylor to receive a monthly payment based on the profits."

"And have you found anything to dispel what Mister Taylor is telling you?" the Home Secretary now asked.

"We're fairly sure that Wolfgang Brandt has connections with Freiheit as well," Sir Tavish said, "but we have no actual proof to question their story."

"And without that proof, Sir Tavish, I must insist that you back off from pestering Mister Taylor any further. Good God, the man is Chief Executive of one of the major companies in Europe."

And no doubt, thought Sir Tavish, *a major contributor to the Tory Party.*

"What makes you think we've been pestering Mister Taylor?" Sir Tavish now asked.

"Sorry?" said Maudling.

"You said we had to back off from pestering Mister Taylor. Why do you think we've been pestering him?"

"You sent someone to question Mister Taylor when you had no real right to do so," Maudling said. "Unless you come up with some evidence against him, I must insist that you now leave him alone. Do I make myself clear?"

"Very, Home Secretary," was all that Sir Tavish could bring himself to say.

Underneath, however, he was thinking plenty. Thoughts he knew were best kept to himself. He finished his tea and was allowed to leave. He felt dirty as he walked out of the Home Secretary's office and the first thing he did, when he got home, was dive under the shower.

After he had washed and changed he found a cooked meal in his fridge, which he heated before eating. He washed the meal down with a large glass of robust red wine. He then left the dishes in the kitchen and went through to his study. He sat there and finished the bottle of wine.

As he drank, he thought. A plan began to form in his mind. It was a plan that few would have agreed to be a good one. However, it was a plan that a slightly tipsy Sir Tavish thought should now be carried out. It might annoy others but it would make him very happy.

And, at that moment, that was all that really mattered to Sir Tavish.

Monday 18th October, 1971 – MILO HQ, Central London

Sir Tavish was now ready to put his plan into action.

He went to Room 314 and found the file for Julius Podolski. He then went to a small room at the back and photocopied the contents of that file. He returned the file to the bundle in Room 314 and took the photocopies back to his office, where he folded them and placed them in a large, brown envelope. He then set the envelope aside until the clock on the wall had ticked around to nine.

Sir Tavish picked up the phone and dialled the number he had looked out for Gerald Taylor. This would be the first risk in his loose plan. He had given the Home Secretary his word that he would have nothing to do with Gerald Taylor, unless he had proof of wrong-doing, and yet here he was trying to make an appointment to see the man.

A brief chat with Taylor's secretary concluded with the call being passed through and soon Sir Tavish was speaking to the Taylor himself.

"So sorry to bother you so early on a Monday morning," Sir Tavish began, "but I've been asked by the Home Secretary to apologise for the fact MILO came to interview without proper cause."

"Oh, that's quite alright, Sir Tavish," Taylor said.

Sir Tavish could sense the smugness in the man's tone

It angered him even more. He had to fight to hide his true emotions as he spoke again.

"Only, I didn't want to just apologise over the phone, Mister Taylor, I wanted to do it face to face. To that end, might we meet this afternoon?"

He could almost see Gerald Taylor fluffing up his feathers and enjoying this 'victory.' He wasn't going to give up the chance to see Sir Tavish Viewforth squirming in front of him. Of course, he'd agree to a meeting.

"How about three o'clock?" Taylor then said.

"That would be perfect, Mister Taylor. I'll see you then."

Sir Tavish put the phone down and smiled. Part one completed. He picked the phone up again and dialled a number he rarely used, but never forgot.

"I have a job for you," he said.

"Usual meeting place?"

"Yes."

"Time?"

"Meet me at midday and we'll have lunch."

"I'll be there."

And with that, the receiver was replaced again.

*

Lunch was spent at one of Sir Tavish's clubs. He did not eat alone. In fact, his guest was causing quite a stir. He was in the company of a woman whose beauty shone like a beacon. Although not banned, females were rare in the dining room of the Club and more than one pair of eyes kept glancing in her direction throughout the entirety of the meal.

What was said was of little importance, other than the brief instructions Sir Tavish passed on, along with the large brown envelope and a typed note.

When the woman left the Club, she knew exactly what to do next. Sir Tavish waited a little longer before making his way to Gerald Taylor's office.

Part two had now been completed and it was time for part three.

Not that it was really a plan, more a collection of ideas that came loosely together. However, if it all worked out as Sir Tavish hoped, then all had not been lost in the MILO investigation into Varga and the circle around him.

Sir Tavish arrived early for his meeting with Gerald Taylor. He sat in Hannah Kennedy's office until the clock ticked around to three, at which time the door to Taylor's office opened and the man himself, came out. He came towards Sir Tavish, hand extended and a smile on his face. He was looking forward to receiving a personal apology from someone as important as Sir Tavish.

"Would you like a coffee, or tea perhaps?" Taylor said.

"No thank you, Mister Taylor, I've not long finished with lunch."

"Very well, do come in," Taylor then said. "No interruptions please, Hannah," he then said to his secretary.

The two men went into Taylor's office and the door was closed. Sir Tavish sat down and waited while Taylor made his way round his desk and flopped into a large, leather chair. He then looked at Sir Tavish somewhat expectantly. The words of apology would be music to his ears. However, it soon became apparent, as Sir Tavish began speaking, that the outcome of the meeting might not be what Taylor had been expecting.

"We've been watching you, Mister Taylor, and we intend to go on watching you."

Taylor sat forward, his expression changing.

"I thought you came here to....." he began.

"Apologise?" said Sir Tavish. "Oh, I'm sure that *is* what your close friend, the Home Secretary, would like me to do and if anyone asks why I'm here, that is what I shall say. However, the truth is, Mister Taylor, that I think you're crooked. I think you have connections to Freiheit and I think your role with the Varga Corporation is no more than a front for other activities. There were two bank raids in London recently and I wouldn't be at all surprised if you had been involved in their funding. However, as I said, I have no proof, just a lot of suspicion."

Taylor stood up. "Then I must ask you to leave my office."

"I think you'll want to hear me out," insisted Sir Tavish, "otherwise you'll never be able to stop looking over your shoulder."

Taylor now looked concerned. "What do you mean?" he said, slowly sitting down again.

Sir Tavish smiled. "As I was saying, I aim to get my proof and the only way I can do that is by watching your every movement from now on."

"You can't do that," said Taylor.

"Just watch me," Sir Tavish added. "I aim to have all your phones bugged and to have cameras in every property you either own at present, or buy in the future. If you go out, I'll have you followed. If you do anything around the home, I'll have it recorded and filmed. I'm sure your romantic moments with Mrs Taylor will be greatly affected by the knowledge that MILO will be recording everything that happens. Do remember and let her know, it *would* seem only fair."

Sir Tavish had the expression of someone who was really enjoying the moment. Taylor looked like he would burst.

"You can't come in here and threaten me like that," Taylor then said.

Sir Tavish merely grinned. He then spoke again.

"I believe I just did. You won't have a moment's peace, Mister Taylor, and I feel certain that one day you will say, or do, something that will give you away and when that happens I'll be there to pounce. You will pay for your crimes, I guarantee that."

"I haven't committed a crime, Sir Tavish, it's all in your warped little mind," Taylor then said.

"My mind may be warped, Mister Taylor, but all I have to do is create smoke and others will find the fire. A few half statements
floating around could go a long way to making life, for you, a whole lot harder than it should be."

"But you can't do that," said Taylor. "I'll sue."

"Sue away," said Sir Tavish, sounding like that was a really good idea. "Once in a court of law, I'd be able to say even more, be able to create even more smoke around you. I don't need proof, Mister Taylor, I just need to spread my suspicions and others will do the rest."

Taylor was now looking really worried. His expression then seemed to brighten for a moment.

"Even if you thought you had something on me, Sir Tavish, you're tied by the Official Secrets Act, you wouldn't be able to say anything to anyone."

Sir Tavish laughed out loud. "Bugger the Official Secrets Act, Mister Taylor, I would be doing nothing more than airing my suspicions. Take me to court and I'd gladly put meat on the bones of those suspicions."

Gerald Taylor was seething inside. "That is tantamount to harassment, Sir Tavish."

Sir Tavish positively beamed with delight.

"Excellent, you've understood the true meaning of what I've just said."

The fury building inside Taylor was close to boiling over. His fury was mixed with a feeling of helplessness, as there was clearly nothing he could do to counter these threats. He also knew that these were not idle threats; Sir Tavish would ensure that every word would become an action, Taylor could have no doubts about that. Of course, he knew that Sir Tavish couldn't possibly allocate resource to following him around all the time, but the problem was there would always be the *chance* that someone was following him, or that a room had been bugged. Taylor could never be sure that his every word and action wasn't being taped, or filmed.

For a brief moment, he thought about contacting one of his high-powered friends, but quickly dispensed with that line of thought. It would be his word against Sir Tavish's and Sir

Tavish did not, usually, have a reputation for threatening anyone, let alone a top businessman, such as Gerald Taylor. No, if Taylor made any more of this, he'd just be attracting attention to himself and possibly forcing Sir Tavish underground in the process. In other words, Sir Tavish would just find other ways to annoy him. Whichever way he looked at his future, it was bleak in the extreme.

Taylor tried a more general form of defence.

"You won't get away with harassing me."

"Ah, but I will, Mr Taylor because harassment can come in many shapes and forms and I have access to all of them."

Taylor's fury finally erupted. "This is beyond belief, Sir Tavish. You cannot possibly be talking about tying up huge resources, simply to get back at me."

"As I said, Mister Taylor, I may tie up resources or I may not. The fact remains, that you wouldn't know one way or the other. What I will say, however, is that I will be watching you very closely, Mister Taylor and *will* take every opportunity to make your life a misery. I aim to get a lot of pleasure from that, by the way."

Taylor's anger was subsiding. He could go on arguing; he could call Sir Tavish all the names under the sun, but the reality was he couldn't shake MILO, if as an organisation they made a concerted effort to go after him. Just one month of MILO watching his every movement would be too damaging to both the legal and illegal world he moved in. Much as he hated the notion, Gerald Taylor knew that he was beaten.

"You seem to have gained the better of me, Sir Tavish."

Sir Tavish stood up with a look of contentment on his face. "Yes, I do, don't I?" No need to get up, I'll see myself out."

As he made his way down to street level Sir Tavish could not remember ever having felt quite so good in a very long time.

*

Back in his office, Gerald Taylor was regaining his composure. He poured himself a drink and sat, thinking for a moment. Finally, he made a decision that he simply couldn't skirt around. He couldn't effectively do anything for Freiheit if there was even the slightest chance that MILO were standing at his shoulder. He would have to cut all ties, forthwith and, at least for a little while longer, concentrate on the legitimate business of working for the Varga Corporation.

He finished his drink and told Hannah that he was going out for a while. Later that afternoon, he was on the phone to Fritz Wagner, explaining the situation he now found himself in and saying he would have to be replaced as the Tongue of Great Britain.

"Is there nothing we can do to stop you having to leave us?" Wagner had asked.

"I just feel that the authorities are too close, they'll have eyes on me all the time and I don't want to place our organisation in any more harm."

"Very well, I will aim to find a replacement for you, as soon as I can."

"In the meantime," added Taylor, "just before I call it a day, I will arrange to pay money in to the Freiheit account, from our little banking ventures. I can assure you, Fritz, that it will be an amount to make your mouth water. I feel sure that Gerd will be delighted when he sees the kind of money we've been able to amass."

Taylor could sense Wagner smiling down the phone.

"Nothing like going out on a high, eh Gerald?" he then said.

"It's the only way to go," said Taylor and the call was brought to an end.

Gerald Taylor went off to begin the next phase of his life and Fritz Wagner sat back in his chair. He was tiring of having to make changes to their organisation, even when he knew they were changes that simply had to be made. As soon as anyone attracted attention they knew it was time to move on, knew it was time for a slight change of direction and for someone else to take over.

Wagner knew he would have to update Heinz Franke, but that was a call he'd rather make later. He hoped to be able to offer the Grand Master a few suggestions by the time he did make that call.

For the moment, it was time to give the matter more thought. Whoever took over in London would have to be able to hit the ground running. Gerald Taylor, after his latest banking venture, would be a hard act to follow.

Friday, 22nd October, 1971

That morning, The Washington Post printed a story about Toby Reinhardt. They told the American people that Reinhardt's real name was Julius Podolski and that he was a war criminal. They also printed details of those crimes and questioned why no one, in America, had ever considered it necessary to take a form of action against the man. The word 'cover-up' was never actually used, but the implication was there for all to see.

In the White House, Richard Nixon sat and quietly fumed. He wasn't really that bothered about Podolski, as such, but he was angry at the fact that someone had chosen to ignore his implicit instructions to leave Podolski alone. Nixon had instructed his Chief of Staff to contact Abner McQueen and seek assurances that the leak had neither come from him, nor anyone else on his team. Abner was able, with hand on heart, to say that he knew nothing about information being sent to the Washington Post. What he didn't say, however, was that he had a bloody good idea who *had* sent the information, but as that individual worked thousands of miles away, there seemed no need to mention it.

The information had travelled those thousands of miles in the possession of four, different people. It had taken a convoluted route and spent most of the time concealed within suitcases, or briefcases. By the time it found its way on to the editor's desk at The Washington Post, word was already permeating through the Capitol that Toby Reinhardt might not be the person everyone thought he was. Sir Tavish had wanted a groundswell of interest to already be in place before the Washington Post printed their story.

It worked. The FBI had no other option but to investigate the report and, of course, in the process gained access to the same material seen by the newspaper's editor. It would just be a matter of time before Reinhardt was facing justice, all be it twenty-five years late.

In London, Sir Tavish sat in his office and pondered on all that had been achieved. After being so despondent with Ben, a few days earlier, he was now in better spirits. He knew that a war criminal would be sent for trial and that Gerald Taylor would now be slinking off to the business equivalent of the back benches.

Two successes, all be it of the kind that no one else would know about. Both matters would be viewed in isolation by everyone except Sir Tavish. He knew they were linked and he felt no regret for what he had done.

He sat back in his chair and smiled.

There were times when a success couldn't be properly celebrated; times you just had to sip a cup of coffee and reflect on the actions you'd taken.

Sir Tavish was not a smug man normally, but there were times when smug was acceptable.

This was one of them.

Friday, 5th November, 1971 – New Freiheit Headquarters, Hamburg

Freiheit's new Headquarters in Hamburg were still little more than a building site. The property had been acquired a month ago, but required a lot of work to upgrade it to the level at which it could be properly used. One room that had been finished, however, was the Board Room, the meeting place for the Grand Committee.

A special meeting had been called by Heinz Franke and so, at ten o'clock that grey and rainy morning, seven men sat around a table of polished oak, papers strewn in front of them and a coffee waiting to be drunk. Two secretaries, looking smart in their white blouses and black skirts, scurried about, ensuring the final items were all in place. One then clarified with Herr Franke as to when he wanted lunch brought to them. A time was agreed and one of the secretaries left the room. The other took a seat behind Franke and prepared to take notes.

Those in the room with Franke were; Fritz Wagner, Gerd Seeler, Sebastian Diefenbach, Helmut Breitner, Emmerich Kassmeyer and Rudolf Froese, who was about to become their new man in London. This would be the Grand Committee for the foreseeable future with the immediate future of Freiheit lying squarely upon their collective shoulders.

The meeting opened with Gerd Seeler running over the accounts and passing on belated congratulations for the money Gerald Taylor had paid in prior to his retirement from the organisation. It was agreed that Taylor would be a great loss, but Franke also took the opportunity to welcome Rudolf Froese to the table. Froese had been a suggestion made by Wolfgang Brandt; in a brief telephone conversation he had had with Ralf Dinger. As no one else had other suggestions, Franke agreed to speak with Froese and the two men hit it off from the start.

Rudolf Froese had agreed to move to London. Franke knew it was a risk asking a German to take over as the Tongue of Great Britain. He was bound to attract instant attention from MILO, in particular, but Franke was convinced that the fact Froese already had a successful and legitimate business, his cover story would be sound and MILO would back off after a brief investigation. Froese knew what he was letting himself in for and was fully prepared.

After the accounts, the Committee then moved on to future business. Franke returned to a theme he would continue to push for a long time to come; he sorely wanted a foot in the Eastern half of Europe and he was now prepared to work all the harder to achieve that.

A name had been suggested; Otto Witt. Witt already ran a business, which had outlets either side of the Wall. He travelled between West and East a lot and was well known to the guards on either side of the border. Over the years the guards had become less formal with Witt and his coming and going now passed off with little interest being shown in him. He seemed the perfect candidate to help spread Freiheit's message in the East.

Fritz Wagner was instructed to contact Witt and sound him out. Witt was already a member of Freiheit, already contributing financially to the cause. It was to be expected, therefore, that he would be more than happy to contribute on other levels as well. Wagner was to speak with Witt, as soon as possible and feedback to Heinz Franke.

Now that all ties with the Varga Corporation had been severed, all meetings of the Grand Committee now needed to be organised separately. Franke decided that they would meet every quarter, with other meetings called if there was a particular problem to be discussed. Financial queries would go through Gerd Seeler and all other queries would be directed to Fritz Wagner.

Franke, himself, would try and stay out of things as much as possible.

It was a successful day for the Grand Committee. It was a day in which Heinz Franke saw that he had a good group of men around him, a group of men who seemed keen to work together for the good of Freiheit. Franke came away feeling that the organisation was in good hands and the future had never looked brighter.

Friday, 26th November, 1971 – The Golden Goose Pub, Central London.

It was a night of sadness, but also a night of celebration. The team had gathered to give Mike a proper send-off. Sir Tavish chose not to be there, feeling he was more likely to cramp their style. He did, however, give money to Ben, asking him to buy a couple of rounds in Sir Tavish's name. Sir Tavish, himself, had spoken to Mike that afternoon and wished him well for the future.

Mike was moving to a desk job in the Home Office. It would provide nine to five stability and also keep him well away from potential danger. Maria had found a job working for a solicitor who had been at school with Mike. Everything seemed rosy for the couple.

There was added sadness for the group in the fact that Amy would be heading back to America. She had enjoyed her time in London and would have been happy to stay on a little longer. However, there was always work to be done at Langley and Derbert couldn't cover it all himself.

Sarah and Paul were in the mood for celebration, more than the others. They were on the brink of moving in together and were already sharing thoughts of settling down as a couple. Paul could still be quite serious at times, but in meeting Sarah he had begun to loosen up a little. He loved Sarah dearly, even if her smoking did continue to annoy him at times.

It was a crossroads for everyone in the team. No one ever knows what lies ahead and all that anyone can do is make the best of the hand they are dealt.

For some there would be good days ahead and for others, not so good.

At the moment, all they could do was enjoy each other's company, have a few drinks, laugh a lot and hope that days like that would outnumber the bad ones.

It was all that anyone could do.

***

www.catchthe22.com

HISTORICAL FOOTNOTE

The Baker Street bank raid did take place, pretty much as I have described it. Four men were ultimately arrested for the crime, though the police never felt that they had caught the 'brains' behind the robbery.

The Moorgate bank raid is pure fiction. I know that to be a fact as I worked in that branch at the time I have set the story. The Moorgate Branch referred to ceased being a Barclays many years ago. There was, therefore not an ulterior motive for the Baker Street raid, at least not as far as I know.

There was apparently talk of an anonymous German putting money in to the planning of the Great Train Robbery. I had created Hans Varga before I discovered that piece of information so my imagination still wins over reality.

In case you missed it at the beginning of the book, £1 in 1971 would be worth around £13 today. Having said that, I can remember being able to do a lot more with a £1 back then than I could ever do with £13 today. My grandmother used to send me a fifty pence postal order and it was like receiving a food parcel.

About the Author

Eric R Davidson spent most of his working life in the Civil Service before having a second career with Grampian Police in Aberdeen. His role with Grampian Police came to an end in 2013, which allowed Eric to concentrate on his main passion, which was writing.

The outcome of having more time to concentrate on his writing has led to a number of novels being written along with one short story.

Eric's other main interest is Crystal Palace Football Club; an interest which makes many a Saturday afternoon either extremely joyous or desperately depressing. He is also a big cricket fan, though can only watch these days as the aches and pains of age prevents him from playing any more.

Printed in Great Britain
by Amazon

11383082R00174